A Summer of Kings

HAN NOLAN

A Summer
of Kings

SCHOLASTIC INC.
New York Toronto London Auckland
Sydney Mexico City New Delhi Hong Kong

ISBN 978-0-545-48253-0

12 11 10 9 8 7 6 5 4 3 2 1   12 13 14 15 16 17/0

Printed in the U.S.A.   40

First Scholastic printing, September 2012

Text set in Sabon
Designed by Cathy Riggs

For Brian, with love

ACKNOWLEDGMENTS

A thousand and one thanks to my husband, Brian, for all the things he does daily to keep me and my writing moving forward in the right direction. Thanks to my brother, Mike Walker, for the music and the memories. Thanks to my readers for their time and encouragement: Brian Nolan, Adrienne Nolan, Lee Doty, Faye Gibbons, and Ann Dorer. Thanks to Rachael Nolan for the daily calls—always a lift to the spirits. Thanks to my agent, Barbara Kouts, and my editor, Karen Grove, for all the time and energy they put into turning my stories into books.

A Summer of Kings

ONE

Last summer a murderer came to live with us. Well, that's what I had called him. Our neighbor Pip and my Auntie Pie called him the cold-blooded killer, but my mother and father said he was just a victim of prejudice and circumstance. King-Roy Johnson, a black boy just 18 years old, was accused of killing a white man down in Alabama. Before anyone could catch him, though, this King-Roy escaped up here to New York, and, with instructions from his mother, who was once best friends with my mother, ended up at our house in Westchester County.

He arrived on a Friday, a day later than we had expected him. He came while my mother was still in the city, at the theater with my brother and sister, who were auditioning for a Broadway musical, and while my father, a director, was at another theater with one of our houseguests, Monsieur Vichy, the snooty avant-garde playwright who hated me most particularly. Our other houseguest, Beatrice Bonham, the actress, was sleeping off a doozy of a hangover after giving her final performance of *Jubilatin'!*, a really, really terrible play, and one that I had to sit through five deadly long times.

Friday was also the day that Auntie Pie, Pip, and I were out scooping up dead squirrels off the road for a couple of injured hawks Auntie Pie had rescued. My mother always disapproved of these outings, saying to Auntie Pie and me more than once, "Do you want the people in this town to think you're crazy? Do you want them to think we're all hillbillies; that we eat those disgusting things?" Which is why we only went out when my mother was away and couldn't lecture us.

We drove the old 1947 Ford Super Deluxe station wagon, another reason why we snuck out when my mother wasn't looking. The wagon was my father's old car, and he treasured it because he had purchased it with the money he made from his first hit play, but Mother believed we looked like beach bums in that car. "It's unseemly for us to be seen riding around in that broken-down bus," she told me once. "I wish your father would burn that thing!"

Broken-down bus was right. The car only ran backward and the passenger door swung open whenever it made a sharp turn, forcing the person inside to hold on to the open glove compartment for dear life. It was the only car Auntie Pie could drive without having to worry about causing too much damage, though, so off we went, traveling backward down the street, past the many stately homes on either side of us, barely missing hitting drivers in their shiny new station wagons and sedans heading in what most people would call the *right* direction, as we kept a lookout for dead animals.

We were in the early days of our summer vacation, and I felt in great need of a new adventure. I looked at the two dead squirrels in the box that sat between Pip and me; looked at same-old Pip-squeak, the boy who lived across the street and was in my class at school, which made him a year younger than I was because I had stayed back a year; looked at Auntie Pie, sweating and twisted around in the driver's seat trying to drive in a straight line even though she was legally blind and wore eyeglasses three inches thick, and I thought, *This is not the adventure I'm wanting to have.*

Every summer of my life had been the same, whether we vacationed in Europe or at home. In Europe everybody in the family got to go on sightseeing trips and have adventures while I stayed in the rental apartment and got tutored so I would be sure to pass all my subjects the following year. If we stayed home during the summers, my younger sister and brother acted in plays or in television commercials or went to a smarty camp while I got tutored so I would be sure to pass all my subjects the following year. Ever since I had stayed back in third grade, Mother had demanded this extra insurance that my summer tutoring provided her, but for me it only made my school year long and boring since I had already galloped through the same subjects the summer before. The only difference for me between a summer in Europe and a summer at home was that at home I had Pip.

Pip thought he was in love with me. He has been in love with me, he said, since he was four and I was five and his mother put us in the bathtub together to bathe us after an exciting morning creating mud pies and throwing them at each other. He told everyone at school that we've bathed together, which is one of the many, many reasons I was *not* in love with him.

That hot, fifth day of July in 1963, sitting in the backseat of the 1947 Ford Super Deluxe station wagon with all but one of the windows stuck shut, in the first summer vacation in forever that I didn't have to be tutored, I decided that this would be the summer of a new me, a more mature me, a more mysterious and exotic me, and I determined that our new houseguest, the murderer, was to play a starring role in my new life. So, when Auntie Pie backed into a spot on the side of the road somewhat near where yet another squirrel had been run down, and Pip and I climbed out of the steamy car to go collect it, walking along the road all the local college students used whenever they walked to town, I told Pip about my plan.

"This murderer, this King-Roy Johnson, he's only 18 years old," I began.

"Yeah, I know. So?" Pip said.

I swept my damp bangs out of my eyes and said, "So, he's just four years older than I am."

"Well, bully for him. So what?" Pip looked irritated. His dark brows bunched together and he clenched his jaw so hard I could see the muscle popping in and out on the side of his face. Anytime that morning that I brought up the subject of the murderer, Pip made the same face.

"My mother and father are four years apart, too," I said. "Mother says a four-year age difference in a couple is just right since men mature a lot slower than women."

Pip swiped the sweat off his forehead like he was trying to mash an insect and fling it, then said, "What are you getting at, Esther? You think you and this cold-blooded killer are going to become a couple? He's a Negro *and* a cold-blooded killer. Are you crazy?"

Pip looked stunned by the idea of it all. His small face and big ears always reminded me of a koala bear, and right then, with his deep-set dark eyes blinking behind his glasses and his mouth open, he looked like a koala bear that had just fallen out of its tree.

I shrugged. "I don't know. He sounds exciting to me, and exotic. Don't you think?" I loved using the word *exotic*. I felt exotic just saying it.

A couple of college girls with perfectly flipped hairdos, looking fresh in their brightly colored sundresses, walked by, and Pip waited a few seconds to let them get out of hearing range, then said, "You think you're going to fall in love with him? With a killer? You can't plan love. It's not a road trip, you know."

We had reached the spot where the squirrel lay flattened and dry upon the side of the road. I heard one of the girls who had passed us, say, "Oh, cool, look," and I knew she had noticed our car. All the college kids loved the 1947 wagon, and over the years several of them had offered to buy the car from my father, but my father always said no. I smiled to myself when I heard the girls behind us strike up a conversation with Auntie Pie.

I wiped the sweat from under my eyes and watched Pip pull a trowel out of the back pocket of his baggy African safari shorts and stoop down to pick up the squirrel. Then, with the dead squirrel lying on the trowel held out in front of him, he looked up at me through his heavy-framed glasses and said, "Love is an affair of the heart, Esther." He put his free hand, the one without the garden trowel in it, up to his heart and said, "Love is a tender thing, not a game, not a toy."

I held out the squirrel box and sang "Love Is a Many-Splendored Thing" in my most dramatic voice, and Pip stood up and dumped the squirrel in the box with a thud, then marched off toward the car without saying anything.

I ran after him. "What? I was just kidding."

Pip stopped and turned around. He was only four feet ten inches tall, although he claimed he'd grown two more inches; but even so, that still made him four inches shorter than I was, and standing as close as we were, he had to look up at me, which he always hated doing. He backed up a little and said, "You were kidding about going after that . . . that killer?"

"No. I was kidding with the song. I'm serious about the murderer. I'm already partly in love with him, anyway."

Pip ran his fingers through his hair, pushing his short bangs off his forehead so they stood straight up, and said, "Esther, you haven't even met him."

I nodded. "That's what's so romantic about it. I've fallen in love with his story, with the story of him, not how he looks." I said this but it wasn't exactly true. I had fallen in love with the idea of falling in love with him, but it was almost the same thing, and anyway I had liked the reaction I had gotten from my girlfriends when I told them about my new love over the phone the night before. Kathy and Laura were both over at Laura's house packing for their summerlong trip to Nantucket. I had only just then found out about the trip, their secret special trip, and that's when I got the idea about being in love with King-Roy.

Kathy and Laura had ganged up on me over the last weeks of school. They told me I acted more like a twelve-year-old than a fourteen-year-old and they claimed we didn't have anything in common anymore. They said they were boy crazy and I wasn't, and they complained that I didn't even carry a purse, as if that had become the major determining factor for friendships.

Well, I had showed them. I told them not to be surprised, when they got back, if I was engaged to be married, and I hung up the phone with them trying to shout out one last question before I did.

I looked at Pip, standing in front of me in his dingy track-team T-shirt he was so proud of and his baggy shorts stuffed with postcards and letters from his many pen pals, looking so out of place with the fantasy of romance playing in my mind, and I said, "Yes indeed, I've fallen in love." Then I looked off into the distance and said, "We're going to have an exotic and enlightened romance, King-Roy and I." I liked the sound of that whole sentence, so I said it again, this time looking straight at Pip. "Yep, an exotic and enlightened romance. A . . . a romance for the times," I added, feeling inspired.

Pip looked back at me through those thick-rimmed glasses of his with such a pained expression it was as if I had just kicked him in the shin.

"What?" I said when he just stood there, with that sad face, not saying anything.

"Do you enjoy hurting me?" he asked. "Do you like hurting my feelings?"

For a second I felt ashamed of myself. Then I came to my senses and said, "You know you don't really love me, Pip. Not romantically. We've never even kissed, unless you count when we were in the first grade and played house out on the playground."

"It isn't because I haven't wanted to, that's for sure," Pip said.

Auntie Pie honked the horn—the one thing on the car that always worked—and I waved to her. "Just a second," I shouted, noticing that the college girls had left. Then returning to Pip, I said, "You just like saying you're in love with me so you don't have to face rejection from every other girl in the school. You think that as long as you can tell yourself and everybody else that you like me, then you don't have to think of yourself as a pip-squeak loser. You're using me, Pip, and I allow it because I like you, but don't act like it's for real. And don't condemn me because I say I'm in love with someone else. I've moved on and maybe it's time you did, too. It's time you grew up."

As I was speaking, Pip's face got redder and redder, and he blew his cheeks up as if they were full of water. Then he let loose with a big burst of air and said, "You know, it's times like this that I don't even like you, let alone love you. Not even a little bit." He squinted up at me. "When did you get so mean, Esther? When did you get so heartless?" And with those words, he threw the trowel on the ground and marched off down the road past Auntie Pie, who honked at him and shouted, "Hey!"

I stooped down and picked up the trowel and called after him, "I was only telling you the truth for your own good. I didn't say no girl would be interested in you; I said *you* thought no girl would be interested in you. I said *you* thought you were a pip-squeak loser."

Didn't I say that? I wanted to think about this, but Pip was getting away. I shouted, "I wasn't saying *I* thought that. Pip! Jonathan! Come on."

I trotted after him, and Auntie Pie honked at me and yelled out the one window that worked, "Get in the car already; I'm burning up in here," when I passed the car, but I kept on going.

Auntie Pie started the engine and backed the car up

and followed me while I followed Pip, who had started to run.

"Have fun with your colored boy," he called back to me. "Have fun with your cold-blooded killer, Esther." He stopped and turned around and walked backward so that with Auntie Pie driving backward and him walking backward, I was the one who looked out of place. I stopped walking and Auntie Pie pulled up beside me.

"Hey, just remember to invite me to your wedding, okay?" Pip said. "Would you do that? Invite me to your wedding? 'Cause that I've got to see." Pip jabbed his index finger in the air for emphasis, and then, jerking his head sideways as if his neck were in sudden spasm, he said, his glance returning to me, "You know, why would anybody be interested in you? Huh? Did you ever think that maybe I pretended to be in love with you because I knew no one else liked *you*?" He stopped walking and brushed at his eyes a second. Then he said, "All the guys make fun of you. You may be cute and all with your big brown eyes and all those freckles and your so-called million-dollar smile your old grandfather's always going on about, but like your parents said, you're not photogenic, and anyway, you're a . . . a goofball. Yeah, that's right." Pip nodded to himself and started walking backward again. "You're always saying the wrong thing and knocking into people and making a total fool of yourself, and your hair is always in tangles like you just came out of the jungle or something. The guys make fun of the mass of knots in your hair you think you're hiding with that headband."

I put my hands up to my hair and adjusted my new pink headband. "That's not fair. You know I have trouble keeping the tangles out. It hurts. You know blond heads are more sensitive."

Pip wasn't listening. He said, "Didn't you ever think that maybe *I* was protecting *you*? Huh?" He was still walking backward, and when he said "Huh," he tripped and fell back on his bottom. He popped up again like it didn't happen and said with his voice cracking, "Think about *that,* why don't you. You made me say it. You made me tell the truth. How's it feel? How's it *feel,* Esther?"

Pip turned back around and ran off so fast that he was out of sight before I could even think of a response.

Finally one came to me.

"Oh yeah?" I shouted back.

TWO

"Now, what was that all about?" Auntie Pie wanted to know when I climbed back in the car with the box of dead squirrels in my arms.

"Oh nothing," I said, even though my heart was pounding and my stomach was churning. Pip and I almost never fought. We were best friends, really. Pip was the only reason I even survived staying back in the third grade. Everybody else made fun of me and called me lame brain, or moron, but not Pip. The first day of school, he took my hand and we walked together to Mrs. Mahoney's class and Pip walked right up to the teacher and said, "I'm Jonathan Masters. My father is the president of the college, and this is Esther Young, and we want to sit together."

Mrs. Mahoney had smiled at Pip and frowned at me. Then she said, "Yes, I had Esther last year. I hope we're planning on a better performance this year, Miss Young."

"Yes, I hope you are, too," I said in all innocence, thinking she was talking about herself. I realized by the way she had arched her brow, that evil brow, and by the elbow poke Pip had given me that she had meant my performance and not hers, and I corrected myself. "I mean, yes, Mrs. Mahoney, I am."

I hated the third grade—both times. I hated that I wasn't even given a new teacher. Mrs. Mahoney was fat, which wouldn't have mattered if she had kept it to herself, but she liked to threaten to sit on us if we did anything wrong, so it mattered plenty, and it meant I was in constant danger of getting flattened. I think I would have ended up looking a lot like the dead squirrels I had sitting on my lap if it hadn't been for Pip running interference for me all the time. I knew I owed him a lot.

That's what I was thinking, that I owed him a lot, when Auntie Pie said, "It looked to me like the two of you were fighting. Why did he run off like that?"

Auntie Pie had begun backing the car down the road and I was afraid to answer her because I didn't want to break her concentration.

I twisted around in my seat and looked out the back so that I could help navigate and look out for Pip, who most likely took the shortcut through the woods, since I didn't see him anywhere on the road.

"Well?" Auntie Pie said.

"Well, he's mad at me. I think I told him to get lost—kind of."

"Why would you do that?"

Auntie Pie was heading for a telephone pole, so I said, "Pole. Pole. Pole!" She swerved just in time and we were back on the road and she was still waiting for my answer.

"I don't know why I did it." I shrugged. "I guess I just want this summer to be different. *I* want to be different. This is my first summer in forever that I'm free. No tutors and no homework. If I hang out with Pip all the time—I don't know. That's my old life. He's part of my childhood. I need to move on from that."

"Just like that?" Auntie Pie took her hand from the wheel and snapped her fingers.

"Well . . ." I shrugged. "Laura and Kathy have cut me off just like that." I snapped my fingers. "Or at least they're trying to. They think I'm too tomboy or something—too immature."

"Everybody matures at their own rate, Esther. Don't be in such a hurry; your time will come." Auntie Pie took a hand off the steering wheel and patted my knee. We rolled back onto the side of the road and headed toward the stone wall that ran the length of our property. I said, "Wall. Wall. Wall!" Auntie Pie jerked the wheel just in time, and we didn't speak again until we were safely home.

At home, Auntie Pie and I carried the box of squirrels into the gatehouse that stands at the entrance to our property just inside an enormous iron gate.

While Auntie Pie prepared the food for the hawks and let her pet skunk, Earl, out of its cage to run around, I cleaned the hawk squirt off the wall and thought about Pip and what he had said about nobody liking me. When I looked up, still deep in thought, I noticed through the side window the local taxi that waits for passengers down at our train station enter through the gate and roll down our driveway.

Auntie Pie saw it, too.

"Is that him?" she asked, peering out the window at the taxi. "Is that the killer? He's early. First he's a day late, now he's two hours early." She scooted the skunk back into its cage, wiped her hands on her dress, and said, "We're all going to be murdered in our sleep."

I said, "But it can't be him; I'm not dressed yet." I looked down at my dirty plaid Bermuda shorts and my green striped shirt. In my fantasy of our first meeting, I had imagined myself in a more exotic-looking affair. I had imagined myself wearing something out of Beatrice Bonham's closet, something with a lot of fluff and frill. I had pictured myself wearing makeup, with curled hair and high heels. I didn't own any makeup or high-heeled shoes, and the most exotic thing I did own was a black turtleneck leotard that zipped up the back, a leftover from Mother's attempt to either turn me into a ballerina or just plain humiliate me by signing me up to take classes in the city with the School of American Ballet. Mother was on the board there, so they had to take me. I lasted six years (six years!) before Mr. Balanchine himself told my mother that it was pointless: I did not have the body of a ballerina; however Stewart and Sophia, my brother and sister, were beautiful dancers, of course.

Auntie Pie heard my comment about not being

dressed and said, "We've got a cold-blooded killer in our midst and you're talking about your clothes?"

"Mother and Dad said he didn't do it," I replied, placing a towel on the side of the hawk cage closest to the wall, trying to finish up so I could get to the window and see for myself what our new guest looked like.

"Mother said he is just a victim of prejudice and circumstance," I added.

I went over to the window, with my heart racing, and watched as a tall black person climbed out of the taxi and looked around.

"There he is," I said. I took a deep breath and let it out, fogging up the window. I had to wipe it down to see him again.

"Uh-huh, that's him," Auntie Pie said.

The murderer, the Negro boy, the boy I told everyone I was going to have a romance with, looked like a full-grown man standing out there in our driveway. He was dressed in tan pants, a white shirt, brown bow tie, and a straw hat. No boy I knew dressed like that.

I saw him gazing up at the house and whistling to himself, and I knew he was surprised by the size of our house.

Normally, seeing someone admiring our house would give me a real thrill, because if you asked me what I was most proud of about myself, it would be that I lived in this wonderful mansion with my famous director father and my beautiful mother and my gifted brother and sister, but right then I was far too nervous to be thrilled.

I glanced at Auntie Pie, then returned to the window. "Well, all right, then," I said. "I guess we ought to go greet him. Nobody else is home except Beatrice, and she's in no shape to see him. She only got home this morning. She'll be sleeping it off till four at least."

Auntie Pie backed away from the window. "You go ahead, and I'll stay behind and keep watch over things," she said, picking up Rolly Raccoon, then lifting him to examine his bandaged front paw. Her voice sounded shaky. "Anyway, I have to go move the car before your parents get back and find out I drove it."

I turned around to face my aunt. She's really my great-aunt, and even though she's only in her sixties, she acts much older and wears dresses and clunky shoes that have got room for her bunions, with thick stockings she wears rolled down to her knees that she orders from some old-lady catalog. She looks just like an old granny, except for her face, which doesn't have a wrinkle in it.

I said, "You're scared, Auntie Pie. You're scared of a poor boy down on his luck." I moved over to the door and one of the hawks screamed, which, when it's right in your ear, is bloodcurdling.

I hunched up my shoulders against the noise and opened the door. "He's the grandson of Mother's maid from childhood and the son of Mother's oldest best friend. You've heard her talk of her maid Cassie. This is her grandson." I knew she knew all this, but sometimes she forgot things, and anyway, I needed to say those things out loud to reassure myself.

Both hawks screamed when I said grandson, and Auntie Pie and I both jumped.

Then she said over the screams, her voice sounding irritated, "I know who he is. And just because he's from a family of good women, it doesn't mean a thing. He can still be a killer—a cold-blooded killer. You of all people ought to know families don't come out just alike."

"What's that supposed to mean?" I asked, not really wanting an answer. I knew all too well that I was the one in our family who didn't come out right.

Auntie Pie ignored my question and said, "Oh all right, I'll go with you to meet this young man. I guess I can't let you go out there by yourself."

We stepped out of the gatehouse together and saw that the taxi had gone and Mr. King-Roy Johnson was nowhere in sight.

THREE

W here did he go?" I asked. I ran toward the house.
"I see his suitcase on the porch," Auntie Pie
called after me.

I ran up onto the porch and turned around. I called
out, "Mr. Johnson? Mr. King-Roy Johnson. Hello. We're
here on the porch."

Auntie Pie took her time climbing the steps of the
porch, then said, "Why don't you look inside and I'll
keep a watch out here."

I nodded and went inside the house. I stood in the
foyer and called out, "King-Roy Johnson? Mr. Johnson,
are you here?"

"Yes, ma'am, I'm here."

I heard his voice coming from the direction of the
ballroom. I ran through the living room and solarium
and saw that the ballroom doors were open. We always
kept them closed because it was the coldest room in the
winter and the warmest room in the summer. I knew
King-Roy Johnson had to be in there. I hesitated a second before entering, thinking I should wait for Auntie
Pie, but then I thought that maybe my hesitation was

some kind of sign of being prejudiced against murderers or black people, so I went on inside and found Mr. Johnson standing in the middle of the room, staring at all our stained-glass windows.

He turned around when he heard me come in, and the first thing that struck me was that he looked so bright and handsome—not movie-star handsome but still quite handsome. His skin was a pretty copper color, and his face was so smooth-looking I thought maybe he hadn't started shaving yet. He was tall and slender, maybe six feet tall, and he had a nice broad forehead and large, soft brown eyes and a nose that kind of spread out across his face a bit too much and a pretty mouth, full and well shaped. Altogether his face looked gentle and quiet like a pond in the still of the day. He wore his hair cut close to his head, and he had on horn-rimmed glasses that made him look smart. Seeing him, King-Roy Johnson, standing before me, looking every bit like my fantasy of him, made me want to giggle. I felt relief or joy or something rising up in my chest, and I turned away. I wanted to leave, to run get Auntie Pie so I could hide behind her and think about my feelings more, but King-Roy Johnson called me back.

"Hey," he said. "I'm King-Roy Johnson; who are you?"

I turned back around and stepped forward and held out my hand for him to shake. I said, "I'm Esther. I'm Esther Young, and this—this is my house."

King-Roy smiled this easy kind of smile, not forced, and shook my hand. "Pleased to meet you, Miz Esther."

I waved my hand and blushed. "Oh, you can just call me Esther."

"Nice," King-Roy said, and I didn't know what was nice—my name or that he could just call me Esther without the *Miss*.

King-Roy crossed his arms in front of him and looked first to one side of him, then to the other. He said, "Is this apartments or a hotel or what?"

"It's my parents' house."

He shook his head. "It can't be just one house, can it?"

King-Roy's voice sounded smooth like drinking a thick chocolate shake. It was soft and southern—real mellow, like his face. He was all-over mellow. I had never had a fantasy of mine come true, not even a little bit of one, but here was this King-Roy, so handsome and perfect I didn't know what to do. I wanted him to think I was smart and beautiful and glamorous, because that was the other part of my fantasy.

I said, "Lots of people think our house is the college. There's one just down the road. The same architect built both the college and our house, so they look a lot alike— both Tudor style. It's just down the road—the college is." I realized I sounded like a dope, but I couldn't help myself.

"We get new college kids coming here all the time who just walk into the house thinking they've arrived at the college. I guess that's what you did? Just walked in thinking it was a hotel?" I laughed at this, using a practiced Katharine Hepburn kind of laugh, a toss-it-over-your shoulders kind of laugh, and Mr. King-Roy Johnson gave me his easy smile again but didn't answer my question.

I returned his smile, but I felt stupid for laughing the way I did. I could feel its phoniness echoing in my ears. When I had practiced it in my room, imagining our first meeting, with me in one of Beatrice's frilly dresses, it had sounded much better.

"So just one family lives here?" He turned around with his arms held out, taking in the whole of our ballroom.

I looked around. The room was huge, and it was rectangular, with a highly polished wooden floor and rows of leaded, diamond-patterned windows with stained-glass panels at the top. It was, in my mind, a very English ballroom—the kind used in the evening after a day of fox hunting. One set of windows overlooked a stone porch that ran the length of the east wing of the house, and beyond that were the lily pool, rose garden, and pavilion.

"Just one family and a few guests," I said, nodding. "My parents like having company, so you're very welcome here," I said, thinking Mother would be pleased that I said this.

"Nice," King-Roy Johnson said.

I took a step toward him and said, "My mother and

your mother were best friends, so . . . so of course you're welcome."

"That's right, uh-huh, best friends," King-Roy said, his eyes scanning the stained-glass scenes of Viking ships again. He looked back at me. "So, how many rooms does this place have, anyway?"

"Thirty," I said. "Our library is just beyond those doors over there," I added, pointing to both sides of the fireplace. I shrugged, acting as if the house wasn't so grand, even though I knew it was.

"Thirty rooms!" King-Roy Johnson said, shaking his head and peering into the library. "And I bet every one of 'em's as big as most people's whole house." He turned to look at me, then said, "Just between you and me, I'm not so sure how comfortable I'm gon' be staying here."

"Oh it's plenty comfortable here," I said, not really sure what he meant. Then, to demonstrate, I suppose, what a comfortable, easygoing, fun place our house was, I kicked off my Keds and ran over to one of the window seats. My sister and brother each kept a pair of socks on the seat. I put my brother's pair on and then said to King-Roy Johnson, "Watch this." I pushed off from the window seat and skated across the floor. When I was just about to come to a stop, I fell onto my chest and slid some more on my stomach, with my arms spread out like wings on either side of me. I came to a stop in front of the fireplace.

King-Roy laughed an amused kind of laugh, and I

couldn't tell if he enjoyed it or he thought I had just done the stupidest thing in the world.

I stood up, feeling pains in my breasts where I had landed too hard on the floor. I felt my face flood with heat and embarrassment again. This wasn't the way I had imagined myself behaving at all.

I tried to laugh it off with another Katharine Hepburn laugh, then said, "I'm really much too old for that. I'm almost fifteen. Way too old. I don't do floor skating anymore, but Stewart and Sophia still enjoy it. They're my brother and sister. Stewart's ten and Sophia's six going on thirty, as my mother likes to say. They're both really smart, and talented. They're brilliant, really. Mother's had their IQs tested."

"Is that right?" King-Roy Johnson said, his face going quiet again. "So are you brilliant, too?"

I looked out the windows that faced the front yard, where my favorite rock, a giant slab of white granite in the shape of a polar bear, poked out of the earth. The polar bear had been a sort of friend when I was little, an imaginary, rock friend, and I looked to it for comfort before turning back to King-Roy Johnson and answering him. "Well," I said, "Mother says we're all smart, but that's just Mother. She doesn't want to hurt my feelings." I went over to the window seat and pulled off the socks.

King-Roy Johnson walked across the floor, and I noticed his shoes had a good *tap-tap* sound to them. He stopped in front of me, with his arms crossed.

I looked up at him, and he had this gentle, angellike

smile, and he said, "You ever think maybe she's telling the truth?"

"Oh, no," I said, looking up into his face and seeing my own round-faced reflection in his eyeglasses. "Not a chance. She never even bothered to have my intelligence tested like she did with Sophia and Stewart. I stayed back in school when I was in the third grade. That was before I got my eyes fixed. I used to have lots of trouble with reading because I was cross-eyed. No, I have no talents or anything." I sat on the window seat, leaning forward and looking down at the floor with my hands tucked under my thighs. I felt uncomfortable talking to a perfect stranger, a murderer, an eighteen-year-old black boy, about my eyes and staying back and all that. When I had imagined our first conversation together, I thought he would be telling me how mature I seemed for my age, how wise, but after my stint on the ballroom floor, that conversation was down the toilet and instead I was exposing my most tender, most sore, spot. I never talked about my staying back a year in school, not even at home—especially not at home.

King-Roy Johnson shook his head and said, "Shoot, anyone could have crossed eyes and still be smart, even if they were held back a year."

I looked down at my feet and noticed they looked sweaty and swollen. I brought my legs up and sat cross-legged on the window seat so he wouldn't notice. "I read really well, now, at least," I said. "I love to read." I looked up. "Do you love to read, King-Roy?"

"Well, I do now," he said, sitting down next to me and stretching his long legs out in front of him. "But I came late to reading. My brothers and sisters learned early when they were in the first or second grade, but it took me a long time. A real long time. I didn't even start speaking until I was ten years old."

"Did everybody think you were stupid?"

King-Roy said, "Yessum, there were plenty who thought I had no brains in my head, but my momma knew differently. She told all the teachers that she knew in her heart that I was smart and that when I got ready to talk and to read, why, I'd do it, and meanwhile she would read to me and talk to me like I was the smartest boy in town. And she was right. I turned ten, and a few weeks later I was talking up a blue streak and nobody could shut me up. Then I decided I might as well start reading, and sure enough, I could read just fine once I set my mind to it." King-Roy nodded to himself and looked across the room at the fireplace as though it were something different, someplace different. Then he said, "It was my momma having confidence and having faith in me that brought me around to talking and reading."

"Well," I said, "she sure had to wait an awfully long time before you proved her right."

King-Roy nodded. "She had the faith," he said. "I owe her plenty. That's why I'm here, here with y'all. I'm here for my momma. She's always been on my side. She's the only one who believed me when I said I didn't kill anybody. She told me to come here, so here I am."

King-Roy's eyes blinked fast several times, and he turned his head to look out the windows, way off toward the pavilion, still blinking, and I thought he was one of the luckiest people on Earth to have a mother like that. I knew my mother loved me. She had to. But if someone had accused me of killing a man, she would believe him. Maybe she would think I did it by mistake, but still, she'd feel sure that I did it. Everyone in the family, the whole household, would believe I did it. I didn't have anybody, besides Pip, really rooting for me. Everybody was too busy rooting for Sophia and Stewart. They were the stars of the family. Thinking about this made me feel ashamed for what I had said to Pip that afternoon. I didn't tell King-Roy any of this, of course. Instead I said, "Do you know what my sister, Sophia, did last week?"

King-Roy turned back to me and shook his head. "No. What did she do?"

"She drew an aerial view of Central Park on her Etch A Sketch, or 'L'Ecran Magique,' as Monsieur Vichy calls it. Six years old and she's only flown over Central Park once in a helicopter, and she put that on an Etch A Sketch. It's a toy and I can barely draw a circle with one of those things. I'm always turning the wrong knob the wrong way. My father got a book out of the town library to compare her drawing with a photograph of Central Park by air, and her drawing matched it exactly." I looked up at King-Roy. "Now, how do you compete with that?"

"You don't have to compete. You're your own person with your own kind of smarts." King-Roy crossed his legs and pushed his glasses back up on his nose. He did this slowly, carefully, as if he thought the glasses might ram into his eyes if he pushed them too fast. I had never seen anyone adjust his glasses with such care before.

"Now, you take me for instance," he said, bringing me back to our discussion. "I read all the time now, but I can't claim that most of my learning comes from books. A lot of it comes from just watching and living and dealing with what comes my way, and somebody coming up to me and telling me how smart she is with an Etcher Sketch doesn't mean much to me. I'm not so impressed." He stood up and turned to face me and said, "Now, I bet someone like you has got natural smarts. You're easy to talk to, and that takes a natural kind of smarts."

"Really?"

He nodded. "Sure 'nuff. You've made me feel right at home."

"I have?" I asked, standing up and facing him.

King-Roy nodded and looked around the ballroom again. "Coming to a place like this, so big, like a castle or something, well, it feels real strange. It's so grand, it makes me feel like I'm supposed to do something important coming here, or say something real clever, but you make me feel like it's gon' be all right."

King-Roy smiled this warm melt-your-heart kind of smile and I felt my knees go weak. He liked me.

I smiled back at King-Roy and decided that I liked him, too. Maybe I really *could* fall in love with him, and maybe when Laura and Kathy got back from their vacation and saw me walking hand in hand with Mr. Tall-dark-and-handsome, they'd see that I was more mature than the two of them any day.

I hesitated a second, then took King-Roy's hand. "Come on, let me show you the rest of the house. Let me show you your rooms. I fixed them up myself. I even put flowers in your bedroom even though you're a boy—or a man, I mean. Oh, and wait till you see my bedroom. Beatrice—that's Beatrice Bonham, the actress—she's staying with us and she's so jealous of my room it makes *her* cross-eyed."

King-Roy laughed and it sounded like a donkey braying, and that made me laugh, too. It made me want to tell him more. It made me want to tell him everything about my life.

Together we walked back through the solarium and the living room until we came out into the foyer, where we found Auntie Pie standing there. She stood right in the center of the foyer, right in the center of Mother's good jewel-toned Oriental rug. She stood right there, waiting for us—waiting for us with a gun in her hand, aimed right at the two of us.

FOUR

Esther, get out of the way," Auntie Pie said, using the gun to gesture with.

The gun looked like a gunslinger's revolver and weighed heavy in her hands. She could barely hold it up straight.

Both King-Roy and I stood right where we were.

"What are you doing?" I asked. "Where did you get that gun? Are you crazy?"

"That's my gun," King-Roy said, his nostrils flaring. "You took that out of my suitcase, yonder." He pointed through the open front door at his straw-colored suitcase. "I don't appreciate that. No, ma'am, I don't appreciate that one bit."

King-Roy's voice sounded as if he could barely contain his anger, and I felt scared—scared of the gun and scared of him.

"I bet you don't. You were planning to kill us all in our sleep. Well, we'll see about that."

"It's not loaded," King-Roy said. "And I don't have any bullets, either. And if I wanted to kill somebody I wouldn't need a gun, but I'm no killer. I thought y'all knew that already. I thought my momma explained all that." King-Roy looked at me for some kind of reassurance.

I stared at him wide-eyed and said nothing. I didn't know what to think.

"I know you were accused of killing a white man," Auntie Pie said. "I know you've got no proof except your mother's say-so that you didn't do it. That's not proof of anything, and here I am with a gun I got from your suitcase. That's all the proof I need."

Sweat was beading up on King-Roy's forehead. He seemed guilty standing there with this wild look in his eyes, and I wondered if for once Auntie Pie was right. What if he really did murder a man? What if he really was planning to kill us all in our sleep? All my romantic thoughts flew out the window. This was the way most of my fantasies turned out—just the opposite of whatever I imagined. I should have known it was all too good to be true.

"That's not my gun," King-Roy said. "You're calling me a murderer, but you're the one standing there with the gun in your hands."

"Don't try turning the tables on me, young man," Auntie Pie said. "You're the one who brought a gun into this house." She brought her other hand up to help her steady the wobbling gun. I could see her wrist was getting tired.

"My friend thought I needed protection, so he gave that gun to me."

"Protection from what? Nobody around here is going to shoot you. Sounds like you've got a persecution complex, if you ask me. Everybody just goes around accusing you of murder and wants to kill you for no good reason, yet here you are with the gun."

"Oh they've got reason, all right, ma'am," King-Roy said, flashing his eyes at Auntie Pie. "I'm black. I'm a Negro, and that's reason enough, isn't it?" King-Roy's smooth milk-shake voice sounded angry or bitter or both.

Auntie Pie let go with one hand and waved the gun around again and said, "If this isn't loaded, why don't you just come take this out of my hands, then? If it isn't loaded."

I was ducking and swaying every time Auntie Pie swung the gun toward me while she spoke, but I noticed King-Roy stood right where he was.

"Because, ma'am, I'm showing you the respect I wish you'd'a' shown me and my belongings," he said. His glance shifted back and forth between the suitcase on the porch and the gun in Auntie Pie's hands.

He said, "If you want to see the gun isn't loaded, just—"

Auntie Pie didn't let him finish his sentence. She waved the gun around again and said, "You'd like that, now, wouldn't you? I get busy checking for bullets, and you dart forward and overpower me and shoot me dead. I didn't just fall off the turnip truck yesterday, you know."

King-Roy and my aunt stood staring at one another for a good half minute, and then King-Roy said, his voice softer, gentler, "Well, then, ma'am, Miz...?"

"That's Auntie Pie—my aunt," I said, feeling like maybe I shouldn't be helping him.

King-Roy nodded. "Miz Pie, I think I will just have to remove that gun from your hands and show you myself that it's not loaded. Otherwise we're going to be standing like this all day."

King-Roy stepped forward, and Auntie Pie raised the gun up to eye level and said, "Stand still or I'll shoot," just like she was on *Gunsmoke* or something.

King-Roy tiptoed over to Auntie Pie and spoke to her like he was trying to calm a lunatic. "It's all right. Now, I'm just gon' show you it's empty. It would be nice if you could just hand me the gun. Could you do that, ma'am? Just hand me the gun?"

"Not on your life," Auntie Pie screeched. By this time, King-Roy was right up on her, and Auntie Pie dropped the gun on King-Roy's foot and ran out the door, back toward the gatehouse, shouting, "Run, Esther, run for your life!"

I didn't know what to do, so I stood right where I was, listening to the sound of my heart pounding in my ears. I watched King-Roy bend down and pick up the gun. "My oh my," he said, shaking his head. "I don't know about this."

He opened the gun and turned around to show me. "See, no bullets. I wouldn't bring a loaded gun into your house. I never owned a gun in my life—never even fired one."

I stepped forward and stretched my neck to see the empty gun. I let out a big breath of air and smiled at King-Roy.

"I knew it wasn't loaded," I said.

"That Auntie Pie's dangerous," King-Roy said, with a touch of anger still in his voice. "I don't know about staying here with someone like her running around loose and getting into my things. What gives her the right?"

"Oh, she's all right, really—most of the time. You just need to make friends with her."

King-Roy walked over to his suitcase, on the porch, and I followed him, standing over him while he crouched down to open the case. He used great care to tuck his gun underneath his folded shirts. Everything in his suitcase was folded to perfection. He had three shirts, all of them white, and two pairs of trousers, both brown, a shaving kit, a newspaperlike thing that said MUHAMMAD SPEAKS across the top, and a flyer with MALCOLM X written on the front of it in red letters. The name scared me. I didn't know much about Malcolm X except he hated white people and wanted to blow them all up. Seeing the flyer made me scared again, and I backed away.

King-Roy closed the lid and stood up with the suitcase in his hands. He turned around to face me. "Now, then," he said, "how am I gon' make friends with your Auntie Pie?"

I studied his face for a second, trying to read him, trying to decide if he was a good guy or a bad guy. I knew even murderers could be handsome, but I remembered our conversation in the ballroom and how sweet and gentle he seemed, and I said, "Well, it's simple. First, it helps if you like animals, because she's got a bunch of them down at the gatehouse. They're wild, wounded animals, and she fixes them up and sets them free again. But if you don't like animals, then just give her something sweet, like candy or a pie or cake. She's got a real sweet tooth."

"Is that so?"

I nodded. "It's easy as pie—literally," I said, hoping I wasn't betraying my aunt to a murderer. I shrugged off the thought and said, "Come on, I'll show you to your rooms."

King-Roy nodded, adjusted the suitcase in his hand, and held his hat in his other hand; then together we climbed the stairs.

"Is that how your aunt got her name?" King-Roy asked, stopping on the steps to look back at the foyer a second. "It can't really be Pie," he said, returning to me. "What's her real name?"

"Hyacinth," I said, running my hand along the curving banister. "I couldn't pronounce Hyacinth when I was little, so I called her Pie and it stuck. It suits her. I can't ever imagine her being called Hyacinth. It's too flowery, and Auntie Pie is not a flower; she's too full of piss and vinegar." I put my hand to my mouth and looked at King-Roy. "Oh, sorry, I shouldn't have said 'piss' in front of you."

King-Roy laughed his donkey laugh, then said, "You haven't said anything I haven't heard before."

I said, "It's not very ladylike, though," knowing how much my mother would disapprove. I glanced over at King-Roy and I could see a twinkle in King-Roy's eyes and I knew he really didn't mind, so I added, "But that's okay, because I'm never ladylike; just ask my mother."

"You don't like pretty dresses and jewelry and stuff?"

We were at the top of the stairs by this time, and I pointed with my thumb to the right.

"You're in the north wing with my brother and Mr. Vichy," I said. "My parents are in the wing to the left, and Beatrice's rooms are just beyond that door." I pointed to the door to the left of my parents'. "She gets the whole servants' quarters to herself—seven whole rooms—and she still complains. And, no, I don't like dresses and jewelry. If they would let us, I'd wear pants to school every day. I mean if boys can wear pants, why can't girls? All we can do is wear shorts under our skirts." I decided to come clean and tell the truth about myself. I was glad I hadn't had time to change into Beatrice's things. I was starting to get the feeling that King-Roy might like me just the way I was. "And perfume and colognes make me sick—literally," I added for good measure.

We walked down the hall past my sister's tidy pink

room. I kept talking. "A couple of years back I had real bad BO because my mother didn't notice that I was growing up and needed deodorant and—and things—so I sprinkled my father's English Leather cologne onto my slip so I would smell good and so Martha Reed at school would stop following me and telling me how bad I stunk. I always loved how my father smelled, so I thought that it was a good idea, but that stuff's strong. It was so strong, everyone in the school could smell me coming a mile away. I ended up getting sick from it in the middle of math class. I threw up right beside my desk and I got sent home, and Martha called me the Little Stinker that whole year, even after Mother got me the deodorant and everything. And Martha had braces on her legs, so she wasn't one to speak, if you ask me. But I never said anything about her braces."

"Well, you acted better, then, sounds like to me."

"Honestly?" I said, stopping in front of my bedroom and looking up into King-Roy's handsome face. "Not really. If I had been the better person, I wouldn't have even thought about her braces. Lots of times I thought about calling her bracey, or even tubby because she was also kind of plump. I didn't do it. I didn't call her anything out loud, but I thought it often enough."

"How come you didn't say anything, then?" King-Roy asked, setting his suitcase down as if he thought he was going to be staying in my room. "Were you afraid to?"

I shrugged. "Maybe a little. It wouldn't have been

very nice, would it? And I figured she probably called me the Little Stinker because she wanted people to see she wasn't the only one with problems. She only went to our school for a year. She didn't know me when I had my crossed eyes, thank goodness. Anyway, this is my room. I just thought you'd like to see it."

Most of the time my room was messy. Not a bad messy—with dirt and cookie crumbs and cockroaches or anything—but a good messy, with books and papers and clothes and sports equipment. I had cleaned it before King-Roy arrived, and as long as he didn't look in my closet, my room looked as neat as Stewart and Sophia always kept theirs.

King-Roy whistled. "This room's like a palace," he said.

I pointed out the real gold used to paint the carved work in the wood molding that runs around the top of the walls, and the way one side of my room looks just like a stage, the way it bows out with the floor-to-ceiling windows overlooking the lily pool and pavilion. King-Roy crossed the threshold and went over to the windows to look out.

"Nice," he said.

"That's why Beatrice Bonham, the actress, wants my room," I said, joining King-Roy at my windows. "She loves gold and diamonds and fur coats, and, of course, she loves the stage. My room is the most fancy room in the house except for my parents'. Look." I turned and pointed to my bed and chest of drawers. "That's all hand painted—those flower bouquets and the gold."

King-Roy crossed his arms in front of him and examined the furniture a moment, then said, "I don't know, maybe, but it doesn't seem like you and this room go together."

I shrugged. "My mother chose this room for me, so it's special even if I don't really care for it. I think she thinks if I live in a feminine room, I'll become more feminine. I think she worries about that—that I'm not turning out right or something." I shrugged. "Anyway, I like that Beatrice wants this room and I have it. It drives her crazy. She's always scheming to get it away from me." I looked up at King-Roy and felt this giddiness travel through me. I couldn't believe that here we were talking about school troubles and my room and what I liked to wear and about my mother. My jaw trembled with the excitement of getting to tell about myself to someone, knowing that he was listening.

"You know what?" I said. "I believe you're going to be the first houseguest I've ever really liked."

King-Roy smiled, then turned back around and gazed through the windows. I watched him staring down at the lily pond. I studied his face and noticed how flat his nose looked from the side and how sad it made him look somehow, and I knew somebody as gentle and sad-looking as King-Roy could never be a killer. I smiled to myself and joined him looking down on the lily pond and the fields and gardens. After a few minutes King-Roy turned his head and said, "You ever had a day, or maybe just a moment, that changed your life forever?"

I shrugged and crossed my arms in front of me. "I don't know."

"Oh, you'd know it if you did. It happens and then all of a sudden you aren't thinking the same about anything anymore. Everything's changed."

"What happened? What was your moment?"

Before he could answer me we heard footsteps on the stairs, and I tensed up. "That's her," I said. "That's my mother. Please, don't tell her I said 'piss,' okay? She doesn't like me talking like that."

King-Roy nodded. "All right," he said.

We moved over to the doorway of my room and watched my mother walking down the hallway. I could tell by the company smile she wore that Auntie Pie hadn't told her about the gun yet. If she had, I knew King-Roy would be out the door and on his way back to Alabama and I wouldn't be able to bear it. I liked this King-Roy Johnson, and for some reason I couldn't explain, even to myself, I felt most desperate for him to stay.

FIVE

I watched my mother coming down the hall and wondered what King-Roy thought of her. Had his mother told him how beautiful she is? Did his mother even know? Our mothers had been best friends up until the third grade, but then they had to stop being friends in public because people in town didn't like it. Mother said King-Roy's mother could have gotten hurt if they were seen playing together, so they had stopped and only saw each other on occasion and in secret, and eventually, they drifted apart.

Most people say Mother looks like Jackie Kennedy, only prettier. She's tall and slender, with a small waist and perfect posture, and she's a brunette and she has almond-shaped brown eyes and her rounded chin sticks out just the slightest bit at the end. My little sister is going to grow up to look just like her, as far as I can tell.

I waited until my mother got close enough to us that I didn't have to raise my voice before I said, "Mother, this is Mr. King-Roy Johnson." My mother didn't like me to raise my voice. She always said my voice was so loud it could shatter glass.

Mother's smile broadened and she extended her hand toward King-Roy. "I'm so pleased to meet you," she said. "I'm sorry I wasn't here to greet you when you arrived. You're early today, I believe, and yesterday, when you were supposed to come, you got lost?"

Mother tilted her head, still smiling, and yet I saw in her eyes a flash of annoyance. I hoped that King-Roy didn't see it. The look came and went so fast, and I figured since King-Roy didn't know Mother yet, he wouldn't catch it; but I saw by the way he drew back from her, even taking a step back with one foot, that he had.

"Yes, ma'am, I got lost in New York City yesterday, and today I'm early," he said, without stammering or looking away. "I didn't know how long it would take me to get here. I'm sorry if I arrived at an inconvenient time."

"Not at all," Mother said, even though her eyes said, "Of course you did."

Mother turned to me. "Esther, I went shopping on my way home. Would you go downstairs and unload the groceries, please?"

"But I was showing King-Roy the house. I wanted to show him his rooms. I wanted to be the one to show him."

Mother closed her eyes a moment, then opened them again. "The ice cream is melting, Esther. I'll show Mr. Johnson his rooms."

I didn't want to leave. I wanted to show King-Roy the house. I was so proud of our house—my house. Someday, I would own this house. That was my dream.

I knew that my parents didn't hold out much hope for my success in life, but my dream, my fantasy, was to someday walk up to my parents and surprise them with buckets of money and say, "I'd like to buy this house from you—in cash."

I saw Stewart and Sophia coming down the hallway, still in their audition outfits of matching stretch pants and tops, looking both so adorable. Sophia was a miniature of my mother and had her hair pulled up in a perfect little bun, and Stewart, with his mop-top head of golden curls, looked like a little prince. I saw my mother's eyes light up. She lifted her head and said, "Ah, here they come." She held out her hand, and Stewart and Sophia trotted up to Mother. "Mr. Johnson, these are my other two children. Sophia, Stewart, say hello to Mr. King-Roy Johnson."

Sophia, being the little charmer, curtsied and said, "*Roy* is French for 'King,' so your name is really King-King, did you know that?"

Before King-Roy could answer, Stewart said, "Of course he knows that; everybody knows that, even Esther." He held out his hand and said, "It's very nice to meet you," all in his sweet high-pitched little voice.

King-Roy leaned forward and took each hand and shook it saying, "It's nice to meet y'all. Miz Sophia, you're mighty pretty, and, Mr. Stewart, you look right tall for a boy of ten."

King-Roy had said just the right thing. Sophia and Stewart both beamed.

Then Mother said, "Stewart, Sophia, I'd like you to show King—"

I knew what was coming and I tried to head it off by jumping in and saying, "But Mother, *I* was showing him the house. Please, please let me show it to him—please."

"Esther, enough. Sophia and Stewart can show—"

Again I didn't let her finish. I raised my voice to block out hers. "No! Mother, please, let me show him." I could hear the whine in my voice and I knew I sounded like a baby, but I just wanted to be the one. I wanted King-Roy to be my special friend. Mr. Vichy thought Stewart was the greatest boy child in the world, brilliant and handsome and complex, and Beatrice doted on Sophia. Everyone always doted on the beautiful little genius, Sophia. I wanted King-Roy to like me, especially me. I wanted him to tell me about the moment that changed his life and for it to be a secret between us. For once, I wanted a visitor to like me best.

I felt tears stinging my eyes. I blinked several times, refusing to cry. "Mother, I can run down and put up the groceries and then show him the house. I'll be really quick and—"

Mother took a deep breath and then in a firm voice said, "Esther Josephine Young, do as you are told!" Then she glared at me as if she wanted to rip my throat out of my neck. I knew she was more furious than usual because I had created a scene in front of our new guest. Mother hated scenes, particularly mine.

I swallowed hard and nodded. "Yes, Mother. I'm

sorry." I looked at King-Roy, who stood with his head bent and his arms down in front of him, one hand folded over the other, his hat dangling between two fingers, as if he were praying. I said to him in a voice that imitated my mother's exactly, "I'm sorry for my behavior, King-Roy. You must think that I am very silly. Stewart and Sophia will show you your rooms while I put up the groceries. If you will please excuse me."

I broke through the group standing there, pushing aside Stewart and Sophia just the littlest bit to get through, and headed toward the stairs. I moved slowly, listening to my mother make her excuses for my behavior.

"She just gets herself so wound up sometimes. I'm sure she talked your ear off. I'm sorry if her little scene has upset you."

"No, ma'am. Miz Esther has been good company and I've been most glad to have it."

When I heard King-Roy say that, I wanted to make the biggest scene ever. I wanted to turn around and run down the hallway to Mr. King-Roy Johnson and throw my arms around his neck. Even if he didn't mean it, even if he said it just to be polite, he had contradicted Mother. He had stood up for me. I made a run for the stairway, quickly, before I found myself making a scene that would get both King-Roy and me in trouble.

SIX

I had just put away the last of the groceries, hiding the cookies and pies so Auntie Pie wouldn't find them and dig into them before anyone else had a chance to eat any, when Beatrice glided in with the Beast in her arms.

Beatrice Bonham, the bottle-blond actress, had arrived with her enormous bosom and her pesky dog, Prissy, a shih tzu, three years ago, and, as far as I knew, had no intention of ever leaving.

The shih tzu was the devil herself and tore up my favorite pair of sneakers—a pair of boy's Converse All Stars that I had found in the lost-and-found at school. They hadn't been claimed in over a year, and Coach O'Keefe said I could have them. I could have strangled the little Beast for eating those sneakers, and I refused to allow Beatrice or the Beast in my room, but I knew she came in anyway when I wasn't there. I once found one of little Prissy's red hair ribbons on the floor of my room, and on that same day, my 1922 silver Peace Dollar disappeared out of my piggy bank—my only silver Peace Dollar. Mother had once warned us that Beatrice could be a little light fingered, and apparently she was. If she could figure out a way, she'd steal my bedroom right out from under me while I slept and leave me lying in the mud.

Beatrice came into the kitchen that afternoon dressed in a shimmery peignoir set just when I was finally free of the groceries and could rush out to the gatehouse and try to convince Auntie Pie not to tell Mother about finding a gun in King-Roy's suitcase. I couldn't bear it if Mother found out and sent him packing. I just couldn't bear the thought of it, but Beatrice liked getting attention, needed attention, and even though I was always her last and worst choice for somebody to talk to, I was there and I could see she wanted to talk, so I stayed put. Before she could open her mouth, though, I said, hoping to hurry her on her way, "You know Mother doesn't like the Beast in the kitchen, near the food."

Beatrice sniffed. "And I don't like my little Prissy being called the Beast, especially today. Don't you have any sensitivity at all?"

I had forgotten. Last night had been Beatrice's last performance. She was officially out of a job, and as I had learned the last time she was between plays, nothing was worse than Beatrice with time on her hands.

"Sorry," I said. "I forgot. How did it go—your last performance?" I glanced out the window, checking to see if Auntie Pie was coming. She wasn't.

Beatrice slid into a chair at the kitchen table and set her bosom and the Beast down on top. "I got a standing ovation, as a matter of fact. Too bad no reviewers were there to see that!" She fiddled with her flowing gauzy sleeves and watched me while I hunted around for a hiding place for the last bag of cookies, then she said, "Hey, how about handing me some of those. Might as well have a few before Auntie Pie gets hold of them. And some tomato juice, if you've got any. Would you do that for me, hon?"

I set the bag on the table and the Beast crept toward it as if she thought it was an exploding dog turd. Before she could figure out it was something to eat, I shoved the bag toward Beatrice and got out the tomato juice.

"Oh, by the by," Beatrice said. "I noticed the old station wagon was out of the garage. I notice those things, you know, since all my rooms overlook the garages and the porte cochere—the servants' view, you know. You'd better get your aunt to move that old bus out of sight before your mother finds it. I don't think I could stand your mother in one of her moods today. I'm just too tired." Beatrice put the back of her hand up to her forehead and added, "It's been a ghastly week."

I set a glass and the can of juice on the table and said, "Too late. Mother is already upset with me."

Beatrice picked up the can and set it down again with a bang, which I knew hurt her with her hangover more than it hurt me. "You and your scenes. Honestly, Esther, when are you going to grow up?"

I ignored her question, figuring it was rhetorical, and said, "I'd better go find Auntie Pie and warn her—uh, tell her—about the car."

I turned to leave, and Beatrice grabbed my arm. Her hand was cold, and her glossy pink nails dug into my flesh.

"Wait," she said. "Has Mr. Johnson, that Negro, arrived?"

I nodded and removed my arm from her grasp. "Yes, he did. He sure did. He arrived early, before Mother got back from the auditions."

"And? What's he like? Is he handsome?"

"I think so," I said with my face turned toward the window so Beatrice couldn't see me blush.

"Oh really?"

I heard the curious tone in her voice and turned around.

Beatrice had sat up and was patting the back of her over-sprayed coiffure. I watched her glance slide sideways—her scheming and conniving look. "Hmm," she said, finally. "Too bad he's a Negro, but just the same..."

I stepped away from the window and glared at her. "You'd better leave him alone. I know just what you're thinking," I said. "You think you're going to have some kind of—of exotic romance with him or something—a summer fling. Well, you'd just better give it up," I said, disgusted with her all of a sudden. "Just leave King-Roy alone. Anyway, he's not your type."

"Oh? And whose type is he? Yours, perhaps?"

I felt my face flush again and I turned back to the window. "He's only eighteen years old. He's way too young for you, and anyway, men fall all over themselves to get at you. You don't need to chase after King-Roy."

Beatrice sniffed and said, "Just how old do you think I am?"

I turned to look at her. I figured it had to take at least forty years to build a bosom like hers, so I said, "Forty, forty-five, maybe."

Beatrice's eyes almost fell out of her head. "I'll have you know I am just thirty-three years old, thank you very much."

"Well, that's still too old for King-Roy."

Beatrice shrugged and her peignoir slipped off her right shoulder. She didn't fix it. "Some men prefer older women," she said.

"Yeah, well, he's not one of them, so leave him alone."

"Honey pie, I don't know a teenage boy alive who isn't interested in an older woman showing him the ropes, so to speak."

Beatrice always turned everything into some kind of sex-talk innuendo thing and I hated it. I wanted to tell her to go wash her filthy mouth out with soap, but before I could say anything I heard Mother coming down the back stairs and I sprang away from the window. I didn't have a reason. I hadn't done anything wrong that I could think of, but I made a quick inventory of my actions over the last half hour to be sure.

Beatrice jumped up from the table and grabbed the Beast. "I wasn't here," she whispered, before scurrying toward the other end of the kitchen, where the laundry room and another set of back stairs that went to the servants' quarters were.

When Mother opened the door at the bottom of the stairs and entered the kitchen, she saw me standing in front of a plate with one cookie left on it and a half-drunk glass of tomato juice. I hadn't had a snack that day, but it was close to dinnertime so I knew she wouldn't be pleased.

She sighed when she saw the snack on the table and said in a voice that told me she'd had enough of me for one day, "It's close to dinnertime. You know better than that. When are you going to grow up?"

I shrugged and stood there like a dumb stick.

She grabbed up the plate with the cookie and carried it to the sink. Then with her back to me and ice in her voice, she said, "That was quite a little scene we had upstairs."

"I'm sorry, Mother," I said, "but it's just that I was the one who had fixed up his room for him. Even though I thought of him as a murderer then, I fixed it up nice. I made his bed real neat, with hospital corners, and I picked flowers from the garden and put them in a crystal vase, and I dusted the table and plumped the pillows in his sitting room and vacuumed—I did it all. I just wanted to show him what I had done."

"If you had paid that kind of attention to your schoolwork this year, maybe your report card would have been better. You realize, don't you,"—Mother turned around—"I've just given up on you, Esther. I've given up. No tutors this summer. You're on your own in school next year."

"Yes, Mother, and I appreciate it, I really do."

That seemed to infuriate her. I could tell by the way her face broke out in red blotches.

"You appreciate it? I tell you I've given up on you and you appreciate it?"

I knew if my mother could only see things from my side, she'd understand. I was free. This summer would be my first real vacation since my second third grade. Being on the receiving end of too much of my mother's attention was too much of a bad thing in my book, but I could see from my mother's point of view that she was wanting to make me feel ashamed of myself, so I'd try harder in school and she wouldn't have to give up on me. I didn't want to encourage her, so I just stood there and said nothing in response. Mother didn't need encouragement. She went on without it.

"You got a C in French," Mother said. "With Mr. Vichy living with us and speaking French all the time. It's shameful."

Since the only thing Mr. Vichy said in French were insults to me and praises for Stewart and Sophia, I didn't pay much attention to him or his language.

"Okay, Mother, I'll try harder next year," I said without feeling.

"I'm sure you will," Mother said, turning to me and forcing a smile—the sign that her pick-on-Esther jag was over for the moment.

"Now come on and help me get dinner ready. Our Mr. Johnson has not started off on the right foot here, has he? First he gets lost between getting off the bus and finding the train station, and then he arrives early today, when Daisy has the day off, and when we're not ready to receive him properly."

"But you cook great, Mother, just as good as Daisy, and the house is still clean from yesterday. Anyway, he can't help it if he got lost. He did his best to get here real fast. You said he had to get out of town," I said, glancing out the window for Auntie Pie, then following my mother to the refrigerator. "You said he'd been on the bus all day and all night to get here and he had almost no money and nowhere to go, remember? I bet he was scared last night, lost in a big city like New York."

"Esther, don't tell me what I've said. I know what I've said. The whole thing's just very inconvenient." Mother handed me the broccoli and a bunch of carrots with the tops still on. I carried them over to the counter.

"You sound like you don't trust him all of a sudden, when you were the one who said he was okay, and, Mother, he is," I said, turning back to the refrigerator and taking the swordfish out of Mother's hands. "He's great, just like you said he was going to be." I set the fish in the sink and dug a broiling pan out from under the counter.

Mother grabbed a bib apron and tied it over her green shift with the belt that cinched in her waist so it looked real small and gave her skinny hips some shape.

"I know I never said he was great, Esther. Do I speak like that?"

"You know what I mean. You said you loved your maid Cassie and her two children more than anybody. You said Cassie was like a mother to you and her girl Luray was your best friend when you were little. You said any kin of theirs would always be welcome in your house and you said—"

"Esther, what did I just get through telling you?"

"Not to tell you what you said?"

"Exactly. Now, Cassie has been very honest with me about King-Roy's troubles at home and—"

I interrupted, "And you said it was up to us to show Mr. Johnson that not everyone who comes from the South is prejudiced against Negroes." I nodded.

"And I meant all that." Mother returned to the refrigerator. "I don't cotton to people who judge others by the color of their skin or where they came from or how much money they have, and I don't expect you to, either, Esther."

Whenever we talked about the South, Mother's southern accent got stronger and deeper, and she used words like *cotton to,* and *fixin' to,* and *terectly.* I always liked her best when she let go of herself enough to let her Alabama roots show.

Mother continued, "There are lots of people in the South who feel the way I do. Unfortunately, we're the minority down there."

I turned from the sink, where I had begun chopping the carrots, and saw my mother coming toward me. I felt so proud of her for being so unprejudiced and letting King-Roy come stay that I just turned and grabbed her in a big bear hug, not realizing until it was too late that she had a blueberry pie in her hands.

"Esther! Let go of me," Mother said, her voice muffled by my shoulder.

I let go and stepped back. I knew I had upset her, but I didn't yet know why.

"Now look at this! Just look!"

I did look and I saw that Mother's chest, the bib of the apron, and parts of her dress were covered in blueberry pie, and Mother's face looked furious.

"Oh, Mother, I didn't see. I didn't mean to—I—"

"No, of course not!" Mother said. "Esther, sometimes I wonder where your head is. I found this pie in the vegetable bin."

"I was hiding it from Auntie Pie. I'm sorry, Mother, really. I was just wanting to give you a hug and I didn't see."

Mother set the remainder of the pie down on the counter, then moved to the sink and dabbed at her chest with a sponge. "Esther, at your age and height you can't afford to be clumsy and thoughtless. You've ruined my dress, do you see that?" She glanced at me a second and I nodded.

"I'm so sorry, Mother. I am."

Mother calmed down a little and shook her head. "You're a big girl, Esther. You're not Sophia. You can't just grab me like that, you understand?"

I didn't need anyone to remind me that I wasn't Sophia, but I didn't have time to dwell on that thought or on the stains on Mother's dress; Auntie Pie was coming. I saw her through the window, marching straight for the kitchen, looking like she had something to say, and I knew just what it was.

SEVEN

I left Mother in mid-sentence, still dabbing at her dress, and ran out the kitchen door to catch up with Auntie Pie. I heard Mother calling after me.

"Esther, what in the world! You come on back in here."

I ignored Mother and ran down the driveway toward Auntie Pie. I caught up to her and said, "You didn't put the car back. Beatrice saw it."

Auntie Pie held her chin forward and her thin lips pressed hard together. She kept walking toward the kitchen door.

"Did you hear me? We've got to go move the car and I've got to talk to you."

"And I've got to talk to your mother," she said.

I stood in front of Auntie Pie, walking backward, trying to keep her from seeing Mother at the kitchen window. "What about?"

Auntie Pie tried to brush me aside. "Get out of my way, little girl. I am on a mission of mercy. If we're not careful we'll all be shot dead in our sleep. He must think we're as stupid as pudding."

"Auntie Pie, he's not like that."

"What do you know?"

"I know there weren't any bullets in that gun. I saw with my own eyes." I kept walking backward and Auntie Pie kept aiming for the kitchen door. I felt desperate. We were almost at the door. "Auntie Pie, stop!" I said, holding up my hand and stopping in front of her.

Auntie Pie stopped and put her hands on her hips. "Let me by."

"I know what's really going on here," I said, standing firm. "You're prejudiced. You're afraid of colored people." I said this not really believing it, but when I saw Auntie Pie's expression I changed my mind.

Her face had turned almost purple.

I pointed at her. "It's true. You are! Why, Auntie Pie, you're prejudiced."

She swatted at my hand. "Don't you point your finger at me. I like our Daisy just fine. I have no problem with her or any other Negro person, but this man is a stranger and he's been accused of murder and he has a gun in his suitcase. I have a right to be concerned about the safety of this family."

"But he's not a murderer. That was just some white men putting the blame on him. He didn't do it. You know he didn't. You're acting just like the KKK blaming him. You might as well just put a sheet over your head and carry a flaming cross."

"That's enough. I'm not listening to you. Get out of the way, now."

"No, I won't let you. You can't tell."

Auntie Pie tried to push me aside and I pushed back. "I want him to stay. Auntie Pie, I need him. Please!" I didn't know why I felt so desperate. I couldn't explain it if I had to, but I did feel desperate. I needed him. I needed him for so many reasons.

Again Auntie Pie pushed me and I pushed back, but this time she fell. She fell down onto the gravel.

"Oh, Auntie Pie." I stooped down to help her up. "I'm so sorry. I didn't—"

Auntie Pie caught hold of the front of my shirt and pulled me forward. I didn't know if she was trying to get up or trying to fight me. I landed on top of her and she yelled and pounded on my arms and back. "Get off of me, you—you . . . gorilla!"

"What in heaven's name is going on here? Esther, get up off of your great-aunt this instant. What has gotten into you? I am appalled!"

Mother stood on the stoop behind us with a chopping knife in her hand. I made a move to get up, stirring the gravel with my hands as I did, hoping to make enough noise so that Mother wouldn't hear what I was about to say. I whispered into Auntie Pie's ear, "If you tell, I'll tell Mother how you left me there with him and the gun when you thought it was loaded. She'll be furious with King-Roy, and then King-Roy will be after you."

"Esther Josephine! Did you hear what I said? Get off of your aunt this instant. I am ashamed of you!"

I rolled off of my aunt and stood up. Then I leaned forward, offering my hand for her to take so I could help her up.

Auntie Pie didn't take it. She rolled away from me and eased herself up onto her knees and then stood up, using a hand on one knee to brace herself. Her hair, usually in an old-lady bun, had come undone. I was surprised at how long her hair really was. It ran all the way down her back.

"I do not know what to think," Mother said. "Esther, you go to your room and you don't come out until you can explain yourself."

I looked at Auntie Pie, then over at my mother. I couldn't tell by Auntie Pie's expression whether she would tell or not, but I knew just what my mother was thinking. She looked ready to spit in my eye.

"I don't need to go to my room, Mother. I'm ready to explain right now." I pinched my lips together and squinted mean-eyed at my aunt for a good long second. Then I turned around and said, "I need to tell you what happened this afternoon."

Auntie Pie came up behind me and shoved her shoulder into my arm and said, "No, I'll tell her what happened."

I looked down at my aunt, standing beside me, and tried to guess what she would say. Was she going to tell about the gun? She was hard to read. I couldn't take a chance.

I began, "You see, this morning we were out collecting dead squirrels and—"

Auntie Pie shoved me so hard, I fell to the ground. "I said, *I*'d tell it!" she shouted.

Mother held her hand with the knife in it up in the air and said, "Stop it, both of you." She looked at me sitting on the ground wiping the gravel out of my palms and said, "Esther, go to your room and stay there until I tell you to come out. And Auntie Pie—well, I can't send you to your room, but I'd like to. I never thought I'd see the day when I'd see you sink to her level."

Auntie Pie wagged her finger at Mother and said, "Don't you talk to me like I'm one of your children, Nora."

I stood up and waited to hear what else Auntie Pie would tell Mother, but Mother saw me just standing there and she waved her knife at me. "Go on, now, Esther. I won't tell you again."

I marched off toward the front of the house, and the last thing I heard was Mother saying to Auntie Pie, "Now, what was so important that you had to tell me?"

EIGHT

Mother didn't come get me for dinner, so all through the dinner hour I wondered and worried about King-Roy Johnson. Had Mother asked him to leave? Did Auntie Pie tell on him? I tried to be patient while I waited for everyone to come up to bed. I read Dr. Norman Vincent Peale's book, *A Guide to Confident Living,* and his chapter on how to avoid getting upset, and I listened to my transistor radio, waiting for *Surfin' USA* to come on. I wasn't allowed to own any Beach Boys records because Mother said she would not have music in our house by a group of teenaged boys who promoted hedonism as a lifestyle. I tried to explain to Mother how she was costing me my friendships with Laura and Kathy because they didn't want to come over to our house anymore.

The last time I had tried inviting my girlfriends over, Laura had said, "It's just not fun at your house. You don't have any cool record albums, and I've kind of grown out of the secret rooms and Nancy Drew stuff."

Kathy had agreed. "Yeah, Esther. Your house was fun when we were kids, but what's there to do there anymore? And your house is too far away, anyway."

When I told Mother this, she had said, "If all those girls want to do is ruin their minds with loud hedonistic music, then you're better off without them," which showed how much she knew about my life. Without Kathy and Laura, all I had was Pip, and Pip was just one more reason why they didn't want to come over anymore. "Why's Pip-squeak always over there? He's so immature," Laura had said.

"Yeah, Esther, he's so immature," Kathy had agreed.

So I listened for *Surfin' USA* on the transistor and listened for footsteps in the hallway. It seemed like no one was ever going to come up to bed. At one point I heard Sophia and Stewart singing "Dites Moi" from the play, *South Pacific,* and that at least gave me hope that King-Roy was still there. Mother always had my brother and sister entertain new guests.

At last I heard footsteps, and I jumped off my bed and ran to my doorway to listen. First came Sophia and Mother, and soon after I heard the footsteps of Beatrice and the Beast and a few minutes later, Stewart's and Auntie Pie's footsteps, and then that was all and I thought King-Roy must have left. Mother would never have left a new guest downstairs in our house alone. Despite Dr. Norman Vincent Peale's advice, I was upset. I couldn't stand not knowing what had happened, so I scooted on down to Auntie Pie's room and knocked on her door.

"Auntie Pie, it's me."

"Go away."

"Auntie Pie."

There was silence and then finally, with a sigh, "Come in."

I opened the door. Auntie Pie was sitting up in bed, with a tray on her lap, eating a piece of rum-nut cake and reading one of her Gothic romances.

She looked up at me and said, her voice cross, "What do you want? I'm right in the middle of the denouement."

"What did you tell Mother?" I came over and sat down on the edge of Auntie Pie's bed, sending her plate sliding to the far side of her tray.

"Hey there, you! Get up off my bed. You're making me spill."

I stood up. "Well? What did you say?"

Auntie Pie took a large bite of her cake and mumbled, "About what?"

"About King-Roy. About King-Roy, Auntie Pie. What did you tell Mother? Come on, you know what I mean."

Auntie Pie smiled and a piece of walnut showed, stuck between her front teeth.

"I told her about the gun, just like I said I would. What did you think? You think you could blackmail me into not telling her? Are you a blackmailer now?"

"Oh, Auntie Pie, you didn't. How could you?" I flopped back down on the bed, forgetting about the cake.

"Hey, watch it! Now look what you've done."

The cake and all its many crumbs had slid off the

tray and onto Auntie Pie's bedspread. She held her hands up in the air and looked down at the mess with dismay.

"I'm sorry, Auntie Pie." I felt tears stinging my eyes, and I tried to blink them away while I helped her clean up the mess.

"I hate this day. I hate everything about it," I said, giving up and letting the tears fall. "I thought—I had hoped—well, it doesn't matter. King-Roy's gone and that's that."

"He's not gone. Did I say that he was gone?" Auntie Pie had gotten out of the bed and was helping me brush the crumbs off the bed and onto the floor.

I looked across the bed at her and said, "But you said—"

"I said I told your mother, but he's still here."

"But . . ." I looked toward the hallway.

"But nothing. As it turns out, our Mr. Johnson had already told your mother everything. He said he didn't want the gun in the house, and your mother took it and threw it in the trash. The end." Auntie Pie stood looking at me with her finger in her mouth, trying to dislodge more nuts from her teeth.

I reached across the bed and grabbed her and gave her a peck on the cheek. "I knew he was a good guy. Thanks, Auntie Pie."

"Would you let go of me and get out now?" she said, exasperated.

I let go and she fell forward, reaching her hands out to catch herself before she landed face-first on the bed.

Her right palm landed in her plate of cake and smashed it flat. "Now look," she said. "Honestly, you're just like a white tornado. Get out before you bring the ceiling down on me."

I hurried out of the room and ran to the top of the staircase to listen for King-Roy. I wanted to see him one more time before I went to bed. I just had to see with my own eyes that he was still there.

I leaned over the banister and stretched my neck and listened for him. I heard voices. Monsieur Vichy and Dad were home. I heard King-Roy say, "Yes sir, same to you, good night, now."

I clapped silently and bounced on the balls of my feet and listened for King-Roy to climb the stairs.

There it was, the *tap-tap* of his footsteps. I heard him approaching, and I stood back at the top of the staircase to wait for him. Then, just before he rounded the corner, just before I saw him again, I looked down at myself and realized all I had on was a T-shirt and my underpants, which is all I ever wore when I went to bed. I squealed and ran down the hall.

I heard Auntie Pie call out, "Get to bed, Esther," as I passed her room, and Sophia called out, "You okay?" as I passed hers. I didn't answer either of them. I ran into my room and jumped back into my Bermuda shorts, then I ran back into the hallway and crashed right into King-Roy on his way down to his room. He held a can of paint in each hand, and these were what I hit up against when we crashed. Both cans knocked into my hips and I knew I'd get some ugly bruises from them but I didn't care. King-Roy was there. I could feel my heart pounding. After we both said, "Omph," from the crash, King-Roy clutched the paint cans to his own hips and said, "Well, hey, there you are. I missed you at dinner."

"You did?" I looked into King-Roy's face to see if he was being sincere. He looked sincere, there in the yellow glow of the night-light Mother always turned on before bed. His face, ocher from the night-light, held that quiet expression he had worn when I first met him.

He held up the paint cans. "Your momma gave me work to do. I'm to paint the laundry room. Imagine that, a whole room just for laundry." He shook his head.

I nodded. "You could park four limousines in that laundry room and still have room to skate around in it. It's that big," I said.

"Well, I'm not complaining, I need the work. I need to make me some money. Does she pay well?"

"If you do a good job she does, but Mother's a perfectionist, so don't take any shortcuts."

"Thanks for the tip. I'll do her a good job, all right. Well, good night, then."

He started to leave and I grabbed hold of his shirt. "Wait. Uh—this afternoon you were going to tell me about the day that changed your life. Remember?" I didn't want him to leave yet. I wanted something from him, but I didn't know what. I just wanted him to come into my room, sit down, have a talk. I wanted to get to know him, figure him out. Mother always said I made people uncomfortable, the way I looked at them, the way I sort of attacked them like I wanted to crawl inside them and get up in their heads. She said I unnerved people. Maybe she was right. I could see King-Roy pulling away.

"Tomorrow sometime," he said, withdrawing his arm from my grasp.

I let go, tried another tack. "So, how was dinner?"

King-Roy wrinkled up his nose. "You want the truth? Your momma's been up north too long. She cooked New York food. Tasted like cardboard with baking-soda sauce." He shook his head. "First time in my life I ever sat down to supper with white folks."

"Really?" I said.

King-Roy lifted his hand and, with the paint can hanging from his palm, scratched his nose. "Where am I gon' eat with whites in the South? I can't even look out the same window as them down there." King-Roy lifted his chin. "So where were you, anyway? Why weren't you at dinner?"

I shrugged. "Auntie Pie and I got into an argument, and I lost. Mother sent me to my room."

"Too bad. You must be hungry. I would have been happy to save you off some of my supper."

"I'm starving, but that doesn't matter, as long as you can stay here. You *can* stay, can't you? Mother didn't tell you to leave or anything—because of the gun?"

King-Roy shook his head. "No, it's all right."

I grinned from ear to ear. I know I did. "I'm so glad," I said.

King-Roy said, "Yeah, it's all right," but he didn't look so happy about it. He said, "Now you go on and get a good night's sleep. We all wore ourselves out today, sure 'nuff."

"Oh, I'm not tired. I never sleep much. My father says I have the Young curse. Everyone on his side of the family tends to burn the candle at both ends." I knew I was just talking, trying to keep him with me just a little longer.

King-Roy nodded. "Well, good night, now. Be seeing you in the morning."

I touched King-Roy's sleeve. "Good night, King-Roy. See you tomorrow."

I watched King-Roy walk down the hall, and I noticed he was walking funny, like he had a leg ache or something. He reached the end of our wing and was just about to turn left to go to his rooms when I heard a thud and saw something fall out of the leg of his pants. I couldn't tell what it was because his pant leg was still covering most of it, and even with the night-light, the hallway was too dim to see well.

King-Roy said, "Shoot," and looked back at me.

I ran forward. "I'll get it," I said, thinking he wanted me to pick up what he had dropped.

King-Roy panicked. "No!" he said, starting to bolt, then, I guess, remembering the object on the floor, he stopped and stooped down, still with the cans of paint in his hands. Before he could release the handles, before he could reach down and pick up what he had dropped,

I was there, on the floor, and I grabbed it up for him. I had only wanted to help. I had only wanted to be his friend, but when I saw what I held in my hand, when I felt the weight of it, the coolness of it against my skin, I knew I had made a mistake.

"It's—it's your gun. The one Mother threw away in the trash. Auntie Pie said so." I looked at him. Our heads were almost touching, we were so close, stooped there in the hallway. I could smell his sweat. I could see fear in his eyes.

"I sure wish you hadn't seen that," King-Roy said. He pulled the gun out of my hand, moving slowly, being really careful, as though it was loaded. Then he stood up and tucked it back into the waistband of his pants.

"Can we just pretend you didn't see that?" he asked me, whispering.

"I—I don't know," I said, standing up with him. "I don't understand. How come you took the gun back?" I kept my voice low, and when I said *gun*, even I couldn't hear it, but I knew King-Roy understood.

"Because it doesn't belong to me. I'm gon' have to give it back someday."

"Whose is it, then?"

He studied my face and asked, "Can I trust you?"

I nodded, wondering what he was about to tell me. I felt scared. Standing with King-Roy in that narrow, dimly lit hall felt dangerous all of a sudden. The hallway didn't look familiar to me anymore; it didn't feel safe. In my heart everything felt dangerous.

King-Roy lowered his head so that it was closer to mine and said, "I met someone on the bus on the way up here. A man. We rode together for two days. For two days this man—Ax is his name; short for Accident—he told me things. He told me things I'd never heard before. Things I could hardly believe, but it made a lot of sense."

King-Roy stopped talking and picked the paint cans back up as though that was it, that was all he had to say, so I asked him, "What did he tell you? Was it about the gun? Why did he give it to you?" Again, I only mouthed the word *gun*.

"For protection. That's all, just for protection."

"But from what?" I asked, wondering what kind of protection someone needed in our little town.

King-Roy lowered his head again and said, "From the white devil."

I pulled my head back. "What's that?"

King-Roy looked to his left and right and leaned in toward me. "I shouldn't be telling you this."

"Sure you should," I whispered, too curious to let him stop now.

I could see a look of doubt in King-Roy's face, so I took hold of his wrist and tugged on him to follow me. I led him back to my bedroom and we went inside and I closed the door behind us.

NINE

King-Roy turned around at the sound of the door clicking shut. His eyes were wide and his head was shaking as though he was saying no.

"This isn't good. I can't be in your room at night with the door closed," he said.

"Why not? It's okay. Nobody cares," I said, moving around him, then turning to face him.

King-Roy backed up toward the door. "People care aplenty." He spoke with his voice just above a whisper, so I did, too.

"Not here, they don't. Not in New York. Not at my house," I said, moving closer to King-Roy until I saw him backing away from me again, then I stopped and we just stood facing each other. King-Roy still had the paint cans in his hands, and I thought the handles had to be digging into his palms.

"At least you can put the paint cans down," I said.

King-Roy shook his head. "No, I'll hold on to them. I can't be accused of doing anything with my hands full of paint, can I?"

I moved over to my bedside table and turned off my

radio. "So what's the white devil?" I asked, hoping to get him away from his fear of getting caught in my room and back to what we were talking about.

King-Roy looked miserable. His eyes were all over the place, glancing at the door, at the windows, at my closet door, at me. Then he said, "You're not the right person I should be talking to about that."

"Why not?" I asked, sitting down at my study table and wishing King-Roy would join me. I didn't understand anything. King-Roy's face wore two lines between his brows and they deepened when he said, "Because you're white. Don't you see? You're a white girl, a white devil."

"Me? A white devil?" I asked. "But you don't need protection against *me*. At least not gun protection, do you?"

King-Roy said, "I don't rightly know who I need protection from. It's different up here in New York. The rules for black and white are different up here, but Ax says just because I can sit down with y'all at the same dinner table and sleep under the same roof with y'all, that I'm not to let that fool me, and I know he's right. Shoot, maybe he's right about a lot of things." King-Roy paused a moment, pushed out his jaw, and squinted across the room at the windows. Then he said, "I was raised in a Christian home, a good Christian home, but now, that's not right for me anymore. Things have changed." He glanced at me for a second, then back to the windows. "My whole life has changed."

I tilted my head. "What do you mean, King-Roy?"

King-Roy spoke as if he hadn't heard. "It started changing before I left Birmingham, and it's still changing. It seems every day I'm waking up into a brand-new life. It's getting so I'm afraid to go to sleep at night for fear of what I might wake up to."

"Is that why you need the gun, because you're afraid to go to sleep?"

He nodded, still squinting at the windows as though he could see his friend Ax standing there, and he said, "Yeah, I think old Ax has got something there."

"Got what? Where? What do you mean?" I asked, staring up at his face.

King-Roy didn't shift his gaze. He stared steadily at the windows and said, "Ax said the white devil wants to keep us ignorant and make us feel bad about ourselves, like we're dirty and no good, so he makes up all these stories to keep us ashamed of ourselves. He said the white devil doesn't want us to know that Negroes were the first people on Earth. He doesn't want us to know that we were the original masters of this planet."

"Who says so?" I wanted to know. "Ax? How does he know?"

King-Roy looked at me as though he had just realized I was sitting in front of him, and he nodded. "Ax told me all about this Nation of Islam group and a man named Elijah Muhammad. And he gave me some things to read about it on the bus. They're articles by Elijah Muhammad, who said that all our struggles for equal rights are a waste of time. The white devil will never give us what we're due. He'll never give us our basic human rights."

"He won't?"

"Nuh-uh." King-Roy shifted one of the paint cans up under his arm. "We got to go on and take what we want and stop begging for it. We got to have us a revolution and set this world right again, with the black man back on top. That's what Ax told me."

"A revolution? Then is that why you need a gun? For a revolution? Are you planning to shoot us all dead?"

King-Roy shook his head. "I don't know what all it means. I'm just learning about it. But I want to know more because I know the way we're living's not right. And I know I don't want any part of the white devil's world anymore." King-Roy brought the paint can into his hand again and stared down at his feet. He said, "This Elijah Muhammad writes all about the Nation of Islam and being a Muslim. It's the one true religion, he says. It's the black man's religion. And he says our God is Allah, the one true God."

"What else does he say?" I asked when King-Roy just stopped talking and stood looking at his feet some more. "How does he know all this?"

King-Roy glanced at me, then went back to looking at his feet. "Elijah is Allah's messenger. He was sent by Allah to tell us how to live and what we should do to get our power back from the white man. For instance, he says don't smoke and don't drink liquor." King-Roy shook his head at his feet and said, "The white devil loves to see us throw away our money on his cigarettes and liquor. He loves to see us get stoned so we don't know what Mr. Charley's putting over on us."

"This Elijah guy makes us sound so mean," I said. "We're not like that, really."

King-Roy's head shot up, and his mellow face suddenly looked pained like I had just slapped him. "Is that what you think?"

"Yeah." I shrugged and added, "Well, maybe," and King-Roy, looking like he might cry, said, "Y'all have a whole history of mean and nasty, Esther. Starting with taking us in chains from our homeland in Africa and stealing our names and giving us all your white-devil names instead. Elijah says if we're ever going to be free of y'all's oppression, then we've got to take back our names."

I shook my head. "But how do you know what your name was. If it's not King-Roy Johnson, then what is it?"

"Ax told me that it's better we take the last name X, if we don't know our names, than to keep on using a name given to us by the blue-eyed devil."

"Like that man Malcolm X? But—"

"And Ax told me," King-Roy interrupted, his voice getting a little louder, "that black and white can never live together peacefully. He says we shouldn't even have friendships with Christians or Jews and we should form our own nation. It's the only way we'll ever really be free." King-Roy licked his lips and then bit down on the side of his mouth, looking like he was mulling over what he had just said.

I stood up, and moving closer to him, I said, "Then you mean we can't be friends? My mother and your mother can't be friends? Is this Nation of Islam your new religion now? Do you hate us white people?"

King-Roy took a long time answering me. He rocked back and forth on his shoes awhile, then finally he said, "That's what I've been thinking about. I've been thinking about what I should do. I'm thinking maybe I shouldn't stay here, no matter what my momma says." He shook his head and made a tapping sound with his shoes as he dropped forward on them. "I'm thinking about moving on after I do this paint job for your momma. Yeah, I'm gon' move in with Ax. I'm gon' move on to Harlem." He nodded to himself. "That's just what I'm gon' do."

TEN

King-Roy didn't want to talk anymore after he had made up his mind that he was going to be moving on to Harlem, so he left and I stayed awake in my room a long time. I couldn't sleep. I couldn't read, either, and I didn't even want to listen for *Surfin' USA* anymore. The music sounded too happy, and I wasn't in a happy mood. I needed to think. I lay in the dark, in my bed, with so many questions running through my mind, like, where did this Nation of Islam religion come from? Why hadn't I ever heard of it before? And what did King-Roy mean by "a revolution"? Were black people going to come storming through our streets with guns and bombs and things, killing off all the white devils?

King-Roy had sounded so angry before he left, so different. There I had been planning out how we could maybe be boyfriend and girlfriend someday, while he had been planning out how he hated us and how he wanted to move on to Harlem to live with a man named Ax. He almost looked like he hated me when he left my room. He couldn't even look at me.

I thought about the gun. He wouldn't shoot us,

would he? I wondered what the real story was behind King-Roy being accused of murder. Mother hadn't said. All she had said was that a group of men had accused him of killing one of their friends and that his momma, Luray Johnson, had shoved King-Roy onto a Greyhound before these men could do anything about it.

I decided I needed to ask him straight out what the whole story was. Who were those men? Why did they think King-Roy had killed their friend? I just needed to ask him straight out. Or maybe talk to Pip about it. Pip was good at straightening my thoughts out for me. I nodded to myself and rolled over on my back. Yes, I could ask Pip what he thought about King-Roy and his gun and stealing it out of the trash. I could ask Pip what he thought about this Nation of Islam—that is, if he would still talk to me.

My head was reeling with all the thoughts and questions I had, but then I realized that I was still so hungry and I was really feeling light-headed, so I got out of bed and crept downstairs to get myself something to eat.

Once I reached the bottom step, I saw that the kitchen light was on and I knew that Dad and Monsieur Vichy were still in there. I came into the kitchen, squinting in the bright light. "Hi, Dad," I said, shielding my eyes. "I'm glad you're home. I missed you tonight."

My father and Mr. Vichy were standing over the enormous black cast-iron stove that filled up one wall of the kitchen. Dad was eating a sandwich and drinking milk while Monsieur Vichy was drinking a gin and tonic

and smoking his cigar. We never used the stove for anything except to set things down on: schoolbooks, scripts,
mail, and food. We had a modern stove on the other side
of the kitchen for cooking.

My father set down his sandwich and spread his
arms for me to hug him when he saw me come in. "Hey,
muffin, how's my girl?" he asked.

I hadn't looked like a muffin kind of girl since I was
about two, but I liked that my father still called me that.
When he called me muffin, I knew that he was in a good
mood. My father was moody, more so than my mother.
He was either all lovey-dovey and wanting you to take
his hand or give him a hug or rub his back, or he was
yelling at you for breathing too loudly. He was always
the director, whether he was at home or in a theater, or,
as Auntie Pie likes to say, "All the world's a stage, and
Herbert Nelson Young is its director."

I needed a hug badly, so I rushed into his arms and
wrapped my own arms around his neck.

Monsieur Vichy snickered behind me. "Like zee little
child, still, Esther, running to your papa like zat. When
will you grow up?"

I broke free of my father and whirled around.
"When you learn to speak English correctly, I suppose.
You've lived in this country since you were twenty, for
Pete's sake, and I'm tired"—I took a breath, trying to
stifle a sob—"I'm *sick* and tired of everybody asking me
when I'm going to grow up. I am who I am."

Out of all of our guests, Monsieur Vichy was the

most hateful. He was a fat, pasty-faced man with very small feet. He reminded me of a bowling pin when he was standing still and a penguin when he walked. He smoked cigars all day long and carried around an old candy-mint tin for his spittle. His hair, what little was left of it, was the same color as that spittle. Monsieur Vichy wrote and puffed in his room all day, stinking up the whole house with his cigars, and came out at dinner-time to join us and glare down his pince-nez at me whenever I opened my mouth to say something. He thought my little sister, Sophia, was delightful and such *une fille intelligente*. He told my father that she and my brother, Stewart, would both be famous someday but I, alas, was to be nothing extraordinary. In his eyes, I was plain to look at, frivolous in my speech, and a poor student in school. I was likely to become the family scandal, he declared to my father one night out on the pavilion, when he thought I couldn't hear. But I did hear, and right then and there I determined that I would someday, somehow, become the family hero and show him a thing or two; but so far he had been right in his estimation of me, and that irked me to no end.

My father patted my head, trying to calm me down. "All right," he said. "It's late, no fighting, you two."

I turned to my father. "He's the third person today who's asked me when I'm going to grow up. Well, when's he going to write a *real* play? I could write what he writes—all those actors walking around in cardboard boxes, saying nothing that makes any sense."

"Oh, you *sink* so, do you?" Monsieur Vichy said, snickering and talking out of one side of his mouth so he could hold on to his precious cigar with the other side.

"Yes, I do," I said.

I thought his plays were too pretentious for words, and I didn't understand why my father would bother with them.

Monsieur Vichy smirked when I told him that I could write a better play than he, and he said to me, "Why don't you prove it? You talk so big all the time. Why don't we see what you can write, eh?"

"I don't have to prove anything to you," I said, and my father said, "That's enough, you two."

"*Non, non, non.* Let us see zis child write even a play, good or bad. I do not believe she can do it. She is lazy and *stupide.*"

"Henri, you've gone too far! That's enough!" my father said, his voice booming, not caring, I guess, that it was the middle of the night.

I ignored his indignation, even if it was on my behalf. I was used to fighting my own battles, especially with Monsieur Vichy. I said, "Oh yeah? I'll show you a play. I'll give you a play, and my play will have a plot, a real plot, with a beginning and middle and end. You ought to try it sometime."

Monsieur Vichy nodded his head. "*Oui, oui, oui,* we shall see. By the end of zis summer you will show me your rough draft, *non?*"

"I don't need a rough draft. I'll show you a polished-to-perfection play."

"Esther, let's not promise what we can't produce," my father said, his voice more angry than concerned. I knew he didn't like that he wasn't directing this scene between Monsieur Vichy and me.

"I *can* produce it, Dad. Don't you think I can't, because I can," I said. "I'm going upstairs right now to start writing it. I'll show you who's lazy."

I stormed out of the kitchen without food and with Monsieur Vichy laughing behind me.

"At least get some sleep first," my father called after me.

Up in my room I sat at my desk with my light on, wondering how I had managed to get myself into such a fix. I couldn't write a play if my life, or at least my dignity, depended on it. And who wanted a writing assignment during summer vacation? I could have kicked myself for opening my big fat mouth like that. I sat at my desk, with my notebook from last year's French class opened to the blank pages in the back and a pen in my hands, and just stared at the blank page. I sat like that for a long time, trying to come up with even an idea. Then I thought, *Wait a minute!* Monsieur Vichy opened his mouth, too, but he doesn't have to prove himself. I should tell him that he has to write a real play, too. I should tell him that he has to write one with a plot. Why should he get out of doing anything all summer?

I got up from my desk and headed back downstairs

to the kitchen, thinking that he probably would say that he had no intention of writing a play for me and that would let me off the hook, too. Why should I write a play for an old penguin who calls me lazy and stupid, anyway?

I could hear Dad and Monsieur Vichy talking, and I heard my name. I tiptoed around to the other entrance, going through the butler's pantry to listen at the swinging door there.

"... always baiting her. I *don't* like it, Henri." Dad pounded the stovetop for emphasis, something he did often. It scared people until they got used to his flaring tempers.

"But it will be good for her, *non*? You need to keep a young *fille* like your Esther busy or she will get into trouble, I know."

"She'll get frustrated and angry with herself. She can't write a play. She needs to be busy in sports. She can play ball. You should have challenged her in something that she could succeed in."

"But we were not talking ball; we were talking plays. She has insulted my play. It happened *naturellement*. What could I do?"

"You didn't have to sink to her level."

Mother and Dad must have discussed this sinking-to-my-level thing before, since it seemed to be their catchphrase for other people's behavior when they interacted with me, and I didn't like it. And the whole play-ball thing just sent me through the roof. That's all anyone thought I could do. "You'll make a nice gym teacher someday," my mother has said to me smugly, time and again, thinking she had put me in my future place all neat and tidy. She wasn't going to worry about me. I would play ball the rest of my ball-bouncing life!

The sad truth was, I wasn't all that good at ball sports. I was just better at it than I was at just about anything else. I mean, I could kick a ball or hit it with a bat or occasionally sink it in a basket, but I was no great athlete like Babe Didrickson.

Listening to my father explaining to Monsieur Vichy how I could never write a play made me feel so low I wanted to just curl up in a ball and let someone use me for basketball practice. I didn't want to hear any more of their discussion, so I swallowed hard, stood up straight, and pushed through the swinging door of the butler's pantry, and entered the kitchen.

"Hey," I said, glaring at Monsieur Vichy, my voice louder than I intended and the swinging door making a *thwunk, thwunk* sound behind me. I knew I had startled them both, and I was glad.

I said, "If I'm going to write a play, then you'll have to write one, too. And with a plot for a change. A real plot, not your whacked-out weirdo intellectual stuff, but a real plot. Okay?"

I waited for Monsieur Vichy's protest. I waited for him to talk his and my way out of this whole deal. I saw him glance up at my father and wink. Then he looked at me and said, "*Mais bien sûr,* but of course. I will write my play with a plot, as you say, and you will write yours. We shall shake on it, *non*?" He held out his sweaty, pasty hand for me to shake.

I stuck my hand out and shook his with one quick shake, then I let go and rubbed my hand on my shorts.

"And the due date will be?" he said.

"Um." I hesitated, wondering how I had managed to dig myself into it even deeper than before. How could I not write a play if he was going to write one? It would be like cheating. "How about the last week in August?" I said, finally. "Rough draft," I added, hoping that he wouldn't hold me to my previous claim of being able to produce a final draft in a little over two months.

"*Très bien.* It's a deal, as you say." Monsieur nodded, removed his cigar from his mouth, and spit into his candy tin. And with that, the deal was sealed.

ELEVEN

Back up in my room, I decided to climb into bed, prop myself up with my pillows, and work on my play all night. Since I didn't know what King-Roy had planned to do with the gun he'd pulled out of the trash, I figured I had better stay up and listen, in case he decided to shoot everybody in their sleep. Not that I thought he really would, but if he did, it would be my fault and I couldn't live with a murder rampage on my conscience. I thought I would listen for his door creaking open or his footsteps in the hallway and scream bloody murder and wake the household up if I heard anything.

That was my plan, to stay up all night, but I must have fallen asleep, because I found myself waking up to the sound of birds outside my window and the weight of something heavy pressed against my back. I opened my eyes. Someone was sleeping on my bed with me. King-Roy Johnson's face flashed into my mind, and I sprang from my bed and spun around and shouted, "Aha!"

Pip lifted his head up from my bed and said, "Wha—?"

"Pip, what are you doing here?" I asked, relieved that it was just Pip.

He sat up on his elbows and said, "You people never lock your doors at night."

"That's because we don't have any keys. But Pip, what are you doing here?"

Pip pointed to the front of his track-team T-shirt and said, "Training for cross-country, remember? You said you'd train with me. Or is that off, too, now that we're fighting?"

I smacked my head. "I forgot all about that. What time is it?"

Pip sat up and yawned. Then, looking at his watch, he said, "Five fifteen; we're fifteen minutes late for the first day of training. I wrote up a schedule; you want to see it?" Pip reached back into the waistband of his shorts and pulled out a sheet of paper.

"Wait a minute and let me get dressed first." I ducked into my closet and pulled the string above my head for some light. I searched on the floor for some loose-fitting shorts and a bra and a T-shirt and put them on. While I dressed in the closet, I said, "Hey, Pip, I'm sorry about yesterday. That was stupid—*really* stupid. What I said came out all wrong and I'm sorry."

I had hoped that he would apologize, too, and say that the boys at school really didn't make fun of me and my hair, but he didn't.

All he said was "Yeah, it was stupid," and the way he said it made me think he hadn't even heard me.

I stepped out of the closet and saw Pip reading from my notebook the one sentence I had managed to write for my play. When he saw me he smiled, then read the sentence out loud.

"*As the curtain rises on a dimly lit stage, there is the distant sound of the ocean.*" He looked up. "What's this?"

"I really stuck my foot in it this time," I said. "I told Monsieur Vichy how even *I* could write a play better than his silly stuff, and now I have to write one to prove it. You know I've always loved the sound of waves crashing. What do you think?"

He looked at me sitting on the floor putting on my socks and sneakers and said, "What comes next?"

"I don't know. I can't think of anything except waves. You're good at writing," I said, standing up and making sure I had on the same shoes. One time I went to school with two different shoes on by mistake, and my homeroom teacher kept me after school for two days because, she said, I was trying to be a smart aleck, and she didn't care for class clowns.

"You could help me write a play, couldn't you, Pip?"

Pip set my notebook back down on my desk and said, "I don't write fiction; I write letters. I don't make things up, and anyway"—he turned around and looked straight at me—"I thought you didn't want me around this summer."

I sighed, pulled the rubber band I wore off my wrist, and grabbed my hair into a ponytail. "Pip, if you were listening, you would have heard me. I said I'm sorry about yesterday. I didn't mean what I said. I *do* want you around. I always want you around. It's just—well, I want something this summer. I don't know what it is. I want to feel something—something different." I wound the rubber band around one more time to make the ponytail extra tight and headed for the door.

Pip shoved his glasses up on his nose. "You really want me around, then?" he asked, following me to the door.

I smiled at him. "I need you, Pip. I have something I want to tell you—about King-Roy."

"Oh, King-Roy. So what's this killer like, anyway?"

"I'll tell you outside while we're running," I said, whispering since we had stepped out into the hallway.

Once outside, we stood together beneath the porch light, and Pip pulled his running schedule out of the waistband of his shorts. He unfolded the piece of paper and said, "My New Zealand pen pal wrote me about this incredible coach they have there. This coach trained Peter Snell and Murray Halberg."

Pip had pen pals all over the world. He collected them the way other people collected stamps. He loved letter writing, and he loved having friends from so many different countries. They were always telling him about the latest and greatest things going on in their countries and Pip would tell them about President Kennedy and life in these United States as he saw it.

When he said the names Peter Snell and Murray

Halberg, Pip's eyes flashed owllike at me, as if this were the greatest news he'd ever shared with me.

"Who are they?" I asked.

Pip's eyes got even wider. "Who *are* they? They're only the two nineteen sixty Olympic gold medalists in track. Look at this." Pip handed me his schedule. "I plan to run fifty miles a week."

"Fifty miles! What for? You only race two or three miles, don't you?"

Pip nodded. "That's the beauty of this plan. You run big miles, like fourteen miles in one run." He pointed to week six of his training schedule, where he had placed fourteen miles beneath the word *Saturday*. "You get faster by running longer. My pen pal Leslie now runs faster than I do, and he used to be slower. This is his exact schedule. Just think. I might be able to beat out Pete Finny next fall."

I looked at Pip's dreamy expression. "I can't run that, can I?" I asked him.

Pip blinked. "You don't have to. You can run the first two or three miles and get me started, and I'll run the rest. I build up to it. See?"

He showed me his schedule again, and I saw that his longest runs in the first week were four miles long. The second week they jumped to six, the third week they jumped to eight miles and so on, up to fourteen miles by week six. I said, "If you're going to do it, then I'm going to do it, too."

Pip's mouth dropped open. He said, "But you can't.

You just said you couldn't, and anyway, girls can't run too long or their plumbing will fall out."

"Our plumbing?"

Pip's face turned red. "You know, your . . . your uterus. It falls out. Isn't that why girls can't run? That's why girls don't have a track team, isn't it?"

I was laughing and pointing at Pip. "You should see your face. You look so embarrassed. Our plumbing!"

Pip didn't join in. He had on his serious face, which somehow always made his glasses look way too big for his head. "But isn't that true? It will fall out?"

I stopped laughing. "If you're running fourteen miles, then I'm running them, too."

"But what's the point? You can't use it for anything." He folded up his schedule. "I shouldn't have shown you this. I should have just run on my own. Now it'll be my fault if you lose your, you know, uterus and can't have a baby."

"A baby! Who wants a baby? I'm fourteen, for Pete's sake."

Pip ran his hand through his hair, making it stand up on top. "We're going to want a baby someday, aren't we? I mean, aren't we?"

"Pip!" I said, turning away from him, then turning back.

"Well, aren't we?"

"You never give up. I'm not marrying you. It would be like marrying my brother."

"Well, I'm not your brother." Pip turned and ran

down the porch steps, out toward the polar bear rock and the woods beyond.

I ran after him. "Pip, wait."

"I suppose you're going to marry the killer, then, huh?" he shouted back over his shoulder.

"Pip!" I ran as fast as I could to catch up with him, so I was panting hard when I said, "I wanted to talk to you about him. About King-Roy."

Pip slowed down. "What about him," he said with anger in his voice.

"I don't know if he's wonderful or scary or what." We were almost to the woods, and I could smell the pines and the clean moist smell of the bark and new leaves on the maples and poplars.

"So what's so wonderful about him?" Pip asked, slowing down even more, so that we could hold a conversation while we ran.

"I didn't say he was wonderful. I said he might be. I don't know. I think he understands me. We understand each other, or, well, he talks to me. He talks to me like a grown-up, not like a child."

Pip brushed past a bush, and I followed behind for a second until we had entered the woods and were on the path leading to the big and little ponds. "I know you better than anybody," Pip said, the pitch of his voice rising. "*I* understand you. *I* talk to you. What can he know in one day?"

"It's just, I don't know. There's something in him— we're alike, I think. We're like two peas in a pod."

Pip picked up his speed again and I stayed with him, keeping my eye out for roots and rocks along the path so that I wouldn't trip over them.

Pip asked, "How are you alike, exactly?"

"Oh, Pip, I don't know. We've both had struggles with school and reading and all that. You know, when I stayed back."

"When you stayed back? What kind of thing is that to build a relationship on? That's history, anyway. That happened a long time ago. You're a great student now, and you're smart, too."

"I'm okay. I'm just an okay student." We were on a steep hill that led up and around a boulder, then down toward the big pond. I was in front, which I knew Pip hated because he said he couldn't see around me, so I slowed down and let him pass.

As Pip caught up, then ran by me, he said, "Maybe compared to a genius you're just okay, but you're smart, Esther. You practically make straight A's every year, and you're wise. Stewart and Sophia aren't wise. If you ask me, that Sophia's going to end up in a nuthouse one day, and Stewart's going to be a ballerina no matter how hard your parents try to shove him into musicals instead."

"Auntie Pie says I'm already crazy. She calls me the white tornado." I caught up with Pip again, where the path widened, and we ran side by side.

"You're the only sane one in your family, Esther. Don't you know that?"

I glanced at Pip. His glasses had slid down to the end

of his nose. "You're blinded by love, Pip," I said, "and anyway, that's what's so great about King-Roy." Pip had picked up his speed so that we were almost racing when we got to the pond.

Pip waited until we had reached the tag boulder, a large rock that the winner around the pond had to tag first in order to claim the win, and then he said, panting, "What? What's so great?"

I tagged the boulder and kept running, and Pip followed.

I said, "It's our history. You say it's old news, my staying back in school, but it's not to me, and King-Roy gets that. He understands. I live with staying back every day—in school, with all the kids in my old grade looking down on me and calling me stupid, and at home, with Mother making me take summer lessons, or now giving up on me and telling me I'm going to be a gym teacher."

"Gym teachers are smart. I might want to be a gym teacher someday, maybe," Pip said.

I swatted Pip. "No you won't. You're going to work for the United Nations or that new Peace Corps thing President Kennedy started. You said so, remember?"

"I can be a gym teacher, too, if I want," Pip said, "and anyway, if you think you and King-Roy share a history, then maybe you *are* crazy. Don't you know what's going on down there in the South? Just last month little kids were getting torn apart by dogs and sprayed with fire hoses all because Negroes want the right to vote and eat in restaurants. Believe me, you don't share any history with a Negro."

I clicked my teeth. "You just don't get it, Pip," I said. I felt irritated with him. I hated it when he got logical on me. I knew what I meant, and I didn't want to have to try to explain it to Pip. I picked up my pace and tried to run ahead, but Pip picked up his and stayed right there with me. I sped up some more and so did Pip until we were all-out racing again, up and down and around through the woods, crossing over our property boundary to the little pond, around the pond and back through the woods, taking a different path toward home. We ran neck and neck, shoulder to shoulder, until I jammed my foot into a root and went flying. When I landed, I skidded along the ground for a couple of feet and finally stopped. I lay still for a few seconds, breathing hard and taking note of what hurt. My hands, elbows, hip bones, and knees burned and stung, my left shoulder ached; and my nose was running or bleeding, I didn't know which.

Pip knelt down beside me and touched my head. He always had the lightest, gentlest touch. "Are you okay, Esther?" he asked, panting near my ear. I could feel the heat of his body above me.

I rolled over, wiping my nose as I rolled, to see if it was bleeding. It wasn't. I sniffed. "I'm okay."

"What hurts?" Pip asked, looking down at my bloody knees.

"Everything," I said. I sat up and lifted my arms to show him my hands and elbows. "Everything hurts."

"That was dumb of us," Pip said, sitting back on his legs. "We weren't even halfway through today's run and we were racing. From now on, no more racing."

"Sorry," I said. I started to get up but Pip held me back. "Just sit there a minute, why don't you."

I sat back down. "You said yourself that we still had more than half the run left. I don't want to get cold."

"You can take it easy just for a second," Pip said, taking my hands in his and turning them palms up to look at them. They were bright red and smudged with dirt, but the skin wasn't torn.

Then out of the clear blue sky he said, "What's scary?"

I took my hands back. "Huh?"

"You said King-Roy was scary, too. What's so scary about him?"

I brought my knees up to my chest and wrapped my arms around them. I could smell the blood and dirt embedded in them. It smelled like rust.

I lowered my voice as though I thought King-Roy might be hiding behind a tree and said, "He brought a gun with him. He's got a gun."

"A gun!" Pip sprang back, falling off his knees as though I were holding the gun on him right at that moment. "Do your parents know?"

"They know he brought a gun, but he gave it to Mother to throw away. But then he took it back out of the trash and hid it in his pants, and they don't know that. I'm the only one who knows that."

Pip stood up and glared down at me with his hands on his hips. "What?"

I nodded and stood up, too. I brushed myself off, gave my knees one last glance, then I said, "Let's run," and we were off again. We turned right and headed along the path toward the pavilion, moving at a gentle pace, and I started from the beginning and told Pip everything about the gun and white devils and the Nation of Islam—everything.

By the time I had finished, we had almost reached the edge of the woods and I could see our lawn and fields, green and moist and pretty. Once through the woods, we slowed to a walk and took our time going through the lower fields. Up ahead were the grape arbor and the pavilion, and beyond that, the rose garden and the house. We hadn't planned on slowing down. Usually our final tagging spot was the stone porch outside the ballroom, but for some reason, without saying anything to each other, we both just started walking.

We had stopped talking, too, and I suppose we were both deep in thought about what I had told Pip about King-Roy and the gun and everything that had happened the night before, so we didn't hear the tapping sounds until we were almost up to the grape arbor. We both heard it at the same time and we stopped to listen. When we stopped, the taps stopped. Then we heard someone talking. It was King-Roy and he was talking to someone inside the pavilion.

TWELVE

The low pavilion walls were made of stone, and thick wooden pillars supported the roof. Between the roof and the walls was open space, so we could hear everything anyone was saying inside. We heard King-Roy say, "I didn't think anybody else was up at this hour."

Then another voice, Beatrice Bonham's flirty voice, said, "Let me set you straight about this place, King-Roy, there's always somebody up, at any hour, day or night. So if you've got any secrets, you'd best hide them well, and don't count on the distance of the pavilion from the house to keep your secrets for you."

"Yes, ma'am," King-Roy said, "I already found that out."

"Well, your tap dancing will be our little secret."

That was the sound we'd heard when we came out of the woods, tap dancing! I heard Beatrice say those words and I got so excited, I jumped out of hiding and started for the pavilion, but Pip caught hold of me and pulled me back behind the grape arbor. "Hold on," he whispered, "or they'll see us out here."

I looked at Pip's frightened expression—as though we were in some grave danger—and did as he said. I crouched down with him and peered up through the grapevines at the pavilion. From our new position, closer to the action and with a view of the open entrance, I could see King-Roy pretty well. He stood shifting from one foot to the other the way some kids at school do when they're nervous giving a book report in front of the class. He kept his hands in his pockets.

"You're quite good," Beatrice was saying. "Ever think of taking it to the stage?" Beatrice stood with her back to us, so I couldn't get a good look at her face, but I could see that she had on the same sexy peignoir set she wore the day before and she had silver slippers on her feet, with their puffs of white fur on top.

King-Roy shook his head. "There are three things I won't ever do for a living. I won't pick up other people's garbage; I won't do any of those yes-ma'am-yes-sir kind of jobs, like butler or chauffeur or bellhop; and I won't be a tap dancer. There's no dignity for a black man in any of that."

Beatrice shrugged one shoulder and said in her sexy, smoldering voice, "Mr. Johnson, if there's dignity in the man, there's dignity in the job."

"Well, ma'am, I don't quite see it that way." King-Roy's voice sounded bitter, and I waited for him to say more, to explain his bitterness, but he didn't, and Beatrice asked him, "What about acting? You're handsome enough. You could be an actor if you had the proper coaching."

"No, thank you, ma'am. I'm not interested in the stage one whit."

Beatrice ignored this and said, "Of course, I wouldn't be the one to coach you. Nobody around here takes my acting seriously."

I supposed her idea about dignity being in the man, not the job, didn't hold true for a woman, and I figured she probably didn't mean what she said in the first place but was only using it as a way to work the subject around to her, which is what she did.

King-Roy had started to say, "I wouldn't know about that, ma'am. I only just got—," when Beatrice jumped in and said in a pouting voice, "I've been here almost three years. Three years right under Herbert Nelson Young's nose, and he's never once suggested I audition for one of his plays." Beatrice let out an exasperated-sounding sigh and added, "He doesn't take my acting seriously at all. It is so frustrating I could scream. Really, I could."

Pip nudged me and rolled his eyes.

King-Roy said, "Well-uh, I-uh, don't rightly know about—"

"No, you wouldn't understand how desperate an actor gets when they're not performing if you've never been on the stage before. I tell you, King-Roy, one taste of the stage and you never want to leave it. Never! And here I am, right here in this house with Herbert, and soon he'll be casting for his next play and I know I'd be perfect for the part of Vera." Beatrice held out a rolled-up script she had in her hands and shook it at King-Roy.

"Well," King-Roy said, drawing his head back out of the line of her script. "I don't know about acting, but I've been on the stage before and you can take it. I don't want any part of it."

Beatrice lowered her script. "But I thought you said you'd never been on the stage."

King-Roy shook his head. "I said I never acted, but I was onstage—with my daddy, Johnny 'Shoeshine' Johnson. Maybe you've heard of him? He's who taught me to dance. We used to travel together some, and he put me up on the stage to draw the crowds."

"Then, you know," Beatrice said, moving in closer to King-Roy. "You know how it is to be born for the stage. I don't know how I'm going to cope. I hate being out of work. I need to work. I need the stage, King-Roy."

Beatrice took another step closer and sort of leaned against King-Roy, and I couldn't stand it any longer. I didn't want to hear Beatrice prattle on about her pitiful career. I wanted to see King-Roy dance. I wanted to find out about his tap dancing. I wanted him to teach me. I loved tap dancing. I loved the rhythms. I'd never tapped before, but I loved watching it in old movies on television, like the Shirley Temple movies.

I'd had enough of Beatrice and her flirty ways, so I burst through the grape arbor, ignoring Pip's tug on my

T-shirt, and ran up the steps of the pavilion and said, "King-Roy, could you teach me to tap? I love tap dancing. Could you teach me, do you think?"

Beatrice jumped in the air and squealed when I appeared on the top step of the pavilion, and before King-Roy could answer me she said, "Esther, where on earth did you come from all of a sudden? You scared me half to death." She clutched at her chest for emphasis.

I looked back at Pip and the arbor and said, "Oh, I was listening in on you back there behind the grapevines—me and Pip."

"'Listening in'?" Beatrice stood on tiptoe and looked past King-Roy to the grape arbor. Then she returned her gaze to me and said, "Esther Young, your honesty unnerves me! For goodness sakes, 'listening in.'"

I ignored her, and looking at King-Roy, who stood with his face so calm I couldn't tell what he was thinking, I said, "Please, King-Roy, I'd love to learn how to do tap. I told Mother that I would take tap if she would let me drop the ballet classes, but she said no real lady should take tap lessons, because it makes their knees swell like melons, but I—"

Beatrice interrupted me. "Esther, I was in the midst of talking to King-Roy myself. You can't just barge in on another person's conversation like this and expect anyone to want to do anything for you."

I turned and glared at Beatrice. "I heard what you said about my father, and I can solve your problem for you real quick."

Beatrice crossed her arms in front of her, making the tops of her breasts pop up from beneath her peignoir. "Is that so," she said. "And how would you do that, pray tell?"

"Easy," I said. "Dad does serious stuff, dramatic stuff."

Beatrice closed her eyes. "I think I know better than you what your father directs."

I heard Pip coming up the steps until he was right behind me, breathing on my neck, as though he wanted to protect me from Beatrice's barbs, or from King-Roy, I wasn't sure which, but I didn't need his help. I put my hands on my hips and said to Beatrice, "Oh, you think you know better, do you? Well, tell me this. How come all the sexy actresses and all the comediennes have blond hair? Look at Mae West and Marilyn Monroe. You're like—like some cheap imitation of the two of them. So why would Dad ask you to audition for any of his plays? Dye your hair brown and wear real clothes, for Pete's sake. You look like—like a floozy."

"Esther! I cannot believe I just heard you say that!" Beatrice flapped her arms and looked around at her audience. "Anyway, I am who I am," she added, adjusting the neckline of her flimsy outer robe.

I glanced at King-Roy, whose facial expression hadn't changed since I had arrived on the scene, then I returned to Beatrice. "You're an actress, so act, then. Play the part of a serious actress. Better yet, play the part of Vera. *Be* her. Come down to breakfast fully clothed for a change, and don't put your makeup on at the table. I mean, really, Beatrice, use some basic common sense, why don't you."

"I am not going to stand here and take the advice of a silly ratty-haired girl like you," Beatrice said, moving toward the steps to where Pip stood. "King-Roy, we'll talk later, when we can have some privacy. I told you this house never sleeps."

Pip hopped out of her way, and Beatrice, stepping sideways down the stone steps and holding up the hem of her peignoir, made her exit.

THIRTEEN

After Beatrice left I pleaded with King-Roy to show us some of his tap dancing, but no amount of begging could get him to dance. "I'm not a puppet on a string you can yank around," he said. "And I'm not gon' teach you to tap."

"Why not?" I asked. "Is it because you don't like us? Is it because I'm white? Don't you think white people can tap dance?"

King-Roy shook his head. "Esther, it's not because of you. I don't perform for people anymore, not since my daddy died."

I nodded. "Because it makes you sad to remember."

"No." King-Roy pushed off the wall where he had been leaning. "Because it makes me angry. Before my father saw I could tap just as well as he could, he thought I was too stupid to waste his good money on feeding me. Since I didn't talk, he didn't want anything to do with me. Then one time I got angry at him for pushing my little brother into a wall, and all I could think to do was to dance. I pulled him off my brother and started tapping, doing all his stuff, all his routines, and he just threw his head back and laughed like crazy. He couldn't believe what he was seeing. He had no idea that I had been watching him practicing and had picked up all his steps. Well, after I showed him, he carted me around the South like I was a trick pony."

"Didn't you like traveling with your father?" I asked.

King-Roy shook his head. "No. There wasn't any fun in it. Tap was going out of style. Tap was the going thing in the thirties and forties but not anymore, and the only way my father could get anyone to book his show was if he included me. He used me for the act, then stashed me away in some dirty hotel by myself every night while he ran off with his pals to drink and party with the ladies."

King-Roy crossed his arms and shook his head, then he looked over to where Pip was standing, lifted his chin, and said, "I don't think we've met." He held out his right hand and said, "My name's King-Roy, King-Roy Johnson."

Pip came out from behind me and said, "I'm Jonathan Masters, but people call me Pip. I live across the street."

I could see Pip giving King-Roy the eye. He didn't smile the way he usually did when he talked to people, and I was afraid King-Roy would think Pip was one of those white devils he had talked about, so I said, "Pip's my best friend. He's everybody's friend, really. Everybody likes Pip and Pip likes everybody."

Both of them ignored me.

King-Roy shook Pip's hand and ducked his head to peer out across our property to Pip's house. From where we stood, all you could see of his house was a balcony and the third floor and the rooftops of the house and some outbuildings.

"You live in that big white mansion over there?" King-Roy asked.

Pip nodded. "Yeah, that's it."

King-Roy straightened back up and looked at Pip. "How many people you got living over there?"

"There's just three of us; my mother and father and I."

King-Roy wagged his head. "Shoot, three people in that great big house, and we all live ten to a room where I come from."

Pip, sounding defensive, said, "Well, my father's the president of the college and my mother's a professor, so we have people from the college and from all over the country coming in and out of our house all day and all night long. The whole house gets plenty of use, and anyway, we don't own the house. It's given to the president to use only as long as he's president."

King-Roy raised his hands and said, "All right, all right, I wasn't attacking you."

Pip stood with his legs apart and crossed his arms in front of his chest like he was Yul Brenner in *The King and I* and said, "Well, it kind of sounded like you were. I'm sorry if you're living ten to a room, but it's not my fault, and it's not Esther or her family's fault, either. You can't go shooting people, if that's what you're thinking, just because they live in big houses and you don't."

That took the mellow out of King-Roy's face. He glared at me and said, "Esther, I thought you said you could keep a secret. I thought I had told you all that in private. Now look what you've gone and done."

I stood between the two of them, looking right, then left, then right again at King-Roy. "I just needed someone to talk to about you," I said, "and Pip is the only one I could." I knew I had blown it. I felt sure King-Roy would leave for Harlem that very day.

"Hey, don't blame her," Pip said. "She's scared of you, okay? She doesn't want her head blown off, all right?"

"Pip!" I glared at Pip. "That's not what I said. I said he was wonderful. Remember I said he was wonderful?"

King-Roy pointed at Pip, who was still standing like Yul Brenner, and said, "How come he thinks I'm gon' shoot people? What gave him that idea, huh?"

"Oh, all right," I said. "I told Pip about the you-know-what, but only because I was scared. Wouldn't you be? What if I had a—a you-know-what, or my father had one and it fell out of his pants when he was walking down the hallway? Wouldn't you be scared?"

"I'd mind my own business," King-Roy said.

"Well, I was scared, and I told Pip that I thought you were maybe wonderful but maybe scary, and he wanted to know what was so scary, didn't you, Pip?" I looked over at Pip and Pip nodded, but he didn't look at me. He was watching King-Roy.

"Well, so I told him about the you-know-what, and anyway, that's why I told him."

King-Roy looked at me with this hurt look on his face and said, "I thought you and me were all right. I thought we understood each other. Looks like I was wrong."

I stepped forward and reached my hand out toward his arm, not quite touching it, and said, "I thought so, too, King-Roy. I just wondered about the—the you-know-what. I only wondered is all." I felt rotten to the core.

Then, to make matters worse, Pip opened his big yap again and said, "Hey, don't blame her. You're the one who brought the gun. Don't go making out like everything is her fault."

King-Roy whipped around, puffed himself up to every bit of his height, and looked down on Pip and said, "What did you say? You think it's not her fault? You think it's our fault? Is it our fault we don't get paid same as you for doing the exact same job, only we're doin' it two times better? Is it our fault we build the buildings, plant the crops, lay out the roads and the train tracks all over this country, but we can't get a decent place to live and our own roads aren't paved and the food we get at the grocer is half rotten and full of worms? You tell me that. Is that our fault?" King-Roy glared a second at Pip, then turned around to look out across our field, and he said, more to himself than to us, "Well, just maybe it is because we're fool enough to think they gon' be decent and give us what they owe us. Nonviolence is just a waste of time."

King-Roy's voice had turned down to a whisper, and I moved over next to him to hear him. When he stopped talking I said, "King-Roy, I don't know what you're talking about. All that stuff about crops and roads. I'm sorry for what I said and I'm sorry for what Pip said and I want to be friends. I want us to be close friends. Your mother and my mother were oldest best friends. They still write to each other every Christmas. Can't we be friends, too?"

King-Roy looked at me and said, "My friend Ax said, 'No white devil's ever gon' be best friends with no black.' And he said, 'Don't turn your back on a white 'less you want a knife stuck in it.' And he said, 'Up here in New York it's worse than the South because up here they all act like they're on your side, but they aren't. They're smiling out their faces, but they're still nailing you to the wall every which way they can.'"

"And you believe him all the time? Why don't you just see with your own eyes, King-Roy?" I said.

King-Roy's eyes turned to slits, and he looked out past my head and said, "Oh, I've seen with my own eyes, all right. I've seen plenty with my own eyes." He looked at me and added, "It's you who doesn't see." Then he pointed at Pip. "And you. Neither one of y'all can see the truth, sitting inside your ballroom mansions."

Pip opened his mouth to say something and I could

tell by his expression it was going to be some angry something, so I jumped in first and said, "Then make us see. Tell us. What do we need to see? What?"

King-Roy was staring back out across the field, and Pip and I stared at him. The three of us stood silent together for a minute or two, and then I saw a tear spill out of King-Roy's eye and run down his cheek.

"King-Roy?" I said, almost in a whisper. "Tell me."

King-Roy leaned forward and set his elbows on the stone wall. He looked down and shook his head, and it looked like he was struggling with himself, trying to decide what to tell us. Then, he spoke. He spoke to the stones.

"Last May, right at the beginning of the month, May third, we did this freedom march. Me and my friends, my sisters and brothers, all of us marched. Momma was scared for us. She told me to take hold of my little sister Syllia and my brother Joe-Earl's hands and to not let go. She said, 'If they haul one of you off to jail, they take y'all, but King-Roy, you hold on.'

"I told her I would. Some of my friends had already marched and they were sitting in jail already, but I wasn't worried. None of us were. We all felt brave 'cause we knew we were doing what was right. That's what Dr. King said."

"Dr. Martin Luther King Junior?" Pip asked.

King-Roy nodded, still keeping his head low and looking at the stones.

"Yeah, I've heard about him," Pip said.

I said, "Go on," and Pip came over and joined us at the wall. We stood on either side of him and listened.

"We'd gone to the mass meetings at the church, the Baptist church, and we sang freedom songs, and Dr. King talked to us and asked us if we were willing to fight for freedom, if we were willing to fight for what was right. If we were, then we should step forward and swear that if anything should happen to us, we would agree to turn the other cheek. We had to agree that we would be nonviolent, and if we couldn't agree to that, then he didn't want us to march. Well, me and my friends and sisters and brothers all agreed."

King-Roy paused to blow his nose, taking a handkerchief out of his back pocket, then returning it before continuing with his story.

"On the day of the march, we left the church chanting 'O Freedom,' real soft and quiet, and I was holding my little sister Syllia's hand and my brother Joe-Earl's hand, and we headed downtown with the crowd, but before we could get to the center, the police caught up to us, and they shouted at us to turn back around and go on home or they were going to turn some fire hoses on us."

Pip said, "I read about that in the news," and he said it sweetly, like he was sorry for the way he had been acting. King-Roy kept talking.

"I saw the firemen standing with the big hoses in their hands, and I saw some of the police had police dogs with them, on leashes, and other police had their clubs, and all of them had their guns, but I didn't feel scared, and we none of us turned around to go home."

"Did you get sprayed?" I asked. "Did you get hit?"

King-Roy nodded. "When we didn't leave, they turned on the hoses and it sprayed a group and knocked them down, and then I saw one of the firemen turn round and look straight at me, almost like he had been looking for me all along. He was standing there, standing up against a building, and I was in the street and I heard shouts all around us and rocks were flying through the air, but I didn't look to see who was throwing them because I was looking at this man." King-Roy lifted his head and stared out toward Pip's house. "I never saw such hate in my life," he said. "That man grinned like the devil, and then he turned his hose right on my sister and she was torn out of my hand with the blast of water and I thought my arm had gone with her, it was that strong. She went rolling down the street, and then that white devil turned his hose on my brother and he was torn from my other hand. I didn't see what happened to him because by then a dog was on me, tearing at the sleeve of my shirt. The dog ripped it clear off of my arm, and I looked up and I saw three white men with grins on their faces, watching me while that dog tore at the front of my pants, and that's when everything changed for me. That's when I knew the truth about people, the meanness that lives in their hearts." King-Roy straightened up and said, "Oh, I've seen ugly before, and I've seen cruelty, too, but when I looked in those faces, I saw the truth. We aren't born with goodness in our hearts the way they're always telling us in church. No, we're born mean and ugly, and if you want different, if you want to get to heaven, then you have to change your heart yourself."

Pip looked up at King-Roy and asked, "So what happened to you? What about your sister and brother?"

King-Roy blinked several times and said, "What happened? I'll tell you what happened. I ran. I ran away." King-Roy sniffed. "I ran away and some of my friends saw me run, and they called me a coward. They said I was afraid to go to jail."

King-Roy's face was struggling against the tears that threatened to come spilling from his eyes. His mouth was all bunched up and trembling, and his eyes were blinking and blinking. "They called me a coward."

I reached out and touched his hand, but he didn't feel me touch him. His mind was still far away.

"I had made a promise to Dr. King and I kept it. I didn't fight. If I had-a stayed, if I didn't run, I would have broken my promise. Everything in me told me to fight. It's not right. It's not right what they did, and I couldn't just stand there and take it. I couldn't just stand there and let my brothers and sisters take it." King-Roy wiped his wet cheek with the back of his hand and sniffed. "I had to run away or fight back. I couldn't just stand there."

"So, what about Syllia and Joe-Earl; were they okay?" I asked.

"What?" King-Roy said, turning his head to look at me. "Syllia and Joe-Earl?" King-Roy lowered his head and drew his brows together as though he was trying to remember who Syllia and Joe-Earl were. Then he took a deep breath and let it out again. "I . . . I was so angry I . . . I left them behind." He shook his head and another tear fell on the stones. "All I could think about was that I gave my word to Dr. King, and the only way I could keep it was to run."

"But you gave your word to your mother, too," I said. "What about that?"

King-Roy nodded and glanced up at me, and I saw fear in his eyes. He looked away and nodded. "I know. I can't explain it. I can't explain what happened—how I felt. No one understood. Momma—Momma was so ashamed of me for leaving Syllia and Joe-Earl, and everyone else was on me about running away, and they said I was the only one who ran. Momma, my brothers and sisters, the whole school—everyone was ashamed of me."

"But at least you all came out okay, right?" I asked.

King-Roy twisted up his mouth. He looked down at the tiles, tapped the toe of his shoe on them, and said, "Yeah, everyone came home. Syllia and Joe-Earl came home." King-Roy said this with a catch in his voice, and when he glanced up at me, I saw that same frightened look in his eyes that had been there before. I didn't know what it meant, but it scared me to see it. I knew he wasn't telling us the whole story, but I couldn't bring myself to ask him anything else just then, so the three of us stood there, and we didn't say anything for a while. I watched King-Roy stare down at the tiles, tapping first one toe of his shoe, then the other. Then he said, with his voice so low I could barely hear him, "That was the worst day of my life."

I nodded. "The day that changed your life, like you said to me yesterday, right?"

King-Roy didn't answer me, but he didn't have to.

Another question came to my mind, a question I thought I already knew the answer to, but I asked it, anyway. "King-Roy, what man were you accused of killing?"

King-Roy looked at me a long second, then he said, "'What man'? You know what man. It was that devil with the hose. That white devil who tore my sister and brother right out of my hands." King-Roy turned the palms of his hands up and looked at them as though he could see Syllia and Joe-Earl's little hands resting on them.

I stood facing him there in the pavilion. I stared at his face, saw the sadness I had seen there the day before, and I saw that it was an old deep-worn kind of sadness. I couldn't tell if he had killed that man with the hose or not, but I believed, at the very least, King-Roy knew who did.

FOURTEEN

King-Roy, Pip, and I didn't get to talk anymore because it was time for breakfast and Sophia had come out to get us. Pip stayed for breakfast, but afterward he said he was leaving. "You ignored me all through breakfast," he told me when we stood together on the porch and he was saying good-bye.

"I did not," I said.

"You did. You just stared at King-Roy the whole meal. I saw you."

"I was just seeing if I could tell if he really hated us. He was so friendly and well-mannered at the table, I couldn't tell, could you? I just want him to like us, Pip. I want him to want to stay."

Pip ran his fingers through his bangs, so they stood straight up, and said, "I don't know why. He could be violent. He could just snap again and kill the whole lot of you. How am I going to feel if I keep the you-know-what a secret and something happens to you?"

"But it won't. I know it," I said.

Frustrated, Pip rolled his head around on his neck. "You just said you couldn't even tell how he feels about all of you. He's probably a master at disguising his true feelings. You don't really know what he's liable to do. He could be a real cold-blooded killer, for all you know. He really could, Esther."

I shook my head. "What he told us about that march, Pip, I can't get that out of my mind. He seems so ashamed of himself. Don't you feel sorry for him?"

"I don't know," Pip said. "Maybe he was so ashamed and angry, he went and killed that fireman."

I swatted Pip's shoulder. "Pip, you've got a one-track mind. All you can think about is that he might have killed somebody."

"You'd better think about it, too, Esther, and you'd better not forget it. No telling what kind of dangerous this guy is." Pip jumped off the porch and turned around. "Oh, I left you something, up in your room."

"Pip, you shouldn't have. What is it?"

Pip must have seen something in my face, because he said, "Don't get all guilty feeling about it," which is how I was feeling. "It's just some cream rinse my mother bought for you. She said all the professionals use it, which you would know if you ever got your hair cut at a real salon instead of with me at the barber's."

"They're willing to cut it dry, so it doesn't hurt so much when they comb it. I like the barber's, and Mother doesn't mind my going there as long as they don't make me look like a boy. But thanks for the cream rinse. I hope it works. Thanks, Pip."

Pip just waved and headed off toward his house.

After Pip left, I didn't get to spend any time with King-Roy because I had to go with my sister and brother to the country club for their swimming lessons and a day at the pool.

That's the way it was all weekend long. I took care of my brother and sister and only saw King-Roy at mealtimes, when he wouldn't even look at me, but I was glad to see that at least he hadn't left yet. He hadn't gone to Harlem yet. I still couldn't get what he told us in the pavilion out of my mind. I wanted to do something for him. I wanted to make everything all right, make it so that it was okay that he ran away and left his brother and sister behind. I just wanted to make it right somehow, but I couldn't figure out how.

Sunday night my mother called me to her bedroom to talk to me. Having a talk in my parents' bedroom was never good news, so I took my time dragging myself in to meet with my mother.

"Esther, I called you in thirty minutes ago," my mother said when I finally showed up in her doorway. My parents had the neatest room. It was huge, of course, and it had a secret room hidden behind a wall of books, and a king-sized bed with big fat cherubs—ones you could almost pull out and hold in your hands—carved in mahogany, with fat twisting pillars for bedposts; and they had a pump organ in there that my father played sometimes. It had belonged to my father's mother, and we children weren't allowed to touch it. I looked all these things over as I stood in the doorway, waiting for my mother to get through her lecture on being on time and get down to the real reason she called me.

"Esther, are you listening to me?"

I turned from the organ and looked at my mother. "Not really, Mother, but I know what you were saying and it's not that I can't be on time, it's just, I didn't want to be. I know you're going to tell me something I don't want to hear."

"I want you to look after Stewart and Sophia this week," my mother said.

"See," I said. "Why? Why do I have to watch them all the time? Beatrice has nothing better to do than sleep half the day away; why don't you ask her to look after them?"

"Beatrice has no patience with them, and I need you to take them to the city on Wednesday for another audition."

"Me? Why can't you take them? I hate going on auditions, you know I do, Mother. All I do all day is sit around and watch bratty kids who can't act."

Mother's eyes filled with tears. "Madeline is sick again. I want to go stay with her this week."

Madeline was Mother's other best friend—her best New York friend—and Madeline had cancer.

I rushed to my mother's side and put my arm around her. "I'm sorry, Mother. I'll watch them for you, and I'll take them into the city and everything. I'm sorry about Madeline. Tell her I hope she feels better."

Mother pulled away from me. "Feels better? She's dying of cancer. She's never going to feel better, only worse."

"Well," I said, "I hope she feels better, anyway. I can hope it, can't I?"

So that's the way it was. All week I stayed busy with Sophia and Stewart and I hardly saw King-Roy and I didn't work on my play and Pip and I ran in the mornings, where most of the time we fought about King-Roy, and I wheeled Sophia around in a wheelbarrow and took her and Stewart to the gatehouse to help Auntie Pie with the animals, only they were no help at all. They squealed and hopped up and down when I brought any of the animals out for them to see. I took them swimming, and to Jack's to eat sandwiches and nickel pickles, and we went bike riding, to the movies, to the audition, to a matinee in the city, and to the Metropolitan Museum of Art, where Stewart stared at the Degas paintings and wouldn't leave the room where they were kept, and Sophia stared at the nude-male statues. By week's end I was exhausted and Sunday night came and I had another meeting with Mother and she said she needed me to watch Sophia and Stewart another week. I wanted to complain, but Mother looked a lot more tired than I felt, so I kept my mouth shut and hoped twice as hard that Madeline would get to feeling better soon.

The only good thing about the second week, or so I thought at the time, was that on Friday, when I had to take Sophia and Stewart to yet another audition in the city, King-Roy said he wanted to come with us. He said he had earned himself a day off, and I knew that he had.

While I had been taking care of my brother and sister, King-Roy had painted the laundry room white, fixed the 1947 Ford Super Deluxe station wagon, so it ran forward again, and chauffeured Auntie Pie around in it. He had caddied for my father when he played golf at the country club, listened to Beatrice practice her lines and fixed her hair dryer, so the plastic cap that went on her head was attached to the air hose the way it was supposed to be, followed Monsieur Vichy around with a pad and pencil in his hand and wrote down any great ideas Monsieur Vichy had—which meant writing down anything Monsieur Vichy said out loud—and taught Daisy, our housekeeper, how to make "real" banana pudding.

The only time King-Roy and I had had a chance to really talk again was late one afternoon.

King-Roy was working on the car and I stood watching him, hoping he'd notice how pretty my hair looked. Pip's cream rinse really worked. I twirled a section of my hair in my hand the way I saw my friend Laura do once when she was flirting with Jamie Solo, a junior in high school. King-Roy didn't even look up. When I said hi and asked him what he was doing, he said, "I don't want to talk to you right now, Esther."

"Why not?" I asked.

He glanced at me from under the hood of the car and said, "I shouldn't have told you what I did. I shouldn't have told you any of it."

I said, "I think about it all the time, what you said. I wish I could make you feel better."

"Well, you can't, so go away now." King-Roy unscrewed something under the hood.

"Won't you teach me to tap, at least?" I asked.

"No, and that's another thing I shouldn't have told you about. I talked too much," King-Roy said.

I shrugged. "That happens a lot around here. People are always telling me things they later wished they hadn't. They tell me things because I don't matter. Pip tells me things because I do. Which are you, King-Roy? Why did you tell me what you did?"

King-Roy straightened up, pulled a rag out of his back pocket, and wiped his hands. "You matter, Esther. I told you because, I guess, well, it just came out. You—you're easy to talk to." King-Roy pushed his glasses up on his nose and said, "I guess it's because you're so open and you don't try to be something you're not."

I let go of my hair and shook my head. "Oh, yes I do. That first day we met, I tried to be Katharine Hepburn."

King-Roy chuckled. "Well, see, you're honest and you make mistakes and you make me feel okay."

"I do? That's almost the nicest thing anybody's ever said to me." I leaned forward and gave King-Roy a big hug, and King-Roy quickly pushed me off of him.

"Hey, you can't be doing that," he said, looking left and right. "You want to get me in trouble?" He picked up some kind of wrench tool and pointed with it and said, "You go on, now. Go on and leave me to work."

"You smell like motor oil and soap," I said.

"I said, go on," King-Roy said, hiding his head under the hood.

By the time Friday and the train ride into the city came around, I was really excited about our trip, until I saw King-Roy come down with a filled grocery sack rolled up under his arm.

"What you got in there?" I asked him.

King-Roy grabbed the bag and held it with two hands as if he thought I was going to take it from him and said, "Never you mind."

I looked at him, but he wouldn't meet my eyes. He started walking away from me, toward the kitchen, and I trotted after him.

"Why 'never you mind'? What's in there?"

"I'm not telling, and you just leave me alone about it, Esther."

I stopped and said, "Aren't you coming with us to the audition today?"

King-Roy turned around. "I told you I was going into the city with you, but I'm gon' spend the day with Ax, in Harlem."

I eyed the bag again. "Are you staying, King-Roy? Are those all your clothes in there?"

King-Roy turned back around and walked on toward the kitchen, and he didn't say another word.

FIFTEEN

L ater that morning on the train, King-Roy and I sat side by side, with his grocery bag held under his arm on the side away from me, and listened to the train going over the tracks. We stared out the window at the rain and the towns flashing past and said nothing to each other. We couldn't; Sophia and Stewart were doing all the talking. They had flipped the back of their seat over, so that it faced us, then sat down across from us. The two of them had decided King-Roy needed an inch-by-inch description of every town we rode through, so they gave it to him.

"We're coming to Tarrytown now," Stewart said. "It's named after the settlers who would go into the pubs and tarry awhile."

Sophia, not wanting to be outdone, said, "The Old Dutch Church is near here, too, you know, the one Washington Irving mentions in *The Legend of Sleepy Hollow*."

"And there's a beautiful example of Gothic Revival here, the Lyndhurst mansion," Stewart said, jumping back in.

I had tuned their noise out for as long as I could stand it, but finally I said, "Would you two be quiet? King-Roy can't see anything, sitting in the train, so how's he supposed to get excited about a fine example of Gothic Revival architecture if he can't even see it? You two are just showing off, anyway." I looked at King-Roy to see how he was taking everything.

Sophia swung her leg out and kicked my shin. "We're not showing off," she said. "We're just curious, so we believe others would be curious, too. Not everyone's as uncurious and stupid as you are, Esther." She opened the Jane Austen book on her lap with great dramatic flair as a way of reminding me of her great brilliance, compared to my stupidity.

I was about to say something but King-Roy beat me to it. He wrinkled his nose at Sophia and said, "Girl, being ugly is stupid, and that was ugly. If I were your mother, I'd wash your mouth out with soap for disrespecting your sister like that."

Stewart raised his brows and said, "It's not disrespectful if it's true. Esther is the stupid one in the family and that's a fact. Just ask my parents."

"I don't need to ask them anything. I can judge my own self who's stupid in your family," King-Roy said, looking Stewart up and down like he was seeing stupid all over the place.

I had to bite down on my lips to keep from laughing, but then Sophia burst into tears and stood up and pointed at King-Roy and said, "If I blow my audition, it's going to be your fault. I have lost my focus." She turned to me with her mouth turned down and tears falling from her eyes. She spread her hands out, palms up, and said, "Esther, I've lost my focus!" She looked at me as though she expected me to get down on the floor of the train and look for it like it was a lost bracelet.

I stood up and wrapped my arms around Sophia and pulled her down with me and into my lap. "It's all right, Soph. You'll get your focus back. You'll see. It's all right."

"The heck it is," I heard King-Roy mutter before he stood up and stepped out into the aisle to pace with his grocery sack.

Other people in our car kept giving King-Roy suspicious glances as he passed, so when he reached the end of the car, he turned around and came back and sat down again, crossing his legs.

The four of us stayed quiet all the rest of the way into the city.

Once we got to Grand Central Station, King-Roy went off to find a phone booth, to call Ax, while we waited for him by the big clock. I watched the back of him retreating, his baggy brown pants flapping when he walked, and I wanted to run after him. I felt suddenly that I'd never see him again, but I couldn't run after him because I had to run after Stewart instead.

As soon as King-Roy was out of sight, Stewart said, "I'm not going with you to the audition."

"What? You have to. You're auditioning for the part of Bobby," I said.

Stewart shook his head. "Mother wants me to audition, but I want to take a ballet class over at the school, and if I hurry, I can get in on the ten o'clock class. I've got my ballet slippers and tights in here." He patted the satchel he had hanging from his shoulder, the one I thought held all our lunches.

"I'll meet you afterward, at the theater," he said.

"But you can't! Stewart, Mother would kill me a million thousand ways if she knew I let you go."

Stewart shrugged and started backing away. "I do it all the time. I ride in with Mother and Sophia to the theater, cut out for a class, and get back in time for the audition. She never knows I'm missing."

"Well, you can't do that with me," I said. "What if something happened? What if you got hurt or lost or someone attacked you?"

"Bye." Stewart turned and ran off toward the steps leading to the subway platforms. I looked at Sophia. "Listen, Soph," I said, my hands grabbing her shoulders, "you wait here for King-Roy, and you don't move. I've got to go after him."

Sophia nodded. "Okay," she said, "but you'll never catch him."

"Oh yeah? Watch me."

I ran after Stewart, through the main concourse, feeling constricted in my narrow skirt and good shoes with the slippery soles. I wanted to take the shoes off, but I knew I would tear my stockings. I hiked up my skirt some and just ran. I ran down to the subway platform, past all the people rushing to catch the train that had just come thundering in, and chased after Stewart. I don't know what made him turn and look back—it was too noisy for him to hear me—but he did and he saw me, then took off at full speed. I ran after him, calling out his name, running into people who wouldn't get out of the way fast enough, and finally caught up to him just as he'd reached his line and was trying to slip onto the subway train. I caught him by the collar of his shirt, then by his arm, and I grabbed it tight and pulled him away from the train. "No you don't," I said. "You're coming with us."

The train shot out of the station and another one came in while I struggled to get Stewart under control. People around us stood and watched us as if we were some kind of an act.

"Esther, lay off of me! I want to dance. I just want to dance," Stewart said, when I had full hold of him and he could hardly move.

"Stewart!"

Stewart tried to wriggle away from me, twisting his head so he could reach my arm with his mouth and bite, but I was too fast for him and I changed position, grabbing both of his arms and pulling them back behind him.

"Stewart, stop!" I held him close to me and shouted into his ear over the noise around us.

"I want to dance!" he shouted back.

"Stewart. Stewart, listen. I know you do. I know you want to dance more than anything in the world, I do, and I'll do anything to help you. I'll talk to Mother and Dad. I'll convince them that you have to dance. I'll do it, I promise, but I can't let you go today. Don't you see? I can't risk something happening to you while I'm in charge. Now, please, come on. Right now, Sophia is standing all alone down below. What if something's happened to her?"

Stewart relaxed. "You promise you'll talk to them?"

I let go of Stewart and crossed my heart with my index finger. "I promise I'll do it. Now, come on, let's run."

As we ran back toward where I hoped both Sophia and King-Roy waited for us, Stewart said, "Tell Mother, no more play auditions. Tell Mother I want to be in the *Nutcracker*. Tell Dad that I'm not a fairy. Tell him that long ago men used to dance all the parts in a ballet. Tell him that it takes a strong athlete to be a ballet dancer."

While we ran, Stewart continued telling me what to tell Mother and Dad and I nodded and prayed with everything I had in me that both Sophia and King-Roy would be waiting for us when we got back to the clock.

SIXTEEN

I didn't know who I was more relieved to see when we reached the main concourse again, Sophia or King-Roy, but both of them were there and I had hold of Stewart's hand, so I felt everything was going to be all right. Then King-Roy told me he wouldn't be going to Harlem for a couple of hours yet, so he wanted to join us, and I felt on top of the world.

As we headed for the subways, Sophia said, "I can't believe you caught Stewart. You run really fast, Esther. You'll make a good gym teacher."

I ignored Sophia and smiled at King-Roy, and King-Roy ignored me and smiled up at the zodiac constellations painted in blue and gold in the huge arch high above us.

King-Roy tried to hide it, but I could tell he was excited when we got to Broadway, even if it was in the rain. I could tell he enjoyed seeing all the people walking around, and watching the traffic, and seeing all the shops and theaters. His eyes looked bright, and he walked fast and peppy, bouncing up on the balls of his feet, still clutching his paper sack.

We went down an alley, to the back of the theater, where a lady named Mrs. Holden checked us in. She said we were early, but she let us in even though she kept giving King-Roy suspicious glances. Still, she never said anything and we gathered around Sophia and I made sure she had everything she needed.

Sophia said, "I don't want you back here. You'll ruin my focus. I need to get into character. Go out front the way Mother does and leave me alone."

We had turned around to leave, when Sophia said, "Wait!"

I looked back and saw Sophia staring at another little girl who had just entered backstage.

Sophia ran up to me and whispered, "Who's she?" She pointed at the girl.

I shrugged. "How should I know, Soph? Stewart?"

Stewart said, "Never saw her before, but she's pretty."

That was the wrong thing to say.

Sophia started jiggling herself up and down as though she had to go to the bathroom, and tears spilled from her eyes. "She's prettier than I am. Esther, she's prettier than I am, isn't she?"

Sophia had begun to flap her hands up and down in front of her chest like some baby bird trying to figure out how to fly. Her face had broken out in red blotches.

"Sophia, you're both beautiful," I said.

"No!" Sophia said, her voice rising so that the other girl and her mother, who had been talking to Mrs. Holden, looked over at her. The little girl had a beautiful smile and big round blue eyes with long eyelashes and blond hair with ringlets.

I put my arm around Sophia. "Shh," I said. "It's all right. There's room for more than one pretty girl on the planet, you know. You're prettier than me, aren't you?"

"But, Esther, that doesn't mean anything. I'm prettier than her, aren't I? Aren't I?" Sophia looked up at me, her eyes holding such a pleading look in them.

"Sophia, you're the prettiest, smartest, most talented girl I've ever met," I said, squeezing her. "You're only six years old, and look at you. But you know, it wouldn't matter if you weren't, would it? I still love you, and Stewart and Mother and Dad—we all love you." I thought to include King-Roy in the list of people who loved her, since he was standing right there, but when I looked up at the scowl on his face, I decided to just leave it.

Sophia shot a glance over at the other little girl, who was trying to keep her focus on her script and not look at us, but I could see her peeking sideways at us.

"I'm much prettier, I think," Sophia said, wiping her eyes.

I let go of Sophia and straightened up. "Well, then, see. There you go. Do you want me to stay here with you until your turn to audition?"

Sophia took a deep breath and looked at King-Roy—who stood watching us with his arms crossed, shaking his head—and said, "No. Leave me. I have to compose myself. I've already been upset twice today. If I don't get this part, I'll know whose fault it will be." Sophia glared at King-Roy.

"Sophia!" I said. "That isn't fair and you know it."

Sophia picked up her script and said, "I don't like the way he's always looking cross at me. I don't like him."

"Sophia!" I said, jumping in between the two of them, not wanting either one of them to look at the other. I didn't want Sophia to say anything that would make King-Roy leave, and I didn't want King-Roy to say anything else that Sophia could blame him for later.

I knew that Sophia always got grumpy before an audition, but King-Roy didn't and he said to me on our way out front, "That child's got a problem."

I said, "Oh, that's just the way she gets sometimes. She'll be better when she's through her audition, you'll see."

Stewart said, "No she won't. Not unless she actually gets the part. If she doesn't, she'll be worse."

I didn't want to think about that.

We took a seat right behind where the director was sitting, because that was where Mother always sat so she could hear all the comments, and we got ourselves settled.

Stewart pulled his copy of the script he had for the auditions out of his satchel along with my French notebook from last year, which had my one line in it for the play I was writing, and the book *The Sun Also Rises*. He handed me my notebook and the script, then opened his book up to where he had last left off and started reading, taking advantage of the lights while they were still on in the theater.

"Are you sure you don't want to audition?" I asked Stewart.

He didn't even lift his head; he just shook it and kept on reading.

Other mothers—usually it was mothers who brought their children to these things—came into the theater and took seats behind us. Many stayed backstage with their children, but Sophia hated anyone hanging around her, looking at her or primping her. She needed to keep her focus.

I looked over at King-Roy, on the other side of Stewart, and I saw that he sat on the edge of his seat, staring at the stage as though he expected that any minute a big production was about to begin.

The first auditions were for the part of a girl named Zelda, a fifteen-year-old amnesiac. After more than an hour of bad acting, a very pretty dark-haired girl came onstage to read for the part, and I noticed a bit of motion in front of me, as though the director was interested in this girl. I had slumped way down in my seat, with my knees up against the seat in front of me, and even King-Roy had sat back in his seat with boredom. The girl read her lines, and she didn't seem to be any better than the rest of them. I was in the middle of yawning when I heard the director in front of me say to the woman by his side, "What do you think? I like her. She might fit the part, don't you think?"

I sat up in my seat and leaned forward, and without thinking what I was doing I said, "No, you can't. She's all wrong."

The director turned around. "I beg your pardon? Either be quiet or leave the theater."

"But she is. Zelda is strong and courageous. She's energetic. That girl up there is lethargic. She even talks tired. And her body is all wrong. She's too thin."

"Who are you?" the lady next to the director asked me.

I was busy flipping through Stewart's copy of the script to find the part the girl onstage had been reading.

"And where did you get a complete copy of the script?"

I looked up. "From my father. I'm Esther Young."

"Herbert Nelson Young's child?" the director asked.

"Yeah, look here," I said, pointing out the place in the script. "See where Zelda says, 'Now I remember. I was on the sled and you were there. You were with me, behind me on the sled, and we were going down Bowman's hill.' See that part?" I looked at the two of them. "She's remembering. It's all coming back to her, and that's exciting. She should sound eager and hopeful, and her words should come out faster and faster as she's remembering. She should be like 'You saw the tree, didn't you? I remember. You said, "Look out for the tree." You cried, "Look out!" and then I saw it, too, but it was too late. That's when we crashed.'" I looked at the two in front of me and said, "Now, it shouldn't be read too fast, but, you know, she's been in the dark for so long and here she is; it's coming to her all at once. That girl on the stage, no offence to her, but she's reading those lines like she's scared. Like she's afraid to remember. But see, she doesn't know there's anything to be afraid of yet, right? She's . . ." I stopped speaking. The director and the lady were looking at each other and nodding, and I said, "What?" Then, realizing I should have kept my mouth shut, I slid back in my seat and passed the manuscript over to Stewart. "Sorry," I said. "It's just that it would be a crime for a part like this Zelda's to go to that girl up there."

I slid back down in my seat.

The lady said, "Pretty sneaky way of reading for the part, Miss Young, but it worked. You've got the part."

"Oh, no! I don't want the part," I said, sitting bolt upright in the seat again.

Stewart clapped me on the back and said, "Hey, Esther!"

I turned to look at him and said, "No, Stewart, you know I couldn't."

"Why not?" the lady in front of us asked.

"I can't act," I said, shaking my head and feeling my eyes ready to pop out of my head with the shock of it all.

The director said, "But you just did. Of course you can act. Very well done, Miss Young."

"Excuse me, but is everything all right?" The mother of the girl up onstage had come out to join her daughter and was calling out to the director.

The director looked down at his notes and said, "Thank you, Miss Kelly, we'll be in touch," and the mother and daughter stalked off the stage.

The two faces in front of me stared back at me, expecting me to say something, so I said, "No, you don't understand. My sister, Sophia Young, is here. *She's* the actress. She's reading for the part of Clarissa."

"So, this is for Zelda," the lady said. "Do you want the part or not?"

Stewart spoke up, "Of course she wants it."

I turned on Stewart. "No, I don't."

"But this is your chance, Esther. I never knew you could act. Think of what Mother and Dad will say. They'll be so proud of you."

I said, "But I can't. Think of Sophia, Stewart. I couldn't do that to her. You know it. You know that I can't."

Stewart and I looked at one another, and I knew that he understood. I didn't have to say any more. We both knew that Sophia was too fragile and too young. She needed to think she was the best, the prettiest, the smartest, the greatest, and the most loved one. Someday she would find out that she wasn't, I knew that, but she didn't ever have to know about this. She didn't ever have to know that I could act. Acting was too important to her, and as desperately as I wanted to impress my mother and father and show them I wasn't the dolt they thought I was, I knew acting wasn't the way. Sitting there, I realized that even if I really could act, it would mean nothing to me. I didn't need a stage or an audience the way Sophia did. I didn't need it to go on living, and I realized that Sophia, little Sophia, just six years old, did.

SEVENTEEN

I finally got the casting director to accept that I wasn't going to act in his play, and we settled down again to wait for Sophia's turn. Before long, King-Roy leaned forward and whispered that he ought to be running along to Harlem. He got up to leave, and I got up, too, and followed him to the empty lobby.

We could see through the glass doors that the rain had stopped. The sun reflected off of the wet roofs of the passing cars.

King-Roy moved to the doors and looked up and down the street as though getting his bearings. He still held the paper sack in his hand.

I said, "King-Roy, you'll be coming back, won't you?"

King-Roy turned to look at me. "I told you I would. I'm just goin' for the day, Esther. I'll meet you here at four, just like I said."

I looked at his sack, thinking that maybe it was just his gun and a lunch he had in there, and not his clothes, and he was returning the gun to Ax. That's what I hoped. I said, "Okay, then. Well, good-bye."

King-Roy started to turn, then he turned back to me and said, "You were real good in there the way you said those lines. I wanted to hear you say more of them. With all the other girls, I wanted them to hush up and move on off the stage already, but with you I wanted to hear more."

I smiled and brushed my bangs out of my eyes. "You think so? You think I was good?"

"I think you should have taken the job or the part, whatever you call it, yeah," King-Roy said, nodding. "You know someday your little sister's gon' have to learn that she's not the only shiny apple on the tree."

I noticed two men passing outside the theater with a huge sheet of glass between them. I watched them navigate their way through the stream of people bustling by and then I said, "Sophia won't learn it from me. She loves the stage, King-Roy. She lives for it, the same way Stewart lives for ballet and Auntie Pie lives for her animals and my father lives for directing, and maybe the way you lived for tap until your father killed that for you. Maybe you still love tap that way, or why else do you still do it when you think no one's looking and you have shoes with taps on them?"

King-Roy pushed his glasses up on his nose with his index finger and looked toward the exit doors. Then he turned to me and said, "Well, I'm gon' leave now."

We stared at each other and I felt I was looking at him for the last time. I could see it in his eyes, this distant, already gone look. I stepped up to him and grabbed King-Roy around his waist.

"Whoa," King-Roy said, lifting his arms up in the air, with the bag held high.

I didn't let go. "Bye, King-Roy," I said, squeezing his middle. "Thanks for everything."

"Well, now," King-Roy said, bringing his free hand down and stroking my head a couple of times. Then he said real softly, "Your hair feels real nice, Esther," and when he said that, I knew I was in love. I loved King-Roy for real. My heart just felt ready to burst with my love for him.

"You better let go now," King-Roy said, and I did. I stood back from him a little ways and he said, "Listen here, do you still want to learn how to tap?"

I smiled up at his beautiful, handsome, wonderful face and said, "Really? Yes! Of course I do."

"All right." King-Roy nodded. "We'll start tomorrow. Now do you believe I'm coming back?"

I put my arms around him again and leaned my head on his chest and squeezed him and King-Roy's arms came down around me with the bag pressed against my back and I said, "I love you, King-Roy."

King-Roy didn't say anything, but I thought I felt a little more pressure against my back before he let go of me and turned and walked through the glass doors.

EIGHTEEN

I floated back into the theater and sat down again next to Stewart. All I could think about was King-Roy and hugging him and hearing his heart beating in his chest and feeling his arms around me and smelling his Lifebuoy soap smell. I sat in the dimly lit theater, smiling and dreaming until Stewart leaned over and said Sophia would be up next. I sat up in my seat and noticed that the pretty little girl we had seen earlier that morning was on the stage reading her lines. Listening to her I knew that Sophia had real competition. They were both of a type—one blond, one brunette, but both bright and girly and slender. Both sounded older than they were; both had a similar way of delivering their lines. It was almost as if this little girl had been studying Sophia and was imitating her. In the end, I figured it would probably come down to whether they wanted a blond or a brunette for the part.

I looked over at Stewart and he was shaking his head.

I whispered, "She's good, isn't she?" and Stewart nodded. He leaned in toward me and said, "You should have taken the part, Esther. At least one of us would be in this play and Mother would be happy."

I shook my head. "I don't want you to tell her what happened earlier. Don't tell Sophia, either. Especially not Sophia. I don't want you to tell anyone, okay?" I sat back in my seat and watched the little blond girl trot off the stage. Sophia's name was called and out she came, and I could tell by the way she walked, almost on tiptoe, that she was already in character. Sophia began to speak and I got lost in her performance.

Sophia was good, no two ways about it. I always liked seeing her on the stage. She was different some-how, more normal, I guess. It was like the sharp edges of her personality were gone and in their place was this other character, always a more even, lighter, gentler character than the real Sophia. No wonder she loved the stage. It wasn't just the applause and adoration of her audience. It was the fact that for the time she was up there reciting her lines, she knew who she was and what was expected of her. I knew that life never felt more cer-tain to her than when she was playing somebody else. That day, she was playing the part of Clarissa for all it was worth, and I thought she was better than the other little girl. I only hoped that the casting director would agree.

After everyone had been seen, we waited to see if Sophia would be called back. Even though this was a closed audition, so Sophia and the others had been in-vited to audition, the directors had seen a lot of kids that day and I figured that they'd want to see how well some of the actors they picked interacted with one another, but this time it was different. This time we didn't have to wait. The director told Sophia that she got the part.

When Stewart and I went backstage to get her and congratulate her, I saw the other girl, the pretty blond girl, crying in her mother's arms.

When Sophia saw us, she ran up to us and at the top of her voice she said, "I got the part. I knew I would. I was the best, wasn't I?"

I looked over at the little blond girl and then at some of the other girls and boys still backstage, and I saw them all staring at Sophia. None of them looked happy, and as much as I wanted to root for Sophia, I knew this wasn't the time.

I whispered to Sophia, "Let's wait until we get outside, okay? These other kids' feelings are hurt."

"Why should I be sad when I got the part?" Sophia said, collecting her script and her Jane Austen book and the remains of her lunch and stuffing them into the satchel she had brought with her. "It's not my fault none of them can act."

I grabbed Sophia by the arm and hauled her out of there, saying loudly as we left, "I thought everyone was wonderful. They were the best child actors I've ever seen. You really had some stiff competition." Then I yanked Sophia out the door and Stewart followed us and we were back in the alley where we had begun the day.

Sophia was in a rage. She broke free of me and

shouted, "Don't you touch me. How dare you do that in front of all those people, and they were terrible and you know it! You're just jealous of me. You've always been jealous of me, because I'm six and you're fourteen and I'm smarter and more talented and prettier and everything than you are. You're just jealous."

"Sophia, just shut up," Stewart said.

Sophia looked at Stewart as though he had slapped her. Her brown eyes flashed at him and she said, "What did you say?"

Stewart dug his hands into the pockets of his pants and, staring right at her, said, "Shut up, Sophia, just shut up and stop acting like a spoiled brat. You got the part, so shut up."

Stewart turned and walked away down the alley.

I looked at Sophia, then at my watch. It was almost four o'clock. "Come on," I said, "we don't want to miss King-Roy." The other kids and their mothers were now coming out the door, so I just started walking and hoped that Sophia would follow and not make another scene. Happily, she did follow, and the three of us went around to the front of the theater to wait for King-Roy. While we waited, Sophia talked our ears off about getting the part and how she had thought to play Clarissa one way but then at the last minute changed her mind, and on and on, and she was happy and no one was there to get their feelings hurt, so I was happy for her.

Every once in a while I would look down at my watch. It was ten after four, then twenty after, then four thirty, and still no King-Roy. Stewart was sitting on the concrete ground, leaning against the front of the theater and reading his book, while Sophia paced back and forth in front of us, still going on about how she got the part and picking apart all the other children who had auditioned. I had stopped listening to her. I was looking down the street, hoping to see King-Roy coming. Where was he? It was a quarter to five, then five o'clock, and still no King-Roy. I didn't know what to do. What could have happened to him? I knew Mother would be expecting us home soon. We couldn't just stand around waiting into the night for him to show up. Where was he? I felt all jittery and nervous inside. Stewart looked up from his book. "I think we'd better give up on King-Roy," he said. "I don't think he's coming, do you?"

I didn't want to hear that. I didn't want to think it. Something must have happened. He must have gotten lost again, or maybe he got hurt. Something *must* have happened, because he was going to teach me to tap. He liked me; I knew he did. He wouldn't just leave and not say anything. I decided we had to go look for him. I knew where Ax lived. Well, I knew the address. I had never been to Harlem before, but I knew the subway to take because I had pointed it out to King-Roy before we left the station. I told Sophia and Stewart of my plans, and they both thought it was a crazy idea.

"King-Roy could be lost again or hurt," I said. "I'll just go call Mother and tell her we got delayed. Or I could put the two of you on the train and then go on to Harlem myself."

Sophia was all for that idea, but Stewart didn't want me to go alone to Harlem, so we agreed to stick together. I called home, hoping as the phone rang that Daisy and not my mother would pick up.

It was Auntie Pie who answered. "What's the holdup?" she asked me when I told her we would be delayed. I was a terrible liar, so I said all in a rush, "We're waiting for King-Roy and I'll call you when we're coming home. Tell Mother, okay? Good-bye." Then I hung up fast, before Auntie Pie could say anything else. I looked at Sophia and Stewart and took a deep breath. "Okay, then," I said, "we're off to Harlem." The three of us held hands and we set off down the sidewalk, to go find King-Roy.

NINETEEN

We came out of the subway at 145th Street and St. Nicholas Avenue and we were in Harlem. The sun had gone in again and the day had turned gray. We walked toward Eighth Avenue and everything around us looked gray; the streets, the sidewalks, the litter, the buildings—all gray.

Sophia had a grip on my hand that was cutting off my circulation. People stared at us as we passed—the only white people walking in that part of town—and I thought of how King-Roy must have felt being the only black man walking through our town. Most of the people we passed looked so poor, dressed in worn-out browns and oranges and blues, women in dresses that looked like cotton housecoats, and children in rough-looking bare feet, torn and scarred and looking as if they were coated in a layer of ash. I felt sad and frightened at the same time.

Sophia said, "I don't like this. It's all dirty and ugly here. I want to go home. We don't belong here."

Stewart said, "Yeah, this was a bad idea, Esther."

"It was a stupid idea. Stupid, Esther," Sophia said.

I looked at the two of them, one on each side of me, leaning in close to me, their eyes wide and wary. "You're both just scared," I said. "They're poor, that's all. There's nothing to be afraid of."

"Oh yeah?" Stewart said, looking up ahead.

I followed his gaze and saw a Negro man in a gold-colored suit and shiny black shoes and a white hat, sauntering toward us with a big-bad-wolf smile on his face. When he caught up to us he said, his eyes on Sophia, "Well, well, well, what we got here? You kiddies lost?" The man crouched down to get a better look at Sophia, and I got a better look at his hat, a white fur cowboy hat. "Ain't you a pretty thang." He reached out to paw at Sophia, but she tucked in behind me and said, "Make him go away, Esther." Stewart took hold of my other hand and squeezed it.

I swallowed hard and said, "Uh, excuse me, but maybe you could help us? We're looking for a man named Ax, or Accident, do you know him?"

The man kept his eyes on Sophia, peering around me to get a good look at her, but when I said the name *Accident*, he straightened up, put a hand on his hat, and threw back his head and laughed with his mouth open so wide we could see the gold in his teeth. Then he looked at me and said, "Girl, you don't want to find no Accident and he don't want to find you, that's for dang sure." He held out his hand and said, "Now, why don't you just come along with your Uncle Len and I'll show you—"

"No, thank you," I said, walking fast past him with Sophia and Stewart still clutching my hands. "I have an appointment," I added over my shoulder.

I felt bad for being so afraid of the man. I knew that was prejudiced thinking, but he had a gleam in his eyes that frightened me and I had never seen a gold suit or a fur cowboy hat before, and they scared me, too.

I hurried along the avenue, ignoring Sophia's squeals when we came to a splatter of fresh blood on the curbside and later when we witnessed a man who stepped out from a doorway and vomited right in front of us. Nobody else stopped to see if he was all right, and nobody else stopped for the beggar with the missing eyeball, either. I stopped both times, and the sick man spat at us, and the beggar waved the dollar I had given him in the air and asked if that was all I could give him. When I said yes, he got angry and yelled curse words at us until we reached the end of the block.

When we came to Eighth Avenue and West 148th Street, which was the address King-Roy had mentioned, we found a row of apartment buildings. All of them looked as if they should have been condemned long ago. There were dark holes for windows, some with clothes and rags hanging out of them, some with people sitting in them or leaning out, propped up on their elbows and staring down at the street with bored expressions on their faces.

On the sidewalk a group of girls were skipping rope with a double set of ropes, and a couple of fat women sat outside on a sofa with three legs, smoking and fanning themselves with folded-up newspapers.

I stopped in front of the women and I said, "Excuse me, but could you tell me if a man named Accident lives here?"

"Who wants ta know?" one of the women asked me.

"I do," I said. "I'm Esther Young and this is Sophia and Stewart." I pointed at my brother and sister. "We're looking for his apartment."

"No you ain't," the other woman said. "You ain't lookin' for no Accident." Then she chuckled and said it again, "You ain't lookin' for no Accident."

"Why not?" I asked.

"'Cause he don't got nothin' to do with no gray girl."

"Gray girl?"

"She talkin' 'bout you, child," said the first woman. "Accident, he Muslim. He won't talk to no white devil."

"I'm really looking for our friend, King-Roy, King-Roy Johnson. He was visiting Ax—Accident—today."

"Yeah, we know. We seen him."

The two women eyed each other and smiled, and I knew they thought he was handsome. I just knew that's what they were communicating to each other. I felt relieved that we were at least in the right place. I asked, "Do you know which apartment building he's in? Would it be all right if we went inside?"

Both women found this funny. "Yeah, you can go on inside. He up on the fifth floor of that building there."

She pointed to her right. "Don't got no elevator, though. You gotta walk up."

"Thank you," I said, turning around to find that the girls with the jump ropes had stopped skipping and were staring at us.

One of the girls, dressed in a pink dress and wearing pigtails in her hair, waved at me and I waved back.

"You wanna jump?" she asked. She smiled and shook the ropes in her hands.

I wanted to jump with them. I wanted to learn how to do double-Dutch jumping and maybe impress Kathy and Laura, but I knew it was getting late and we needed to find King-Roy, so I said, "No, sorry. Thanks, anyway, but we've got to go find a friend of ours."

"Some other time, then," the girl said.

"Yeah, some other time." I nodded, wondering if we'd ever see each other again. I turned back around and led Sophia and Stewart along the sidewalk until we came to the apartment building the woman had pointed to. I looked back at the women to make sure I was at the right one, and when they nodded their heads, I nodded back, took a deep breath, and went inside.

The building smelled sour—just like piss and vinegar, exactly like piss and vinegar, and I felt sorry that I had ever described my Auntie Pie in that way.

The stairwell was hot and airless, and the higher we climbed, the more sour the smell. I didn't know how anyone could stand it. The smell made my mouth salivate. I wanted to spit, but I swallowed my saliva and kept climbing.

Sophia was making a whimpering sound that grew louder with each flight of steps we climbed. Once we reached the fifth floor, Sophia said, "I'm going to tell Mother and Daddy on you. Wait till they find out what you've done. You shouldn't have brought us here."

"You're right, Sophia, okay?" I said, knowing she was. "But we're here now, so let's just find King-Roy and then we'll leave."

A tall man with a broom in his hands was coming out of one of the apartments. He looked over at us, and his head jerked back with surprise. "Hey, what's this we got, now? What you three doin' here?"

"We're looking for Ax," I said, speaking louder than usual because there was a couple on the floor below us yelling at each other.

The man slid his eyes sideways at the apartment door across the hall from him. "Ax ain't here."

"Do you know where he is?" I asked, hoping he was telling us the truth.

"You don't want to go there." The man shook his head.

"Yes, I do. I'm looking for our friend, King-Roy Johnson. He's living with us this summer."

"Oh, yeah?" The man said, a smile coming to his lips. "Well, I met King-Roy and I seen him go off with Ax and I know where they gone, but you ain't invited."

I heard a loud noise coming from below us and it sounded like a gunshot. I glanced over at Sophia and Stewart and their big, wide eyes had grown even bigger, and I could tell they were ready to run out of that building, flee Harlem, and get back home, *now,* whether I came with them or not. I knew, too, that I was going to be in big trouble when we did get home, but we were there and I couldn't leave Harlem until I had found King-Roy. I gripped their hands in mine, ignored the noises below, and turned back to the man.

"Could you tell us where they are, please? It's getting late and I *need* to find King-Roy."

The man cocked his head to one side. "What if he don't want to be found?" he asked me.

I looked down at the floor and realized I was standing on a dark stain that looked like old blood. I stepped off of it, and feeling a surge of irritation and impatience hitting me at the same time, I said, "If he doesn't want to be found, then I'll let him tell me so himself." I glared at the man.

The man held up his broom and hid his face behind it. "One Twenty-fifth and Seventh," he said from behind the bristles.

"Seventh Avenue? Is that where he is?" I asked.

"That's what I said. One Twenty-fifth and Seventh."

"Thank you," I said.

The man poked his head up over the top of the broom and said, "I'm gon' kill me some rats."

I turned to leave, pulling Sophia and Stewart with

me and hoping that this man wasn't about to hit us with the broom, thinking we were rats. "Thanks again. Bye, now," I said, fleeing back down the steps.

"Watch out for them rats on the third floor," the man called after us.

Back out on the sidewalk I had to do some quick thinking. I knew it would be easier and faster to take the subway, but I also knew that Sophia and Stewart would insist that we go home and forget about finding King-Roy. I knew they would stay on the subway, and refuse to get off with me, so I decided we had to walk. Twenty city blocks equals a mile, so I figured we had just a little over a mile to go and it was already after six. I looked at my brother and sister and said, "Come on, we'll have to hurry; it's getting late. Sophia, do you need me to carry you?"

She shook her head and said nothing.

I knew Sophia was scared out of her wits, because she clutched my hand and didn't make a sound all the way to 125th Street, even when a gang of boys about Stewart's age followed us for two blocks, taunting us and throwing litter at us from off the sidewalk, and even when we passed an alleyway filled with garbage and too many rats to count, and even when we passed a group of men nodding at us and looking half out of their minds, and even when we passed a white policeman, who kicked a tired-looking man just sitting on the curb and minding his own business. None of us said anything. It felt like more things happened in that long walk to

125th Street than we had experienced in our whole life-
times combined. It was more than any of us could deal
with, so we just kept our heads down and ignored the
comments, the calls, the litter, the rats, the dogs, the
police, the dirt, the beggars, the stoned, and everything
else until we started to notice a crowd gathered up
ahead. I could hear someone speaking, someone saying,
". . . stolen our heritage and the so-called Negro isn't
going to take it anymore."

Shouts came up from the crowd.

We kept walking, listening to the short heavyset man
we saw standing in front of the crowd, wearing a gray
suit with a white shirt and a bow tie. He had a book in
his hand, and he held it above his head when he spoke
and brought it down whenever he paused for breath.

"You don't need bleach creams," he shouted, and
the crowd agreed. "You don't need to get your hair
straightened," he said, and again the crowd agreed.
"And you don't need anything else the white devil is selling in his stores and on the streets and in his churches.
He's selling Christianity, but we don't want it!"

"No sir!" The crowd yelled.

"He's selling us the idea of a white Jesus and a
heaven above, but we aren't buying it."

"We aren't buying it!" the people shouted.

"And he's selling us Cadillacs and trying to get us to
spend more than we got so we're always in debt to the
white devil, isn't it so?"

The crowd agreed, with "That so!" and "Yeah, man!"

"Mr. Charlie's selling us drugs and alcohol and ciga-rettes so we get addicted and go out of our heads and we can't think straight, isn't it so?"

"That's right!"

"Right on!"

"Why are you buying things from Mr. Charlie? Why are you buying things from the white devil? White isn't even real. They aren't even real people. The white man was created in a test tube. He's made of chemicals, bad chemicals, and now we got all these white devils, these bad mistakes, walking the earth."

The man shook his book above his head. "The hon-orable Elijah Muhammad has been sent from Allah to free us, to open our eyes and show us that we've been blind. We're better than the white man."

"Much better!" The crowd agreed.

"We're smarter."

"Much smarter!"

"We're superior to the white man in every way."

"In every way!"

"It's time we acted. It's time we showed them we mean business. It's time we showed them we're not going to let them push us around."

The crowd shouted. "That's right!" "Yeah, man!" "Ain't it the truth?"

"The white devil has stolen us from our country, stolen our African names, and given us their names, like Jackson and Brown and Smith. We ain't no Jackson and Brown and Smith!" he shouted.

The crowd cheered.

"They've raped our women and beaten our men and pushed and shoved us in and out of this place and that. Look around you. Is this how you want to live? Do you want to lose all your children to the white devil's drugs and alcohol?"

The crowd shouted, "No sir!"

"We're not going to take it anymore. We got too much self-respect. We got too much pride. We say enough's enough!"

Everybody shouted, "Enough's enough!"

"If they shove, we gon' shove back. If they strike, we strike back. If they shoot, we shoot back."

This got the crowd really stirred up, and the man at the front smiled and shook his book again. A group of men, standing close by, suddenly took notice of Sophia, Stewart, and me, and looked as if they were checking to see if we were about to strike or shoot, because they were ready, they were ready to fight back.

While this man was speaking, I was looking over the crowd standing there, a mix of well-dressed men and women, in suits and dresses, and men and women dressed like the poor people we had seen back on Eighth Street. I looked for King-Roy, but I kept finding myself listening to this man up front. What he said stirred me. I felt frightened and angry and confused all at the same time. What did he mean by saying white people were created in test tubes? Who told him that? Were white people trying to hurt Negroes by selling them things they couldn't afford and trying to get them addicted to drugs? I had heard stories about the South, about bombing Negro families' homes, and about hanging them and beating them. I had heard King-Roy's horrible story about the hoses and the dogs, but as much as it had upset me, I had felt that it had happened in some far away, unreal place. I had been to Alabama to visit relatives, and I never saw any of those kinds of things happening. It was like hearing in school about slavery, something that happened too long ago and too far away to be real, but as I stood there listening to this man up on the stand, shouting and waving his book, and heard him talking about freedom and how the "so-called Negro" was still a slave, still living with their heads caught in Mr. Charlie's noose, and how they would never be free until they lived in a separate nation from the white devil, I felt the immediacy of what he was saying. Everything—all those terrible stories about the South, and King-Roy's stories, and the stories the man up front was telling us—suddenly felt real and true and close, too close. I was standing in the middle of it. I had seen it with my own eyes right there in Harlem, and as I stood listening to the shouts of the people around me and saw the tired gray looks in some of their faces, all the tragedy and sorrow in the stories I had heard hit me all at once and I felt angry. I felt so angry, I found myself shouting with the crowd. "Enough's enough!" I shouted. "Enough's enough!" I raised my fist in the air and shouted again, "Enough's enough!"

TWENTY

I had gotten so involved in the shouting and in shaking my fist in the air that I had forgotten all about Sophia and Stewart, and even looking for King-Roy, but then I heard a woman close by say, "Ain't nobody gon' hurt you, baby. You all right."

I looked around and saw an attractive chocolate-skinned woman, wearing a pretty aqua dress, speaking to Sophia. I looked at Sophia and saw tears running down her face. Before I could lean forward and say anything to comfort her, the woman in the aqua dress reached down and picked Sophia up in her arms like she was picking a flower from a garden. "You a pretty little thing," the woman said, smiling big.

I was afraid Sophia might demand that the woman put her down and then start showing off how smart she was the way she usually did when people mistook her for a typical six-year-old, but Sophia just wiped her eyes and said, "My feet hurt and I'm tired and I want to go home."

She sounded so pitiful and so little, just like a real six-year-old, and I knew her feet must have been killing her, because we were all three dressed in our good shoes. Her shoes were at least a size too small because she didn't want to get big feet like mine, so she always wore the smallest shoes she could stand. I patted her foot. "Sorry, Sophia. I'm really sorry," I said. "I shouldn't have dragged you here. You either, Stewart."

Stewart stood with his arms crossed and tried to look angry with me, but I saw the bruised-looking circles under his eyes and knew he was more exhausted than angry. I was just about to suggest we go home and forget about King-Roy, when I saw him. I saw King-Roy standing up near the front of the crowd, with a girl in a flowered dress standing next to him and leaning on his shoulder.

"It's him," I said to the lady. I reached for Sophia. "I'll take her now. I've found who we were looking for. Thanks for being so nice."

The woman handed Sophia over into my arms and said, "You take care, now."

With Sophia in my arms and Stewart following close behind, I pushed through the crowd until I reached King-Roy and the girl. "King-Roy?" I said.

King-Roy looked over at me, and the girl turned around, still hanging on King-Roy. She was a tall, light-skinned Negro girl, wearing pink lipstick, with thick frizzed-out hair and long eyelashes that curled way up toward her eyebrows. She looked surprised to see us and so did King-Roy.

"Esther, what are you doing here?" He walked

backward, drawing us away from the crowd and across the street.

"We came to find you," I said, following him. I shifted Sophia higher up on my hip. "You were supposed to meet us at four, remember? It's almost seven and Mother's going to kill me. Why didn't you show up? What happened? What are you doing here?"

I stood staring up at King-Roy, who looked at me with his mellow expression as though he didn't care that we had dragged ourselves all over Harlem looking for him, and I felt tears stinging my eyes. "King-Roy?" I said.

"I'm sorry, Esther," he said, trying to look sorry but not succeeding. "I called your house and I told your Auntie Pie I wasn't coming home. I thought you'd call home, too, and they would tell you that. I'm sorry y'all came out here looking for me. I never would have expected that."

"These the kids you were tellin' me about, then?" the girl asked King-Roy, hanging herself back onto his shoulder again.

"Yeah," King-Roy said. He gestured toward me with his one free hand. "This is Esther and that's Sophia and that's Stewart." He smiled at the girl. "This is Yvonne."

The girl probably wasn't much older than I was, and there she was calling me a kid. Had King-Roy called me that? What about our hug in the theater? Didn't that mean anything to him? I felt furious. I set Sophia down on her own two feet and said, "You told me you would meet us at four. You said you were going to teach me how to tap, remember? Remember, you... you hugged me and asked me if I believed you were coming back and I said yes because you had agreed to teach me tap. Remember? And you hugged me," I said, glancing back and forth between King-Roy and Yvonne. "Remember?"

King-Roy's expression didn't change. He just shrugged his shoulders and said, "Well, things happened and now I'm staying here, here where I belong." He eyed Yvonne when he said the words *where I belong,* and I felt my heart sink into my stomach.

The crowd was breaking up and King-Roy waved to the man who had been doing all the talking, to let him know where he had moved to, I guess.

"Is that Ax?" I asked.

King-Roy smiled. "That's Ax, all right. He's gon' let me stay with him awhile."

"And you?" I asked Yvonne. "Do you live with Ax, too?"

The girl nodded. "I'm his sister." Then she giggled and gave King-Roy a peck on the cheek for no reason at all except that she just felt like it, I guess.

I didn't know how girls got away with flirting like that. I didn't know the first thing about how to flirt, as Kathy and Laura had reminded me often enough, saying, "You're born knowing, Esther. You've either got the knack or you don't, and you don't." I told them I didn't want it. Watching girls flirt, it always looked so stupid I didn't understand why any boy would fall for it, but I could see that King-Roy loved it. He fell for it completely.

"So I guess you'd better get on home now," he said. "You want me to walk you to the subway?"

I knew that walking us to the subway station was the last thing King-Roy wanted to do, and I felt too angry and hurt to want him with us, so I said, "No, thank you. We *kids* are fully capable of getting home on our own. Remember, *I* showed *you* how to get to Harlem this morning."

I grabbed Sophia and Stewart's hands and marched away, and I didn't mind when Sophia said, "I never did like that boy," loud enough for King-Roy to hear it.

TWENTY-ONE

I was miserable on the train ride home. Not only had I lost King-Roy and my dream of an exotic, summer romance, which, I realized, had been a flop right from the start, but I knew what would be waiting for me when we got home. Before we climbed onto the train I had called Mother to let her know we were on our way, and she had asked, "Where have you been? Don't you know we've been worried sick here? Esther, you're old enough to know better. I'm ashamed of you!"

I let her rant on for another minute before I interrupted her and told her that we were going to miss our train if we didn't get going. Mother said, "Don't think this is over, young lady. Not by a long shot. I'm so ashamed of you, I don't know what to do."

I heard more from Sophia on the train ride home until Stewart, seeing how miserable I was, told her to shut her mouth. "You're giving me a headache," he said.

"How come you're on Esther's side all of a sudden?" she asked.

Stewart looked over at me and then back at her and shrugged. "I guess because she's right sometimes, Sophia."

"Well, she wasn't right dragging us to that horrible Harlem. I will never be able to wash all the dirt and poverty of that place out of my hair." She tossed her head back and lifted her eyes to the roof of the train, and I could just see her mind imagining herself onstage, making her dramatic pronouncement and flouncing off into the wings. Since she didn't have a stage to flounce off of, she turned to me instead and said, "Esther, massage my feet; they're killing me."

I had had enough of her for one day and I let her have it, even if she had said all that about Harlem for dramatic effect and was only six years old. "Why don't you think of someone besides yourself for a change?" I grabbed her right foot and began massaging the ball of it. "None of the people living in those apartments gets a chance to just wash the poverty away. They've got to live in it every stinking day of their lives, and it's our fault, too."

Sophia giggled and propped her left foot up in my lap and nudged me to massage that foot, too. Both her big toes and her pinky toes were rubbed raw and blistered from her shoes and the long walk. "You didn't believe that fat old jelly up on the soapbox, did you, Esther? We're not really made from test tubes, you know."

The man, Ax, had made the whole thing with the test tubes sound possible to me somehow, but Sophia made it sound ridiculous. I didn't say anything, though, and the three of us were quiet the rest of the way home.

My father picked us up at the train station, and when

I climbed onto the front seat of the car, next to him, he didn't even look in my direction. He pulled out of the parking space and sped off, and the only thing he said to any of us was "It's after nine o'clock," which he said more to the windshield, really.

When we got home and out of the car, we found Mother waiting for us out on the porch along with Auntie Pie and Monsieur Vichy, who stood staring down at me with a gloating kind of smile as if to say, "I said all along you'd be the family scandal."

"Esther took us to Harlem, Mother," Sophia said as soon as she climbed out of the car. "It was horrible. Negroes were grabbing at me all over the place, and there was blood and vomit, and we heard gunshots, and we saw rats..."

On and on she went, relishing every bit of the tale and the red fury she saw on Mother's face, directed at me.

I finally knew what the expression "She was livid" really looked like, because Mother looked livid. Until then I had always pictured a slab of raw liver when people used the expression, but even though it was raw, all right, it was pure raw anger.

"Stewart and Sophia, you can go to your rooms. We want to talk to Esther alone," Mother said.

The two of them climbed the porch steps and crossed the floor, but then at the door, Stewart stopped and turned around and said, "Esther took good care of us, Mother and Dad. King-Roy had promised to meet us at four but he never showed up. We thought he was lost again. Esther was just doing what you asked her to do. She was just trying to keep us together." He stepped inside the door and added, "I think she did the right thing." Then he turned and followed Sophia inside.

Hearing Stewart defend me to Mother and Dad the way he did made me want to cry. I was full of so many emotions, I wanted to cry anyway, but I didn't. I saved it for when I was up in my room.

I stood with my head bowed, peering up at my parents from under my bangs, while Mother and Dad each had their say about how disappointed they were in me and how I was old enough to know better and how lucky we had all been not to have been kidnapped or worse, and I let their words slam against me and bounce back off again. I was too exhausted and sad and fed up to absorb their words. Dad strode back and forth across the porch, ranting, while Mother stood right where she was and pointed at me, jab, jab, jabbing her finger in my direction, and I watched as though it was a play, a silly play with highly dramatic people all saying their parts. Monsieur Vichy *tsk, tsk, tsk*ed, while Auntie Pie shook her head back and forth the whole time like she had palsy.

When the whole ordeal was over and my parents had announced that I would not be joining the family for the end-of-July barbecue at the country club that next Saturday night, my father asked me if I had anything to say. My parents always asked me that after they yelled at me and I knew they wanted some appropriate response, but I never got it right. I never said I'm sorry right, and everything else I had ever said had been wrong, too. Everything else always made them even angrier. This time when my father asked me if I had anything to say, I said just what was on my mind. "If you think I'm just so immature and stupid, why do you keep putting me in charge? Why don't you just lock me in my room already and throw away the key? I don't care." I stormed across the porch and into the house. I marched up the steps, expecting any second that my parents would call me back to yell at me some more, but they didn't, and when I reached the top of the steps, I ran into Beatrice and the Beast coming out of her servants' quarters, only I almost didn't recognize her. She had dyed her hair a dark brown and she had on a simple navy-blue dress and a pair of matching pumps. Before I could stand back and take it all in, and before I could say anything, Beatrice patted her hair and said, "Don't you go thinking this has a thing to do with anything you said. I don't go taking my advice from the likes of you."

"I know," I said.

"My hairdresser told me the bleach was ruining my hair."

"Okay," I said, turning in the direction of my bedroom. "I don't care what you do, anyway," I added over my shoulder. Then I ran down the hallway to my room and threw myself on my bed and cried and cried, and the last thing I remember before I cried myself to sleep was the cold image of King-Roy's face in front of me, telling me he wasn't coming back.

TWENTY-TWO

I woke up early the next morning determined to forget about King-Roy and all my silly romantic fantasies and to make things better between Pip and me. It seemed that every time we did our cross-country-training runs, we got into an argument. It was always about me. Pip said I wasn't listening to him. He said my mind was always on King-Roy. I told him I *was* listening to him, and I even repeated back exactly what he had said to me, but maybe he was right, because later I couldn't remember any of what we had talked about except that our conversations had always ended with an argument. This time I was going to try my hardest to show Pip that I knew I was lucky to have him as a friend and that I had put all my silly fantasies about King-Roy behind me.

I got myself dressed and ready for our run. I put on the Yankees baseball cap Pip once gave me and the Kennedy for President campaign button with President Kennedy's head on it that he'd also given to me. I pinned it to the one-piece gym uniform, which was way too big on me, so the elastic-trimmed undershorts hung down below the outer cuff almost to my knees. Mother had gotten the uniform large on purpose because it had to last three more years of high school. She had insisted I would grow into it. I figured Mother thought I was going to be an Amazon woman by the time I was a senior in high school. The gym uniform was the only clean item I had left to wear because I had forgotten to bring down my laundry, but that morning I didn't care. I even wrapped the Boy Scout belt Pip had given me around my waist, hoping to lift up the uniform some. It didn't work very well, but at least I would be showing Pip how much I appreciated him.

I was early for our run, so I sat outside on the polar bear rock and waited for Pip. It felt good to sit in the dark with my old friend, Polar Bear, his white granite body appearing ghostlike in the moonlight. I used to like to talk to the bear and tell him my troubles, believing he was listening. I guess I knew better than to do that now, but in the back of my mind I still thought maybe he could hear me, so I talked to him, whispering all my hurts and sorrows.

"I don't know what's wrong with me," I told him. "I don't know why I felt so desperate for King-Roy to like me in the first place. What did I expect, anyway? He's eighteen. He's a man, really, and he's a black man. Pip is right, we're from two different worlds." I took a deep breath. "But I'm scared. I'm scared and I don't know why I'm scared. Losing King-Roy yesterday—I don't know, it means something. I feel like something big and tragic has happened, but I don't know what it is. I don't know what I'm feeling, but it makes me miserable and sad and scared." I patted the rock—a polar bear lying on its side—and ran my hand back and forth along its white body.

A while later the sun began to come up and I knew, without looking at my watch, that Pip was late. He was never late, and I tried to recall if he had said something to me about coming later. I thought about this for some time and then, before I could decide on whether or not to head back inside, I looked up from my polar bear and saw Pip enter through our gate. He had someone with him, and that's when I remembered that he had told me that one of his pen pals was coming to stay with him for a couple of weeks. Every summer Pip had a new pen pal come visit. He had told me this pen pal was from White Plains, the only New York pen pal he had.

I stood up on the polar bear and called out to Pip. He saw me and waved, and the two of them turned and cut across the lawn toward me. That's when I discovered that Pip's White Plains pen pal was a girl, and that's when I saw the two of them walking together holding hands, and that's when my heart started racing in my chest and I felt so dizzy I had to sit back down on the polar bear.

When Pip and the girl—a pretty girl with long straight tangle-free brown hair, with the bangs pulled back in a barrette on the top of her head, and wearing makeup and a matching pink shorts and shirt outfit with strappy white sandals—caught up to me, I stood back up and forced myself to smile. I could hear my heart pounding in my chest, and it was so loud, I had to lean in to hear what Pip was saying to me.

"This is Randy Michaels," Pip said, wrapping his arm around Randy's shoulders and giving me a big grin. "And this is my oldest friend, Esther."

I smiled bigger and gave a half wave at Randy and noticed that she was looking me over and grinning like she was ready to burst out laughing. That's when I remembered what I had on and I looked down at myself with my hanging sack of a gym uniform, and then I heard it—Randy couldn't contain herself. Her laughter bubbled up out of her and she fell against Pip and covered her mouth, and Pip laughed, too, and asked, "What's so funny?"

Randy pointed at me. "What have you got on? Is that your gym uniform?"

Pip laughed some more and said, "That's just Esther; she always looks like that."

I didn't know my heart could pound any louder, but it did. I shouted above it, "I do not! Pip, I do not. I've never worn this silly uniform before in my life. Mother just ordered it because my old one was so worn."

Pip, seeing that I wasn't laughing, closed his mouth, and then Randy said, "We have the same uniform, only ours is gold and they ... uh, fit a little better."

That last bit cracked her up again and she was falling all over Pip laughing.

I said, "My mother bought it big so I could grow into it," and at this Randy looked at me with such a horrified look on her face, I knew she was imagining the monster I would have to become if I were to ever fit into that uniform. Then she burst out laughing again, and I tried my hardest to laugh, too. I knew that normally I would find it funny, but now it wasn't funny to me at all. Inside I felt like something was breaking, and I felt so scared I didn't know what to do. I laughed a fake laugh, which was hard to do because I could hardly breathe and my heart was racing. The sun had come up fully by then and I could see that Randy was really nice-looking. Nothing on her face was too big or too small. She looked perfect. I figured she had probably gotten all A's on every report card since kindergarten. She looked like the kind of girl who skied and rode horses and looked beautiful doing both of these things. I bet her hair never got tangled, even when she had to stuff it up into a bathing cap to go swimming. When she laughed, she opened her mouth wide enough for me to see that she didn't have even one cavity. All her teeth were white and perfect, just like her.

I stood watching her laughing at me, feeling my heart banging against my chest, closing off my air passages, and I thought that if I didn't do something—leave or run or something—I was going to pass out right there on top of the polar bear, so I said, "Are we going to run, or did you come over to tell me you were canceling today?"

Pip wiped his eyes and shook his head. "No, we're running. Randy's going to wait for us." He took her hand in his and added, "She doesn't run."

Pip said this as though her not running was the

cutest, sweetest thing ever, as though no one was as clever as Randy because she didn't run.

Pip said, "I told Randy she could look around the grounds, if that's okay."

I shrugged. "Yeah, sure, I guess so." I looked at Pip and then Randy. They were the exact same height. I looked back at Pip. He looked taller than usual. He looked lots taller. When did he get so tall? I asked him, "Pip, when did you get so tall? You look taller all of a sudden."

Pip ran his hand through his bangs so they stood straight up and said, "I knew you weren't listening the other day. I told you, I've grown two more inches—six inches since Christmas. I'm five-two now, and the doctor says I might grow another two or three inches before the summer's out." Pip glanced over at Randy, then back at me. "He thinks I could be around six feet tall once I reach my twenties." He shoved his thick-rimmed glasses up on his nose and smiled.

My heart pounded. My ears were full of it; I could hear blood rushing around in my head, I swear that I could. I didn't know what was wrong with me. I felt scared. I wanted to run.

"Okay, well—let's run," I said.

I set off toward the woods and waited for Pip to catch up to me.

It took him a minute or so because he had to say his good-byes to Randy, and then when he caught up to me, he said, "Isn't she great?"

"I didn't know Randy was a girl," I said, leaping over a rock and entering the woods.

"That's because you weren't listening. I told you yesterday. I said *she* was coming. I said *she*, not he. I knew you weren't listening."

I picked up my speed, trying to match the rhythm of my heartbeat, and Pip sped up, too.

"No racing," he said. "Remember, we agreed; no more racing on our training runs."

"I know. I remember," I said, already gasping for air. I wanted to slow down but I couldn't. We ran through the woods side by side along the piney trail.

"Randy wants to join the Peace Corps, just like I do," Pip said. "And she's into politics like I am, and her parents both teach at Columbia University, so her parents are teachers like mine. Isn't that crazy how alike we are?"

"Crazy," I said. I ran faster.

"You're racing," Pip said.

"So what," I said. "Let's. Let's race. Come on!"

I took off down the hill and around a boulder toward the first pond, and Pip followed. About thirty seconds later he had caught up to me, and then he passed me. I sped up and reached out to tag his shirt, and Pip sped up. I ran faster and so did Pip. Pip ran so fast, he was getting away from me. I tried to catch up but he was too fast. He was getting farther and farther away, and I wondered when this had happened. When did Pip get faster than me? I pushed myself to run harder, to catch up. I saw his red shirt in the distance. I kept my focus on that shirt and tried to speed up, tried to catch him, but he was too fast. He was leaving me behind. As soon as I thought this, as soon as I realized the truth of what was happening to me, I stopped. I just stopped running. I leaned over and gasped for air, and I could feel tears filling the rims of my eyes. I could feel them spill over as I gasped and coughed and spit the heavy saliva that had collected in my mouth. I straightened up and let my tears roll down my face. I felt a great pressure come down on my chest, and I decided I was having a heart attack. I was having a heart attack because my heart couldn't take it. I knew my heart couldn't take being left behind again. All my life I had been left behind—in school, by my family, then by Laura and Kathy, then King-Roy, and finally, Pip. Even Pip had moved ahead of me. Even Pip had grown up.

Everyone had left me behind and I didn't know how I would ever catch up.

TWENTY-THREE

I didn't want to have my heart attack in the middle of the trail, so I dragged myself, dizzy and panting, off the path, then moved deeper into the woods. Behind a cluster of pine trees, I dropped onto the ground and waited for my full-out heart attack. I wondered if I was going to die. I waited—still panting; my heart still pounding—and listened with my eyes shut tight. The pressure in my chest eased up some, and I rolled onto my back and stared up at the sky. My heart was pounding still, and my hands and legs felt shaky. A tear spilled out of my left eye and ran into my hair. "I've been left behind," I said. "The whole world has left me behind. How did this happen?"

I asked this of the sky, but I knew. I knew how it had happened. It had all started when I had stayed back— no, even before that, when I couldn't keep up with the lessons in class and then I stayed back—and Mother hired the tutors to help me to catch up, but she knew, even then, I would never catch up. That's why she kept hiring the tutors every summer, and that's why she gave up on me this summer. She realized the tutors didn't help; I'd always be behind everybody else.

I remembered the slumber party I was invited to in fifth grade. I remembered going into the woods behind Sara Partridge's house with all the other girls, and Sara pulled out a pack of cigarettes, a pack of Marlboros, and she passed the pack around. No one else looked surprised. It was as if they had all planned this. They had planned to go smoking in the woods and they didn't tell me. Everyone took a cigarette except me. I didn't want one. I didn't want smoke in my throat and lungs. What was the fun of that? I didn't get it. The girls all lit up their cigarettes and sucked up the smoke and choked and tried to look all grown-up and I thought they looked like they were little girls playing at being grown-ups. They were posing and acting like they were so smart and so grown-up, and I thought they had looked so silly. But I had been wrong. That night in the woods was some kind of initiation, and I had missed it. I had passed it up because I thought it was stupid, and then they passed me up and left me behind, holding the Lavoris mouthwash they had used to hide the smell of tobacco on their breaths.

It was always like that. I didn't get it. I didn't get it at all. I realized this, lying there in the woods staring up at the sky. I didn't get how the world worked. Why did we have wars? Why did people hate? Why did white people hate black people? Why did we have to get grades in school? Why did the popular kids pick on the unpopular kids? Why? I didn't get it.

I didn't understand why people had to change. Why couldn't we all just stay the same? Why did boy-girl friendships have to become all about sex? Why did girls have to flirt and boys have to fight? Why did Laura and Kathy go off to Nantucket together and leave me behind? Why did they do that to me? Because I didn't talk about boys all the time? Because I didn't carry a purse? Were those reasons to leave me behind? If I started carrying a purse, would they be my friends again? Did I want friends who wouldn't like me unless I carried a purse?

And why did King-Roy act like he liked me and then like he didn't? Why did he hug me? Didn't he hug me? Maybe he didn't but dumb me thought he did.

What was wrong with me, anyway? That's what I wanted to figure out. I heard Pip calling to me but I ignored him. I was in the middle of my heart attack; I wanted to be left alone.

I looked up through the trees at the white clouds in the sky, and I thought about my polar-bear rock. I didn't want to believe it, but I knew I still did—I still believed the polar bear could hear me. I still believed stuffed animals were real. Logically I knew it wasn't true, but in my heart I knew a part of me still believed. I believed they could see and breathe, and I still treated all my stuffed animals as though they were alive just in case maybe they were—maybe. I still liked climbing trees and running and wearing pants instead of dresses, and I didn't understand why no one else my age did. Why? Why did they have to change, and if they did have to change, why couldn't I? Why wouldn't I? I could wear dresses all the time. I could smoke and wear makeup and carry a purse. I could talk about boys for hours on the phone and play spin the bottle at parties and kiss the boys in the closet. I could do all those things, so why didn't I? What was wrong with me that I hated all those things? What was wrong with me?

"There you are!" Pip said, coming upon me suddenly and almost giving me another heart attack.

"What are you doing there?" he asked.

"Having a heart attack," I said. I sat up and pulled the pine needles out of my tangled hair. I put the baseball cap that had fallen off back on my head and stood up. I guessed the heart attack, if that's what it was, was over, but I still felt light-headed.

"Stop fooling around, Esther. Randy's waiting for us."

Pip said Randy's name and I felt my heart rate pick up again.

I looked at Pip, standing in front of me in his best red T-shirt and his real cross-country running shoes, with his cheeks flushed and his glasses slipped down on his nose, and I asked him, "So are you and Randy boyfriend and girlfriend now?"

Pip shrugged, looking away. "Maybe. She really likes me." He looked at me. "She likes me just the way I am."

I turned away and said, "Well, that's special, then,

and you're lucky, even if you only just met." I started walking. "I've got to go now. I'll see you later."

Pip said, "Say hi to King-Roy when you see him."

"Yeah," I said, still walking away, "when I see him."

Pip called back, "Esther, are you mad at me?"

I stopped and turned around and took a few steps toward him. "No, Pip, I'm not mad."

When I turned to leave again, he said, "Are you jealous?"

I looked back and tried to smile. "No, I'm not jealous. It's great that you have a girlfriend now. Randy's really pretty."

Pip smiled and looked down at his shoes. "She is, isn't she? She's—well, she's perfect. I don't know why she would like someone like me."

"Pip, you're the most fun person I've ever known, and the nicest and everything else, that's why. And anyway," I added, "you're going to be tall, too. It's really great how you've grown all of a sudden," I said, choking on the word *sudden*. I could feel the tears welling up in my eyes again, so I turned away, and looking down, I said, "I won't be running anymore with you, Pip."

Pip jogged over to me and touched my shoulder. "Esther, what's wrong? Are you crying? Why aren't you running with me anymore?"

"I can't keep up," I said, holding my back to him and leaning against a pine tree. "I don't know when it happened, but you're too fast for me now."

"So?" Pip tried to come around to face me, but I kept turning away from him.

"So everything's changed. Everything's different and I can't keep up."

"So I'll wait for you, then."

"Then you won't get faster and be on the cross-country team anymore."

"Well, you can still run with me, can't you? Even if I am faster than you?"

I leaned my head against the tree. "When did you get so fast, Pip?"

"Don't you want me to be fast? Aren't I supposed to be faster than you?"

I stood up straight and turned around. "Why? Why should you be? Who says?"

Pip shrugged. "That's just the way it is. We grow up, and boys get faster and girls get slower, that's all."

"Well, I don't like it," I said. "It stinks."

"So you *are* jealous. You're jealous because I'm faster than you are. I would think you'd be happy for me." Pip scowled at me, his eyes looking dark beneath his glasses. "Thanks a lot, Esther."

"Pip, I'm not jealous. Not like you think. I'm glad you can run fast and you're getting taller and that Randy likes you. That's really great," I said, tears spilling out of my eyes and rolling down my face.

Pip put his arm around me and held me close. "Hey, what's going on?"

I let the tears roll down my face and watched them drop onto the ground. "Why do things have to change? I don't like it. I don't like all the changes. Pip, I can't keep up." I put my head on his shoulder and let the tears flood out of me. "I can't keep up, Pip. I'm falling too far behind."

"In running? Who cares?" Pip said.

"No, Pip, in everything. In everything! I'm retarded! I'm retarded," I said, breaking free of him and running. I ran away through the woods and Pip called after me. I knew he could catch me if he wanted to, but he didn't . . . want to.

TWENTY-FOUR

I stayed up in my room all morning, staring down at the only line in my play that I had written so far: *As the curtain rises on a dimly lit stage, there is the distant sound of the ocean.*

I still couldn't think of what else to write, and I wondered if maybe that could be the whole play. People could sit in the dark theater for two hours and listen to the distant sound of the ocean. I thought about that for a while, trying hard to keep my mind off of my fears so that my heart wouldn't start racing again, and then the buzzer on my intercom phone buzzed. I picked up the receiver. It was Mother.

"We're all waiting for you for lunch in the dining room, Esther."

"I'm not hungry," I said.

"Come down, anyway."

"Why?" I asked.

"Esther, why does everything have to be difficult with you? Just come down. It's lunchtime and I expect you to be at the table."

"Yes, Mother."

I took my dear sweet time getting up and walking down the stairs and into the dining room. When I got there everyone else was already seated: Mother, Dad, Stewart, Sophia, Auntie Pie, Monsieur Vichy, Beatrice, and sitting by her feet, the Beast, chewing on one of my socks. She must have grabbed it out of the laundry bag that I had carried down to the laundry room on my way out to meet Pip.

Everybody, including the Beast, looked at me when I entered the room, and the strange looks on their faces made me think they had been talking about me. But then Mother said, "Esther, what on earth have you got on?"

I looked down at myself, then at Mother. "My gym uniform; the new one. I went running with Pip this morning."

"That's the most outrageous looking outfit I've ever seen."

"Well, you bought it," I said. I pulled some of the material up past my belt, trying to make it look more presentable so Mother wouldn't send me back upstairs to change.

"Now she looks like a marshmallow," Auntie Pie said, chuckling, and Monsieur Vichy said at the same time, "Charming, as usual, Esther dear."

"Is this some kind of a joke, wearing that costume for lunch?" Dad asked, his voice booming as though he were in the theater talking to an actor onstage. "Where did you get that clown costume?"

"She's a droopy drawers," Sophia said, then snickered, and Stewart shook his head and looked disappointed in me. Beatrice just looked bored.

I looked at Mother and then Dad. "I told you, it's my gym uniform. Mother said I would grow into this." I held out the bloomers, pulling on the uniform from both sides, and said, "I've been five feet four inches since the fifth grade, but I guess I'm going to have a wild growth spurt all of a sudden and turn into some kind of mammoth Amazon giant." I turned back to Mother. "Did you call me down to pick on me some more or to eat?" Then, before she could say anything, I pulled out my chair and flopped down in my seat. I could feel everybody's eyes on me, but I didn't look up. I stared down at the white tablecloth and tried not to have a single thought—not a single one, or I knew I would start crying.

"Well, then," Mother said in her prim southern voice, "shall we eat?" She lifted her spoon, signaling the start of the meal, and everyone followed, lifting their spoons and slurping up the navy bean soup Mother had prepared.

While everyone ate and talked around me, I sat still and stared into my bowl of soup. It looked like vomit, with the beans and bits of ham floating around in a yellow-white broth, but I didn't look away. After a while I shifted my gaze to the ham and cheese sandwiches and stared at them. Then I heard Mother speaking to me, and I lifted my head.

"Did you hear me, Esther?"

I blinked at her. "No, Mother, I didn't, unless you meant just now. I heard you say, 'Did you hear me, Esther?'"

Dad rubbed at his balding head and said, "She *said* we've decided to give you another chance. We want you to take Sophia into the city next week for her rehearsals."

I stared back down at my sandwich. "No, thanks. I don't want another chance," I said.

Dad stood up and pressed his knuckles into the table and leaned forward. "Young lady, we're not asking you; we're telling you, do you understand? We're giving you another chance!"

I stood up and threw my cloth napkin on the table. "Yes, Dad, I understand. Believe it or not, I do understand, and I'm telling *you*, I'm not taking her into the city. You all can find yourself another stooge to pick on." I strode out of the dining room, and my father called after me, "Young lady, you come right back here. Don't think you're too big for a spanking."

I kept on marching through the foyer, even when I heard Dad coming up behind me. He caught up to me and grabbed my arm, and that was the trigger; that was the straw that broke the camel's back. I whipped around, yanking my arm out of his grasp, and I yelled at him at the top of my lungs, "Don't you touch me! Don't you ever touch me and don't talk to me, either." I looked past him, through the tears that were pouring out of my eyes, to the startled faces staring at me from the dining room. "Don't any of you ever talk to me again, because I don't want to hear one more mean thing. Not one more mean, awful, hateful, spiteful thing said to me ever, *ever* again. Don't you think I have feelings? You think I'm so stupid I don't even have feelings? You all come to me asking for favors and you talk to me because I'm the only one who'll listen to you whine and complain, or I'm the only one who'll rub your feet or take Soph and Stewart into the city, or put up the groceries or help make the beds, but then when I do, when I do all these things, you make fun of me and yell at me and tell me what a stupid idiot I am. Well, I know that already so, so . . ." I sucked in my breath. I had been yelling and crying at the same time and I had run out of air. I sucked in my breath and said, "So from now on, you don't have to ever tell me again, because I know it. I know I'm stupid. Okay? I know I'm a retard. I know I'll never ever catch up. I know it! I know it! So you don't have to tell me ever again! You don't have to *speak* to me ever again!"

I turned and started up the stairs, when the doorbell rang and I heard Mother say, "Oh dear, that must be King-Roy."

I stopped and turned around while my father went to the door and opened it.

"Ah, King-Roy," he said, after clearing his throat. He rubbed at the bald spot on his head. "Welcome back."

"Yes sir," King-Roy said, peering up at my father with his head bowed. "I'm sorry if I caused y'all any trouble. I'm back till the end of the summer."

My father opened the door wider and King-Roy entered the foyer. He saw me standing on the steps and we looked at each other for a second, and then I shouted as I ran down the stairs toward him, "And that goes for you, too!" I kept going, past King-Roy, straight through the open door and out into the glaring sun.

TWENTY-FIVE

I ran out across our driveway, onto the lawn, past the polar bear, to the stone wall that ran the length of our property. I stared at it a second, then grabbed onto the top of the wall, which is about shoulder height, and climbed up onto it. Then I turned around to face my favorite climbing tree and jumped out toward the lowest branch, catching hold of it and swinging until I could get my legs up around the branch and hoist myself to a sitting position. Then I stood and climbed to my perching spot, a nice thick branch that had a flat section where I could sit and look out over Pip's property on one side and our front yard on the other. That day, I didn't look in either direction. I sat straddling the branch and stared at the bark on the tree and thought about what had just happened at lunch and about King-Roy and Pip and everything else. I felt mean and angry and ugly because of the way I had acted at lunch, but I just couldn't take everybody's hateful treatment of me anymore. Until that afternoon, I hadn't realized how much it hurt. I guess until that day, I hadn't realized how true their comments had been. But that day I saw it all clearly. I knew I was backwards and stupid and that no matter how hard I tried, the world was just going to keep on passing me by. Staring down at the bark on the tree, digging my fingernail in between the narrow ridges, I felt so miserable, I didn't know what I was going to do. I thought about running away, but I knew that wouldn't make me feel any better. I didn't know where I would go.

I thought about taking up smoking, and I wondered if catching up with my friends could be as simple as that. I pictured myself in the school bathroom that fall, with a cigarette in my mouth, drawing on it, then taking it out and waving it about dramatically, as if I were playing a Bette Davis role. But that was just it, I would be playing a role, I would be acting, and that was fine for the stage, but I had been around actors enough to know that offstage that kind of performance looked desperate and pathetic. But I *was* desperate and pathetic. I thought about that for a while and decided that even if I was so pathetic, I couldn't do it. I couldn't even bring myself to carry a stupid purse, so how was I going to take up smoking? It just wasn't me. But wasn't that my problem? Wasn't I too much of me, and not enough of somebody—anybody—else?

I realized that what I really wanted was for everybody to be more like me. I wanted my friends to stay the same way they'd always been. Like Peter Pan, I didn't want to change or grow up, and I didn't want my friends to change, either. So where did that leave me? I knew the answer to that. It was the same answer over and over; it left me behind, and it left me all alone. I leaned my head forward and rested it on the trunk of the tree.

"I guess I'm going to just stay up in this tree the rest of my life," I said to no one.

I pictured myself in a tree house, with four walls and a window looking out over some mountains, and inside, a sleeping bag, a tin cup and plate, and a picture of my family, in a frame. I had always dreamed of living in a tree house, and I asked my parents, once, a couple of years ago, if I could build myself one, but they had said no. They had said tree houses were for boys, and at twelve I was too old for one, anyway.

I was still picturing my life in a tree when I heard someone coming, and I looked up to see my father, his round balding head bent forward as he strode across the gravel drive and onto the lawn toward me. He didn't look happy. I could tell that by the long strides his short legs were taking and the way he had both his hands stuffed deep into the pockets of his chinos, making them hike up, exposing his skinny freckled ankles and his penny loafers.

He walked up to the tree, stopped abruptly, and looked up through the branches and leaves to where I sat. I turned my head and stared out across the road to Pip's house.

"Esther, come down from there."

"I won't," I said.

"You're being childish. Now, I need to speak to you, and this is serious."

"I'm always being childish, Dad, aren't I? You always say that. Everybody always says that, or something like it, don't they?"

"Because it's true. Now, I won't ask you again. Come down from that tree, or do you need me to come up there after you?"

"Go ahead and try."

"Esther, listen to the tone of my voice! I mean it."

I turned and looked down at my father, who stood below me with his hands on his hips. "What's so important that you need to tell me, anyway?" I asked, not moving an inch off the tree branch.

My father let out his breath. I knew he was exasperated with me, but I was exasperated with him, too.

"We need you to take Sophia into the city next week. Your mother will be with Madeline again, and I have to go to California."

"Maybe you should have thought of that before you all attacked me last night. Maybe you should have thought of that before you made fun of me at lunch."

"Esther, don't get smart with me," my father said, eyeing the lowest branch as though he was trying to figure out how he was going to reach it and climb up.

"Why should I do anything for anyone when all I get is some ugly comment or some mean kind of punishment and never, *never* any thanks?" I crossed my arms in front of me and added, "I'm on strike until I get my civil rights."

"On strike! Your civil rights!" my father shouted.

He looked apoplectic. His face had turned the color of a tomato. "Didn't you hear what I said? Now, no more childish games, Esther. Your mother needs your help. You get down from there, and you get down now!"

I reached for the branch above me and stood up. I stared down at my father, who looked like he might try to pull up the trunk of the tree with his bare hands and shake me out if I didn't climb down there right that second, but I couldn't do it. As mean and as wretched as I felt, I couldn't do it.

I called down to him with tears rolling down my face, "And didn't you hear what *I* said? I'm on strike." Then I climbed higher into the tree and waited to see if my father really would climb up after me.

TWENTY-SIX

My father didn't move. He used his I'm-too-angry-to-even-shout voice and said, "Esther, I don't know when in my life I've been more furious and disappointed in you," and I thought, *How about five minutes ago?* He was always disappointed in me, but I didn't say anything out loud.

My father stood beneath the tree, staring up into the branches, and I stayed standing, peeking out from the leaves now and again to see if he was still there.

Finally, he gave up and left, and I suppose I should have felt victorious, but all I felt was sad. I felt so sad, I could hardly stand it. I climbed back down to my good branch and I lay face down on it and hugged the branch with my arms and legs. I hugged the branch and cried. I cried because I knew I had acted awful and childish and stupid, and I cried because I couldn't help how I had acted and because I knew my family hated me. Everybody hated me, and so I cried and let the tears drop onto the grass below. I cried until I had no more tears left and was too exhausted to hurt anymore. Then I let go of the branch with my arms and legs and let them dangle there as though I were a leopard in a tree, and I felt heavy and limp and wet.

I don't know how long I stayed like that in the tree—maybe hours, maybe minutes—but then I heard footsteps crunching on the gravel again and I lifted my head to see who was coming.

It was King-Roy.

I sat up and got myself arranged in the flat of the branch, brushed my bangs out of my face, tucked my hair behind my ears, and wiped at my eyes.

King-Roy walked through the grass as though he were afraid of stepping on flowers or ants or some other delicate thing. He took his time getting to the tree, and when he got there, he didn't look up and try to find me. Instead he turned around and leaned his back against the trunk and stood there with his arms folded. I looked down at the top of his dark head and waited for him to speak. I waited and waited. Finally, when I had given up and had decided that he didn't even know I was there but had just come to spend the time of day standing beneath the tree, he spoke.

He said, "They sent me out here to talk to you."

I swung my legs. "Who sent you out?"

"Your parents. They want me to get you to come on down out of that tree."

"I'm mad at them. I'm mad at everybody. That's why I'm up here."

King-Roy used his back to push off the tree an inch or two, then he fell back against it and nodded.

"Stewart said I got you in big trouble. He said this is all my fault."

I lifted my right leg up to the branch and grabbed it around the knee, letting the other leg dangle on its own. "I don't want to talk about it," I said. "I don't even want to think about yesterday."

"Then what do you want to talk about?" King-Roy asked.

I thought a second, then said, "Tree houses. I wish I had me a tree house. You ever had a tree house, King-Roy?"

"No. What you want a tree house for, anyway; tree houses are for little boys."

I shrugged and set my chin on my knee. "So why did you come back here, anyways?"

King-Roy pushed off the tree again, only this time he didn't fall back against it. He turned around and looked at me.

I sprang up, grabbing the branch above me, and stood looking down on him. I was nervous all of a sudden seeing his face again. His eyes looked sad behind his glasses. His eyelids looked heavy, as though they were too heavy for him to hold open all the way. He looked away and leaned sideways against the tree and said, "Your mother called my momma and told her where I was, and then I called home last night just to say hey, and Momma got on me and told me to get on back out to y'alls' house and stay put till the end of the summer."

"How come she wants you here so badly?" I asked.

"She wants me safe. She doesn't want me to get my-self into any more trouble," King-Roy said.

"So...so, you're not here 'cause you want to be."

"No," King-Roy said, shaking his head.

I sighed and wished I had a pebble or something to throw at his head. "So you still like Yvonne, then, I guess."

King-Roy looked up into the tree at me. "Course I like Yvonne; why shouldn't I?"

I shrugged and pulled apart a leaf I had picked. "I guess you like girls hanging all over you like that. You like flirty girls." I tore at the leaf some more.

King-Roy dropped his head and said, "I don't want to talk about that with you."

"Why not?" I asked, letting the shredded leaf fall down on his head.

He brushed the leaf bits off and said, "I just told you I'm not talking to you about that."

I pulled at another leaf. "Okay, King-Roy, okay, but it's just—it's just that I thought you liked me."

King-Roy pushed off the tree and looked up at me. "I do like you, Esther, but you tell me, what you think is ever gon' come of that, huh?"

"I don't know," I said.

"Well I'll tell you. Nothin'."

I reached my arms over the branch in front of my chest and leaned forward to look down on King-Roy. "Because you're black and I'm white and you don't like white people?"

King-Roy dropped his gaze and didn't answer me.

I crouched and climbed down to the next limb, a limb closer to King-Roy. "You know what I wish?" I asked him. "I wish there was no such thing as black and white. Why were we made different colors, anyway? What's the point of that?" I climbed down to the next branch and sat.

King-Roy said, "I don't know, but I'll tell you what I wish. I wish I had my own life. I wish I could be a man, a real man who wasn't afraid of anything."

"What are you afraid of, King-Roy?" I slid myself down to the lowest branch and swung my legs above King-Roy's head. I knew if he reached a hand up he could touch me.

King-Roy shook his head. "You don't know, do you?"

"Know what?"

"You don't know what it's like for a black man. I'm afraid of everything. I'm afraid I'm gon' sit in the wrong place or drink from the wrong cup or look at the wrong person or touch the wrong thing. Alls I got to do is look wrong at something and I'll find myself with a noose around my neck."

I nodded. "I guess everybody's scared of something."

King-Roy made a face up at me like he didn't believe what I had just said. "Now, what you got to be afraid of?" he asked me.

I pointed my toes and tried to touch his face with my feet. I thought about his question for a minute, and then I said, "I guess, King-Roy, I guess I'm scared I'm always going to like tree houses."

TWENTY-SEVEN

When King-Roy asked me if I planned to stay up in the tree all day, I told him that I would come down only if he promised not to laugh at me.

"Now, why would I laugh at you?" King-Roy asked.

"Just promise me you won't laugh," I said. "Don't even look at me, okay?"

"I'm looking at you right now and I see nothing funny."

"That's because I'm sitting down."

"Esther, are you coming out of that tree or not?"

"All right," I said. I straddled the branch, locked my knees and swung myself around it, then dropped to the grass.

King-Roy crouched down to help me stand, holding me by the waist. We stood back up together. I looked into his eyes and I saw a light in them, the light of laughter just about to break out, and I shouted, "King-Roy, you promised!"

King-Roy let go of me, stood back for a better look, then burst out with a donkey laugh, and I couldn't help myself; I laughed, too.

He slapped his thigh and pointed at me and said, "Esther, girl, what you got on?"

I laughed and said, "You like it? I wore it just for you." I put one hand on my hip and one on the back of my head and sashayed around. "I bet Yvonne never looked so good."

King-Roy laughed up some more donkey brays and said, "Sure 'nuff, you're an original, Esther. You're one hundred percent original."

I stopped sashaying and looked at King-Roy, and I didn't know whether to laugh or to cry. Being an original sounded like a good thing, but living an original life, I had begun to realize, was a lonely, left-behind kind of life.

King-Roy saw that I had stopped laughing, and he stopped, too, saying, "Whew," and wiped the tears from the corners of his eyes.

I wanted to change the subject and think about something happy, so I asked him, "King-Roy, are you really ever going to teach me how to tap?"

We started walking across the lawn toward the house and King-Roy nodded and said, "All right. We'll start tonight, how 'bout that?"

I smiled. "That sounds perfect."

When we got inside the house, Mother was waiting for me and she said, "King-Roy, if you don't mind, I'd like to speak to Esther alone for a minute."

King-Roy nodded and headed upstairs and I followed my mother into the living room, where she had Andy Williams playing on the record player. He was singing

"Moon River" and we had come in just as he was singing the line, "Two drifters off to see the world..." I wanted more than anything to join those drifters if it meant avoiding another confrontation with Mother, but I sat down next to her on the sofa and waited for what she was about to say.

Mother had on her cream-colored dress with the short little jacket, and I thought how smart and pretty she always looked. I marveled at how she never looked hot, no matter how warm it got outside. I brushed my own damp bangs out of my eyes and stared down at her pretty pink-painted fingernails and listened while Mother told me how important it was that she be by Madeline's side that next week.

"She's going back into the hospital on Monday, Esther, and I need to be there to help her, so I see this strike nonsense of yours as a very selfish and defiant act at Madeline's expense. She has no one else, no husband or children to care for her."

I looked down at my own grubby nails, dirty with tree bark, and said, "All I want is a little thanks now and again, a little show of appreciation. All I want is for everybody to stop picking on me."

I looked up at Mother. Her eyes flashed at me angrily, and she asked, "Did you thank me for today's lunch?"

"No," I said.

"Did you thank me for ironing your shirts last week?"

"No."

"Do you ever thank me when you're home sick and I take care of you?"

"Well, I hope I do, but I guess I don't or you wouldn't be asking me," I said.

"The answer," my mother said, "is no, you do not. No one thanks me for driving them to the train station or picking up laundry or buying the groceries or cooking dinner or any of the other million and one things I do around this large household. Even with Daisy coming two times a week to help out, that still leaves me with too much to do, and do I ever get thanked?" Mother asked. She pinched her lips together and stared at me.

I touched her pretty hand. "Mother, thanks for all of those things."

Mother withdrew her hands. "I wasn't asking for thanks, Esther," she said with irritation. "I was just demonstrating to you that being a mother and a housewife is a thankless job, so you might as well get used to it because it doesn't get any better."

I set my hand back in my lap and said, "So you mean you don't ever thank me because no one thanks you? Like a payback? Is it like that, Mother, a payback?"

Mother stood up and shook with frustration. "Esther, no, it is not a payback. Honestly, how you could misunderstand what I'm saying, I don't know. I'm saying," Mother let out her breath, "I'm saying, that someday you, too, will be a wife and mother and no one is going to thank you for all the little things you do for them so there is no use going on strike over the fact that someone didn't thank you. What if I went on strike? How would that be? Would you tell me that? This whole household would come to a standstill."

While Mother was speaking she had begun to pace with her arms folded in front of her, and her pretty cream pumps left small heel dents in the oriental carpet.

I watched her walk back and forth, and when she came to a stop in front of me, after announcing how the whole house would come to a standstill, I said, "Mother, from now on I'm going to make sure I thank you for everything. Thank you even for this talk. Thank you for lunch and for bringing me soup when I'm sick and for taking me to school when I've missed the bus and for doing my laundry, and from now on, I'm just going to remember to thank you."

Mother stood there blinking at me, and I couldn't tell if she was irritated with me still or what, but she couldn't seem to get anything to come out of her mouth except some sputtering sounds, so I added, "And I'll take Sophia to her rehearsals this week if you'll thank me, too, when we get back home."

I could see by the red blotches moving up Mother's neck that this was the wrong thing to say, so I jumped up from my seat and said over Andy Williams's rendition of "Three Coins in a Fountain," "You don't *have* to thank me. I just thought you could, or you might, or . . . or, something. So . . . so, thanks for the talk, Mother, and I'll go now."

The record had ended and was starting over again when I scurried out of the room. I had reached the first landing on the stairs when I heard Andy Williams sing out, "Love is a many splendored thing," and I remembered Pip and how he had said that love was not something that you planned like a road trip, but an affair of the heart, and I thought it must be so, because how else could I explain my love for my mother.

TWENTY-EIGHT

That next week, I took Sophia to her rehearsals, got her settled backstage, and then I took Stewart to his ballet lessons. I hadn't spoken to my parents about Stewart and ballet because my father was out of town all that week, and it never seemed to be the right time to talk about it with Mother. She had enough to worry about with her sick friend, Madeline. She came home in the late afternoons looking so tired and hot—for once in her life she looked hot—it worried me. I did my best to help her out by getting some kind of canned or TV dinner on the table on the days when Daisy didn't come, and I cleaned up afterward, with Auntie Pie's help, and I kept quiet about the lessons. I figured my parents would realize Stewart was taking the ballet lessons when they got the bill for them, but Stewart said Mother and Dad had never said anything to him about any other bill, and he had been sneaking off for lessons whenever he could.

"Maybe since Mother's on the board, they don't charge for the lessons," Stewart had said to me when we discussed it. "Maybe since they donate so much money to the ballet company, they don't send a bill. Do you think that's possible?" he asked.

I guessed that it was, since my parents hadn't ever spoken to him about the extra lessons. So I figured it wouldn't hurt to let Stewart go, as long as he let me take him to the door of the studio and waited for me to pick him up again in the afternoon.

I had never seen Stewart happier than during that week and over the next few weeks, and it was good to see that at least one of us was happy. He came out of the studio each afternoon smiling, his curly blond head bobbing up and down as he pranced along the city sidewalks. He laughed easily and enjoyed teasing Sophia out of her moods, and he helped me any way that he could, and I, remembering my talk with my mother, thanked him for his help.

The high spot in my day, however, came in the evenings when I had my tap lessons with King-Roy.

King-Roy had gotten a job down the street at the college. He worked days in the cafeteria kitchen as part of the cleanup crew, and he had to wear a hairnet over his head like a woman, so that his hair wouldn't accidentally fall out of his head and drop into a soup or a salad or some other dish sitting around in the kitchen. He said none of the white men working in the back had to wear one, just the Negroes, and he said this with a bitterness in his voice that I hadn't heard before.

I took my lessons in the ballroom, where King-Roy and I stood sometimes side by side; sometimes with him

in front of me, demonstrating a step; and sometimes facing each other. King-Roy started me out with simple flap
steps and brush-ball steps, which he made me do a thousand times until I could make the step small and light
and quick instead of big and clumsy. I never knew there
was so much to just tapping my feet. I had to work to
keep my balance while I stood on one foot and flapped
the other one over and over and I had to remember to
watch my hands so that they didn't freeze into clawlike
positions while I concentrated on my simple footwork.
In a way, it was like taking ballet classes, only the steps
were freer and looser and more comfortable to do.

King-Roy always acted patient with me that first
week of lessons, and he seemed pleased with me, too.
He seemed pleased that I was so eager to learn the steps,
and pleased that I never complained when he made me
do the same fl-ap, fl-ap, fl-ap, over and over. I could see
his pleasure in his eyes, the way they twinkled when he
watched me, and one time when I lost my balance, he
caught me when he didn't have to. I wasn't going to fall
on the floor, but he caught me, anyway, and he held me
a few seconds, without saying anything, until it felt awk-
ward for both of us and he moved away and didn't look
me in the eyes the rest of that lesson.

Each night, when the lesson was over, King-Roy
would dance for me. I had brought my record player out
into the ballroom and we put on one of my father's jazz
albums and King-Roy danced.

I had never in my life, not even at the movies or in

the theater, seen such fancy dancing as the tap dancing King-Roy could do. He used the whole ballroom, traveling from one end to the other, or traveling in a circle, jumping up onto the window seats and twirling off again. He tapped and turned and leaped and kicked, and the whole time he looked as if he were skating on ice, the way he glided over the floor. He could do a step on one foot that tapped a thousand taps a minute; that's what it looked like. It was as if his foot wasn't even part of his body. It was like a machine, like a jackhammer. I could sit on the window seat and watch King-Roy and his beaming face dance all night.

I said to him once after he finished all breathless in the center of the room that he looked different when he danced.

"How do I look different?" he asked me, taking a handkerchief out of his back pocket and wiping off the sweat.

"I guess," I said, walking over to him, "you look more like you, somehow. Do you know? More like who you're supposed to be. Like you're this complete, happy person. It's like that saying, 'God's in his heaven and all is right with the world.' You look like that when you dance," I said.

That week was the best week we had had together all summer. Just spending the extra time together made me feel closer to King-Roy. He seemed more relaxed and happy, dancing and laughing with me, than I had ever seen him, and I tried my best to push my own anxieties about feeling left behind and about King-Roy someday leaving us out of my mind.

Sometimes at night, after our lesson, King-Roy would get a telephone call from Ax. I always knew it was Ax because right away King-Roy would have this guilty look on his face and he'd turn his back on me to speak. I felt jealous of those calls because afterward, when King-Roy hung up the phone, he would become so quiet and subdued, he didn't want to talk with me anymore. He'd head off toward his room, saying, "I got me some reading to do," and I'd watch the back of him retreat up the steps, with his hand gripping the banister as though it were supporting his whole tensed-up body.

King-Roy wasn't the only one doing some reading. I had lots of time on my hands while I waited down at the theater during Sophia's rehearsals, so I either stared at the one-sentence play I had written for Monsieur Vichy, trying to figure out how to at least make it into a two-sentence play, or I worried about how I was going to catch up with the rest of the world, or I read.

Ever since King-Roy's story and my trip to Harlem, I was interested in the nonviolent movement going on down south. I heard about the Negro protests and marches, every night on the news on my transistor radio, and when one reporter mentioned that Dr. King was inspired by the nonviolent philosophy of Gandhi, I recalled that my parents had a book about Gandhi in their library, so I took it out and brought it with me to Sophia's rehearsals.

What I hoped to find in that book was some kind of ammunition to use against Ax and the Muslim newspapers that he sent in the mail to King-Roy, because during the second week of my tap lessons, King-Roy had begun acting sullen even before Ax's nighttime calls, and I wanted some way to talk him out of his moods.

King-Roy didn't laugh anymore, or tap for me after the lesson the way he had that first week. He just gave me my lesson on the time step, made his corrections, and looked either mellow or downright somber while he did it. Sometimes when I looked at him at the dinner table or while he washed a dish after he had a late-night snack, I'd see this terrible, sad, almost tortured look come into his face, and I felt so helpless seeing it, I didn't know what to do.

Finally one night, when King-Roy got all snappy at me for not doing my shuffle, ball-change steps just right, I snapped back. I said, "King-Roy, I don't know why you keep talking to that Ax man, when he just gets you feeling so angry and mean all the time. That's really why you're yelling at me. I've been doing some reading, and Gandhi said that you have to love even the meanest of creation like he was yourself. You have to rise above—"

"Rise above?" King-Roy barked at me. "Girl, don't talk to me about 'rise above,' because you don't know what you're talking about." He strode across the room and sat down on the window seat.

"Well, I heard on the radio that they're planning a big march down in Washington DC—a big freedom march," I said, standing still, not moving any closer to King-Roy, who, when I said this, looked ready for a conniption fit.

"You think I'm gon' do another march? Of all days for you to be talking about a march. I don't want to hear about it. You don't know what you're talking about, anyway, so hush up. No march is going to make a difference. The only thing that's gon' make a difference is revolution. Bloodshed's the only thing the white devil understands."

"But Gandhi got all of India free from England's rule just by using nonviolence, and Dr. Martin Luther King Junior is doing the—"

King-Roy lifted his hand up like he would have slapped me if I had been close enough. "Esther! Don't say it, 'cause I don't want to hear it. You think I don't know all about what you're saying? I've listened to Dr. King speak plenty, and I've lived life his turn-the-other-cheek way all my life, you hear? But now I've heard Malcolm X speak, and I know which one's gon' get me freedom *today*, not some hundred more years from now, when I'm dead and buried and it doesn't matter to me anymore."

I opened my mouth to speak, but then King-Roy set his face in his hands and it looked like he was trying not to cry, or maybe he was crying, so I didn't say anything.

I hurried over to the window seat and sat down next to him, and I watched his back heaving and was sure he was crying. I didn't know what to do or what to say.

I had said too much. I had made him cry. I heard his breath coming out in sobs and I put my arm around his back. It was damp and warm against my arm. We sat together like that for a few minutes, and then King-Roy wiped his whole face with his hand, sat up, and said, "Today's my little sister Syllia's birthday."

"It is?" I set my hands in my lap.

"Nine years old." King-Roy nodded.

"Why don't you call her up and wish her happy birthday? Mother and Dad don't mind if you call home."

King-Roy sniffed and ran his hand over his face again. "Can't call a dead person, can I?" He blinked his eyes several times.

"King-Roy, what do you mean? What do you mean a dead person? When did she die? Why didn't you say?"

King-Roy stared down into his lap. "She died after that march. She died after that march in Birmingham."

"But you said she came home. You said—"

King-Roy raised his voice. "I know what I said, Esther." Then he got quiet again. "She got that hose water shot up in her sinuses and it made her sick. The infection moved down into her chest and she . . . she just got real sick." King-Roy dropped his head. "She got sick and died." Then he said real softly, "She died 'cause we promised Dr. King we wouldn't fight. We turned the other cheek and it killed my sister." He looked up at me and said with his nostrils flared and that new bitterness back in his voice, "Now, you tell me. You think that's right? Or do you think maybe, just maybe, we got a right to protect ourselves and fight back? 'Cause that's what I'm struggling with now. And every day I'm struggling with the shame of that march, so don't tell me about some big march they gon' do in Washington." He paused a minute, staring across the ballroom to the fireplace, then he shook his head, and with a look like fear in his eyes, he said, "I don't know—I just don't know how I'm ever gon' get over my shame."

King-Roy set his face in his hands again and took several deep breaths, and I slid in closer and put my arm back around him. I knew nothing I could say would help him feel any better, so I stayed quiet, and when he didn't lift his head up from his hands for a long time I rested my head against his warm back and listened to the sad, slow beat of his heart. Then, after another minute or so, King-Roy reached up to his shoulder, reached up to where my hand rested there, and he placed his hand on top of mine and let out a long, deep sigh.

TWENTY-NINE

King-Roy and I sat huddled together for some time before I noticed a movement outside one of the ballroom windows. I lifted my head up off of King-Roy and caught Pip staring in at us from the stone porch. When he saw me looking at him, Pip leaped back from the window, startled, and took off running. I jumped up and ran to the window, lifted its handle, and flung it open. I called after Pip. I called out his name, but he didn't look back and he didn't stop running.

Later that night I called Pip on the phone. His mother said he was out.

I hadn't seen Pip since the day he brought Randy over to meet me. I had gotten up early as usual the next day, to talk with him before he went for his run, but he didn't come over to the house. He didn't show up the next morning, either, and I figured since I was up and dressed, I would run on my own. While I ran, I realized that I liked running, even if Pip could run faster, and even if I could never run on a cross-country team the way he could. I liked running through the woods and the easy happy way it made me feel, so I kept doing it, but Pip never came back to run and I had decided that he, like everyone else I knew, had gotten fed up with me and didn't want to be friends anymore.

I tried a couple of more times to reach Pip by phone, and I walked over to his house Saturday morning, but his mother said Pip had gone to spend the week with Randy in the Catskills, and I returned home, feeling shaken and upset. I missed Pip. I missed talking to him and arguing with him and running with him, and I missed him loving me and me pretending that I didn't love him. But I did love him. I realized that, walking back to my own house after I had found out he had left with Randy for the Catskills. I didn't know how I loved him, or maybe I mean I didn't know what kind of love I had for him, but I knew that I loved him, and I knew, too, that once again I had messed things up. Pip was gone and I felt lost and even more left behind than before.

On that same Saturday, King-Roy went to Harlem to visit Ax and Yvonne, to fill up on all their white-devil, Muslim revolution talk, and even though he swore he would come back and he reminded me that he had promised his mother he'd stay with us until the end of the summer, I felt anxious about his leaving. I didn't like the way the Muslim talk had started to change King-Roy. King-Roy had said, "You don't like it because you're white, and you white people feel threatened by the power and the anger of the black Muslims."

I thought maybe King-Roy had a point with that, but

his calling me one of "you white people" hurt, and to make myself feel better and maybe less threatened, I went down to our town library and found a book written by Martin Luther King Jr. called *Stride Toward Freedom: The Montgomery Story*. It was about how Negroes were told that they had to sit at the back of the bus and give up their seats to any white person who got on and wanted their seat, but then black people started to refuse to give up their seats, so they got arrested and thrown off the bus. Then the whole Negro community just wouldn't ride the buses anymore and finally, after more than three hundred days of the Negroes walking to work or catching rides in cars, and the buses driving around mostly empty and losing money, the Negroes won the right to sit anywhere they liked.

In the book, Dr. King wrote about how sometimes he would get as many as a dozen threats on his life a day down there in the South, but he still believed that Gandhi's ideas about nonviolence and Thoreau's ideas on civil disobedience were the ways to bring about a peaceful revolution. I loved that. I loved the idea of it, a peaceful revolution.

I carried the book with me to read during Sophia's rehearsals, and I got so excited reading about the boycott and the idea of a peaceful revolution—something I could tell King-Roy about—that I started talking back to the book, sometimes crying and sometimes cheering, and the director had to ask me to leave the auditorium.

That book was the only thing that gave me any kind

of hope those days when everything and everyone around me seemed to be shifting and changing and moving in some new direction that I couldn't keep pace with or even comprehend. I felt as if some giant switch that had kept the world turning in the right direction had been flipped. I could feel the change, feel the slowing of the earth as it got ready to stop and reverse direction. I could feel it in our house, with the way Mother came home each day from the hospital so depressed she couldn't eat or speak to any of us, and the way Father, who had returned from California, couldn't sit still, as if he had some big decision to make that kept him up all night, pacing in his study.

Sophia had daily tantrums at the theater over nothing important, and I suspected it was because Mother couldn't pay her any attention and I had been a poor and impatient substitute for her.

Auntie Pie had released the two hawks she had nursed back to health, and I found her combing the woods one morning as I ran there. She was pale and pinched in the face with worry and had gone out there dressed still in her nightgown and bathrobe. Her hair was falling about her shoulders, looking wild and untidy. She said she had a strong feeling that one of the hawks didn't make it; she had decided in the middle of the night that she had released it too soon, and she was searching the woods for its body. Thursday of that week she found it, and we had a little funeral for the hawk, and then Auntie Pie retreated into the gatehouse and wouldn't come out. She had never made a mistake with her animals before and her mistake had cost it its life.

Beatrice had grown impatient with Dad, who had told her he wasn't sure he was going to direct the Vera play after all, so she took a part in an off-Broadway play, and the experience of working with a new group of people had turned her into a beatnik. She said everything was "cool, man," and she called people "cats" and said "I dig" a lot. She had flattened her hair and had bangs down over one eye. She wore a cotton beret on her head and black slacks with man shoes and a tight pullover top. I had never seen Beatrice in slacks before. She reminded me of a lady spy.

Monsieur Vichy came down from his rooms to meals looking disheveled, dressed in the same black pants and the same muslin short-sleeved shirt and wearing his funny French sandals. His hair looked greasy like he hadn't bathed in forever, and just like everybody else at the table, he didn't have much to say. I decided he must have been having trouble with the new play he was writing, but since I didn't want him to ask me about my play, I didn't ask him about his. All the same, one night he came to my room—something he had never done before—and he asked me how my play was coming along.

I said, "I bring it with me to Sophia's rehearsals every day," which was the truth.

Monsieur Vichy took his cigar out of his mouth and asked, "Do you want me to look it over for you? Do you need perhaps some help with it?"

I should have said something then; I should have confessed that I had nothing to show him, but I didn't. I couldn't bear to have him shame me after all the bragging I had done. I imagined him laughing at me and pointing me out at the dinner table and telling everyone how I couldn't even write a paragraph, let alone a play. How could I stand it? So I said, "No, thank you. I'll keep working on it on my own."

Monsieur Vichy left my room looking disappointed, as though I had deprived him of a good night's entertainment making fun of me and pointing out all my ineptitudes. As soon as he left, I pulled out my play and wrote, *"The lights come up and the sound of the waves, though diminished, remain constant throughout the first scene."* I looked at my new sentence and I realized, staring down at it, that I was stalling. I was stalling because I had nothing to say. I had nothing to write about. How could I write a play when I knew nothing about how the world worked? How could I write about what I didn't understand? How could I write about people's lives when my own life was a mystery to me? The answer was I couldn't. I shoved my notebook under my bed and decided I wouldn't bring it with me to rehearsals anymore, and I thought, sitting there on my bed, how everything I had touched that summer, everything I had attempted, had failed. Even my tap lessons had turned sour.

King-Roy still gave me lessons, but it wasn't fun anymore. He taught me how to do the Shim Sham, but he barely spoke a word. Most of his teaching was through demonstration. Any time I looked at him, his gaze was always looking away, far away, as though he didn't know he was in the room with me, as if his mind was in Harlem with Ax and Yvonne.

I told him about the book I had read by Martin Luther King Jr. and he blew up at me.

"Stop reading all that, Esther!" he shouted. "It's not your business, anyway. It's just none of your business. Peaceful revolution ain't no revolution, you hear me? That's just the old slave-boy mentality, all that peace talk and making nice with the blue-eyed devil. We're no closer to getting our rights than we ever were, or ever will be if all we got is a *peaceful* revolution."

King-Roy was flapping his arms and flaring his nostrils at me, and I couldn't stand it. He sounded so angry. He sounded as if he hated me.

I said, "But Gandhi said that we must be the change we wish to see in the world. That's what Dr. Martin Luther King Junior is doing, isn't he? He's being the change. He's being the peace and the love he wants to see in the world. I think that's a good thing to be, don't you?"

King-Roy marched about the room, his tap shoes slapping at the floor. "He can go on and be all the peace and love he wants to be, but that doesn't stop white folks from bashing our heads in and hanging us by our necks and bombing our homes." King-Roy spun around and pointed his finger at me. "And the only reason you're rootin' for nonviolence is because that way the only people who are getting hurt and killed are black people.

You don't like what Ax and Malcolm X say because maybe y'all in your big white mansions and your all-white towns don't feel so safe anymore."

I jumped back when he pointed at me, and I said, "Well you're right, King-Roy. I *am* scared. I'm scared of how angry you are. I'm scared because you look at me like you hate me, but . . . but you don't, do you? We're still friends, aren't we? King-Roy? Aren't we?"

King-Roy had turned away, to face the windows, and he stood there shaking his head.

"Are you thinking about it, or are you shaking your head no, we're not friends?"

King-Roy sighed. "Esther," he said, then shook his head again.

I moved so that I faced him again, and he folded his arms across his chest and looked down at his feet.

"King-Roy? We're still friends, you and me, aren't we? I mean, you hugged me and you held my hand the other day, and you're teaching me tap. And I'm trying, I'm trying to understand and learn how it is for you. I'm really trying, King-Roy because, well, because, I . . . I love you and you love me, don't you? I mean, don't you? Don't you care about me? Just tell me that you care, okay?" I felt desperate for him to say he still liked me, that we were still friends. If he couldn't say that, well, then, I had lost every friend I had.

King-Roy shook his head some more and held out his hands and kind of shrugged, then said, "Esther," again, and I grabbed one of his outstretched arms and pulled myself to him and hugged him around the waist really tight and I said, "I love you. I love you, anyway, okay? I love you." I squeezed him as hard as I could, and King-Roy tried to pry my arms loose but I wouldn't let go.

"Esther," he said, more calmly, "that's enough, now, you got to let go of me. What if someone came in on us?"

"No one will," I said.

"Someone might, and I'm the one who's gon' pay for it if they do."

"I'll let go only if you tell me you love me," I said, feeling suddenly wild inside. What was I doing?

King-Roy reached back for my hands and tried again to pry me loose but I held on, locking my arms tight around him.

"I know you love me, King-Roy. I know you do and I love you and you have to say it. You have to say it."

I heard King-Roy sigh and I felt the air leave his body. I could hear his heart pounding hard in his chest, just the way mine was doing, and I could smell his Lifebuoy soap and the sweet-smelling stuff he put in his hair. I could feel his warm body up against mine, and I said again, "I love you, King-Roy Johnson," and then King-Roy said very quietly, very softly, with a sigh, "I can't say it, Esther. I can't say what I don't feel."

"What?" I let go and backed up, feeling as if the earth had come to a standstill, as if this moment was the reason why the whole household had become so unsettled. I looked up into King-Roy's eyes and saw nothing familiar there—no light or life, just a dullness that given the slightest push could harden into something cruel. I knew that King-Roy had planned to return to Harlem the next day to attend the unity rally Malcolm X was holding, and I thought as I stared up at King-Roy's blank face that that rally might just be the push.

THIRTY

I felt so sad and frightened watching King-Roy, no longer my friend, leave for the train station the next morning that I didn't know what to do with myself. Everything around me had fallen apart and I didn't know how I could fix it. I didn't know how to make Pip my friend again, or how to get Kathy and Laura to accept me, or how to make my mother happy or my father not worried, or how to calm Sophia down or get Auntie Pie to come out of the gatehouse. Everybody was at loose ends, and I felt responsible for all of it.

I went for a run through the woods and got so sad thinking about how Pip and I used to run together that I couldn't finish and I ended up walking back from the pond to the house in tears.

I put on my tap shoes and practiced the Shim Sham and the difficult kick-back Shoop Shoop dance that King-Roy had made up and taught me, and that made me even sadder as I recalled the first week of tap lessons, when King-Roy and I had laughed and touched and he had danced for me.

After lunch, where we all sat around so steeped in our own miseries that no one but Stewart had anything to say, I went up to my room and stared down at the cover of the bus-boycott book I had gotten out of the library. I thought about Martin Luther King Jr. and the big march he and other Negro leaders were planning to hold down in Washington, and I wished that King-Roy would join them. I wished that he would give nonviolence another chance. Then I thought about Gandhi and how he said that we needed to be the change we wished to see in the world, and I wondered how I could be the change I wished to see in my world, and in my house. I flopped down on my bed and kicked off my shoes. I still had on my saddle oxfords, the ones I had had the shoe repairman in town attach taps to, and they dropped down onto the floor with a slap. When I heard the slap of the shoes, an idea popped into my head. I sat up and another idea popped into my head. I had two wonderful ideas. I jumped up off the bed and ran out of the room to go find Stewart and Sophia.

My first wonderful idea was to put on a show for everybody. Mother loved when Sophia and Stewart sang and performed, and now I could perform, too. I thought I could do my tap-dance routines, and Sophia could sing and do a monologue, and Stewart could dance a ballet.

Stewart had said when I told him, "You mean you want me to do the ballet that I'm learning in class? What will Mother and Dad say?"

"When they see how good you are and how happy it makes you, I know they'll let you keep dancing."

"But what if they don't? Then what? They'll know that I've been sneaking off."

"They're going to find out sooner or later, and besides," I said, "Mother and Dad love a good show. You just have to be the very best you can be. We'll put on the show two weeks from today, that's the twenty-fourth. We'll just have to really practice like crazy until then so that we're perfect."

When I told Sophia about my idea, her face lit up, especially when I said that I was going to try to get Auntie Pie to make us some costumes. Sophia loved costumes—the frillier the better—and I figured if Auntie Pie made the costumes, it would take her mind off of the dead hawk and make the show look like a real production.

I went over to the gatehouse and told Auntie Pie my plans for the show. She was sitting on the floor with her injured skunk curled up in her lap. "Costumes," she said, tilting her head and thinking it over. "In two weeks?"

I nodded. "I know it's short notice, but I thought you could use some old costumes and kind of put things together—you know, the way you know how to do."

Auntie Pie didn't say anything. She just stroked the skunk's back and looked out the window, so I added, "I thought I could wear some kind of roaring-twenties jazz costume."

Auntie Pie looked over at me. "Jazz? That might be fun."

I smiled and knelt down beside her. "Really? Then, you'll do it?"

Auntie Pie stopped stroking the skunk and sniffed. "Yes," she nodded. "Yes, I'll do it."

I was so excited, I hugged Auntie Pie hard and she squealed and woke the skunk, which blinked up at us as if it wondered what all the hubbub was about.

After my great success with Auntie Pie, I decided to go over to the servants' quarters and talk to Beatrice about being our makeup artist. I found Beatrice and the Beast in her sitting room, a room Beatrice had decorated with lots of peacock feathers and orange furniture. She was reading from a stack of old *Playbill* magazines when I knocked on her open door.

The Beast leaped off of Beatrice's lap and barked at my feet. I ignored the barking and told Beatrice about the production Sophia, Stewart, and I were putting on, and I asked her if she would do our makeup.

Beatrice shrugged. "Yeah, sure. I can put some makeup on you," she said, not even looking up from her magazine.

"But I want you to make me look really pretty, Beatrice, okay?" I said, feeling myself blush.

That got Beatrice's attention.

"You're going to be in the show?"

"Yes," I said. "I told you, I'm going to do a tap

dance that King-Roy taught me, and I want to look pretty. Do you think—do you think you could do something for me?"

Beatrice looked so pleased and surprised. "You want me to make you up?" She got up and walked around me as though I were a piece of marble she was hoping to sculpt, and then she grabbed my hands and said, "You know, you might look real pretty. Yes," she said, studying my face. "We'll soften all those freckles with some foundation, put some mascara on those blond lashes of yours, and add some eyeliner, some lipstick, rouge, and eye shadow... Esther, I do believe you're going to look beautiful."

I couldn't help myself, I laughed, and so did Beatrice, and for the first time ever, I felt close to her. I felt as if we were sisters.

Already, in just an hour's time since I had come up with the idea, I could feel the weight of gloom that had settled about the house lifting, and as I tapped my way down the hallway toward my room, I said to myself, "I will be the change."

THIRTY-ONE

My second wonderful idea was even bigger. I wanted to go to the march for freedom and jobs in Washington DC at the end of August. I wanted to see Dr. Martin Luther King Jr. and hear him speak about nonviolence, and I wanted to get as many members of my family to come with me. I especially wanted King-Roy to come. If we could all participate in the march, I thought we could be a part of the change we needed to see in the world. And if groups of friends and families came from all over, black and white together, then maybe King-Roy and Ax and Yvonne and the white people who are prejudiced and think things will never change would see that it could. If enough people came, change could happen. I believed it. That was the way the bus boycott worked in Alabama, and I believed it could work again in Washington.

I knew the only way I could get my parents to let me go and to convince them to go with me was if I could convince my mother. If Mother said yes, then Dad and everyone else would go along—except for King-Roy. He was another problem. I knew he would come back from the Malcolm X unity rally even angrier than when he left, but I had an idea that I thought would get both Mother and King-Roy to go to the march in Washington.

It came to me while I was thinking about King-Roy and how he wanted to go live in Harlem with his friends but his mother wanted him to stay with us. That made me think of my mother and his mother being best friends when they were little, and that made me think of how they hadn't seen each other since high school days. I thought if King-Roy's mother could get on one of the buses I had read in the paper were coming from Birmingham to bring people to the march, then maybe my mother would want to go to see her old friend and show her support, and King-Roy would go to see his mother, and then we'd all be there together. I thought it was my most brilliant idea ever, and I set about right away writing a letter to King-Roy's mother, asking her if she and her family would come to Washington. I enclosed in the letter a twenty-dollar bill, which was two years of birthday money saved up, and was all I had since my 1922 silver Peace Dollar had disappeared. I wrote that I hoped the money would help pay for the family to come to Washington.

That night at dinner Mother announced that her friend Madeline had died that morning. "It's better for her now," Mother said. "She's at peace. No more pain. The funeral will be this Wednesday, and I hope you will all be there. Madeline had only me—I was her only friend. It would be nice if she had a few more people there at her funeral."

When Mother said Madeline had no friends except for her, I felt cold all over. I didn't want to end up just like Madeline someday, with no friends and only strangers at my funeral. I could barely eat the peanut butter and jelly sandwich I had prepared for dinner. Then Dad announced that he had accepted an invitation to direct a film in Hollywood, and everyone got so excited, everyone except me. "Will we be moving?" I asked. "Would we leave this house?"

I looked around the dining room with its pretty bird wallpaper and the cozy alcove where I used to sit on my father's lap while he read the *New York Times* and where I cut out Betsy McCall paper-doll clothes with Mother, and I just wanted to slip down in my chair and under the table in a heap if he said we had to move.

"Well, nothing's certain, yet," my father said. "We'll have to see how this movie goes. If it's a hit—if *I'm* a hit—then who knows; in a couple of years, Hollywood, here we come."

"But you're a theater man," I said. "You've always told me that you were a theater man. It's in your blood—the smell of the greasepaint and all that."

Dad shrugged. "People change, Esther."

Before I could ask why, why do people change, why do they have to? Before I could find my voice again and ask how could this happen, how could he think of leaving New York and the city and this house and the theater, everyone had started talking about Hollywood. Hollywood, Hollywood, Hollywood. The only person who didn't looked thrilled besides my mourning mother was Monsieur Vichy. He looked down through his pince-nez at his peanut butter and jelly sandwich and said nothing.

While everyone talked around me, I stared through the windows that looked out over the front yard to where my polar-bear rock lay and silently asked it why things always had to change. I stood up, on shaky legs, to leave the room, but then Stewart said, "Hey, guess what? We're going to put on a show for everybody." He looked at me. "It's Esther's idea. We're going to sing and dance, and there's going to be some real surprises."

Auntie Pie, who had skipped over her peanut butter and jelly sandwich and gone right to the cheesecake dessert, mumbled over her mouthful, "I'm doing the costumes—roaring twenties."

I sat down in my seat.

Beatrice said, "I'm doing the makeup," and Sophia said, "And I'm the star."

Mother looked over at me and said, "I hope this won't be before this Wednesday, Esther."

"No, Mother. It's in two weeks. It's just to . . . to cheer everybody up because people have seemed so down lately," I said, feeling ready at that moment to burst out crying. I could feel my face turning red as I waited for my mother to tell me that we couldn't have the show and that it was in poor taste considering Madeline had just died, but she didn't say that at all. She said, "That's very thoughtful, Esther. I look forward to seeing Sophia and Stewart's performance."

I smiled and felt suddenly lighthearted. Mother was pleased. She said I was thoughtful. I couldn't wait to surprise her with my tap dancing. I couldn't wait to surprise everyone. King-Roy said I was a quick study. He said I had a real talent for tap.

Then my father said, "That's just what we need, a good show." He nodded and smiled at everyone around the table and took a big bite of his sandwich. He held up the rest of it in his hand and said, "Good sandwich, too. Thank you, Esther, for all the dinners you've made for us the past couple of weeks."

I looked over at Mother and I knew she must have said something to Dad about our thank-you talk. I felt so good, I didn't know what to do. Then Beatrice and Auntie Pie and Stewart, all at the same time, said, "Thank you, Esther," and I lowered my head and smiled. I said real quietly, "You're welcome." And I thought, maybe some change is good.

THIRTY-TWO

The next day, while in the car with Mother, Auntie Pie, Sophia, and Stewart on the way home from church, I brought up the idea of the march in Washington to Mother. I said, "Maybe all of us could go to that march and show our support."

Mother said, "There's likely to be riots. Those things always end up in riots and with people getting hurt. No, Esther, it's nice if you want to support the Negroes' fight for their civil rights, but I think we had all better just stay home."

Sophia said, "Esther doesn't care about the Negroes' civil rights, she's just in love with King-Roy." She looked over at me, all dressed up like an angel in her white taffeta dress and hair ribbons, and I thought she was the devil's own advocate saying that to Mother.

Mother looked back at me through the rearview mirror. "Esther, I don't want you getting any notions about King-Roy. Teenage romances are hard enough without adding racial issues to it."

"What notions? I'm not getting any notions," I said, blushing. "At least not anymore. I just love him like a brother, that's all. I'm not *in* love with him, *Sophia*." I turned and glared at my sister when I said her name, and Sophia stuck her tongue out at me.

I turned back to Mother. "Gandhi said that we should be the change we wish to see in the world, and I wish to see everybody get along and get their fair share and for black people to be treated just like white people, and this march is going to be really big, and Martin Luther King Junior is going to be there, and there'll be singers there and other famous people, and it's a big black-and-white together thing, Mother. I think we should be there. I think we should go and show President Kennedy and all those senate people that we all want Negroes to get their rights."

"No," Mother said. "That's not how we Youngs do things, Esther. You ought to know better than that. We don't get out in the streets and protest. If we feel strongly about something like this, we write a letter to our senators or to the *Times*."

Auntie Pie said, "Big crowds are dangerous. Haven't you read *Julius Caesar*? They turn into mobs and mobs do crazy things. Someone's always getting killed."

"Well, I just thought...," I said, staring out the window at nothing. I let the idea drop after that and decided to bring it up again if King-Roy's mother ever wrote me back and told me she would be going to the march.

When we got back from church, I found that King-Roy had returned from Harlem, and just as I knew he

would be, he was even surlier than before. I had gone up
to his room to talk to him. I wanted to try to get him to
be in our show. I stood in his doorway and explained
my plans and how I wanted to do that fancy Shoop
Shoop tap number he taught me, and I said how I
wanted him to then do something really jazzy for everybody. I said, "I thought you could do a solo and be our
grand finale."

King-Roy sat on his bed, reading from a book called
the Holy Qur'an, and didn't look up or say anything to
me, so I said, "What's that you're reading?"

King-Roy mumbled, "The Holy Qur'an. It's like the
Nation of Islam Bible."

"Are you a Muslim now?" I asked.

King-Roy lifted his head and pushed his glasses up
on his nose in that slow, careful way he sometimes did,
and said, "I am. You can call me King-Roy X now because that's my name until I get a new last name from
the Honorable Elijah Muhammad himself."

"You want to be called King-Roy X?"

King-Roy nodded and stuck his nose back in his
book.

"Like Malcolm X?"

"Um-hmm," King-Roy said.

I said, "X is the mark you make when you don't
know how to write or spell or anything. Why would you
choose that? Won't people think you're illiterate or
something? Doesn't that put you right back where you
started as slaves signing your name with an X? I don't

get why Malcolm X would use that name when he probably had—"

King-Roy's head shot up. "Esther!" he said, his eyes bulging and glaring at me. He opened his mouth, stopped, then shook his head and let out his breath and said, "Esther, just don't bother me now. I'm reading. I've got lots of reading to do. Anyway, I told you; you don't know what you're talking about. You never will. You can't understand 'cause you aren't black."

"I knew you'd come back meaner after that unity rally," I said, turning to leave.

"I'm not being mean; I'm just angry. I'm just really angry."

I turned back around. "At me?"

"At everybody." King-Roy shut his holy book, turned, and sat on the edge of his bed, resting his elbows on his thighs. "You know what they're calling me in Harlem? You know what Ax and them are calling me? The black elite! The black elite, he's calling me. Me!"

I took a step into his room and said, "Why'd he call you that? What does he mean?"

King-Roy took off his glasses and rubbed at them with a handkerchief he pulled out of his back pocket. "He means I'm living out here in rich old Westchester with the nasty, blue-eyed, smelly white man, that's what he means." King-Roy put his glasses back on his face. "That's what Malcolm X said yesterday. He said that the black elite live out in Westchester with their white friends and they never reach back to pull the rest of the

Negroes along with them. And when Malcolm said that, Ax points at my head and yells out, 'Here he is! Here's the black elite.' Now, how you like that? Everybody looked at me like I was the white devil himself."

"That was mean," I said.

King-Roy hung his head and shook it. "My momma's got my hands tied, making me live out here."

"Why is she making you if you hate us so much?" I asked, moving in closer to the bed and King-Roy.

King-Roy lifted his head. "That's just why. She doesn't want me hating white people. She's afraid I'll do something crazy."

"Like what?"

King-Roy lifted his glasses up on top of his head and rubbed his face with his hand. "Like kill somebody."

I drew in my breath. "King-Roy, do you think she thinks you killed that fireman who shot the hose at your sister?"

King-Roy stood up and his glasses fell backward off his head onto the bed. "Esther, I told you when we first met, she's the only one who believes I didn't do it!"

"Okay," I said. "I just thought that maybe—"

"Well, don't think. Don't think about it, you hear?"

King-Roy looked so angry that I just swallowed and nodded and didn't say anything, but I was thinking that it still seemed like, to me, that maybe his mother thought King-Roy did kill that man and she was keeping him out in Westchester with us as some kind of protection from the people down south who were after him. That's what

I was thinking, but I didn't say anything about it. Instead, I changed the subject, kind of, and said that I was planning on going to the march in Washington DC. "You know, the one for freedom and jobs, on the twenty-eighth?"

I expected maybe King-Roy would yell at me some more, but he laughed. He looked at me and pointed at me and laughed. "That silly march? You go on ahead, Esther. You and maybe a bunch of other white folk's all who's gon' show up at that, and you know why?"

I shook my head.

"'Cause as Malcolm said yesterday, you can't find one hundred nonviolent black people anymore. He said we're at war now. This is a race war, and the whole country is on the verge of breaking into violence. The black man isn't gon' just sit quiet anymore while they get bashed on the head and their women get raped. No, ma'am. As Malcolm said, 'What's good for the goose is good for the gander.' If a white man wants bloodshed, we'll give him bloodshed. So you go on to Washington, Esther, but you'll be the only one standing there. We're not waiting around anymore for no white devils to give us what we've deserved all along. We don't want no integration; we want separation. So you go to that march, but if there's any black people there, you watch out because they're gon' be after your blood."

"I don't believe you," I said, feeling tired of King-Roy's all-the-time negative talk. "You know what? All you ever do is talk about what you hate and what you're against, but this march with lots of Negro leaders coming like Martin Luther King Junior, this march is *for* something, and I'd rather be for something than against something."

King-Roy crossed his arms. "Oh, I'm for something all right. I'm *for* the Negro. I'm *for* segregation. I'm *for* a race war that lets every blue-eyed devil know that we aren't gon' just lay down and play dead anymore. That's what I'm for."

"Well, your *for* something sure looks a whole lot like against something to me. Look at you." I pointed my finger at King-Roy. "You can't be for anything with a face like that on. You should see in the mirror what being all full of hate and mean thoughts makes you look like. You've got the face of a monster all of a sudden, or . . . or a bull. You look as mean as a bull. And I don't know how acting like a bull is going to get you what you want."

"That's because you're a child and you don't understand anything at all. You're white and you're living out here rattling around in your big old mansion, not knowing what the real world is like out there. You're sitting on high while we Negroes live in ghettos, ten to a room, just so we can pay the high rent that our Mr. White-devil landlords charge us."

"Oh! *Yakety-yak, don't talk back!*" I yelled at King-Roy in frustration. I couldn't stand any more of his talk.

"What did you say?"

"I said, '*Yakety-yak, don't talk back,*' from the song. Don't you know the song?"

King-Roy laughed.

"What?" I stood with my hands on my hips and watched him laugh at me. "What are you laughing at?"

"You," King-Roy said, wiping the tears from his eyes. "Yakety-yak. Esther, you sure know how to make me feel better."

I smiled. "I do?"

"Yeah, you do."

"Then, you can't hate me completely."

King-Roy grabbed his glasses off the bed and put them back on. "I don't hate you at all. I never said I hated you."

"Well, I'm white," I said. "And you hate the blue-eyed white devil."

King-Roy nodded, "Yeah, I do. I sure do." King-Roy paused and stared down at his feet a moment. Then he looked up with almost a smile on his face and said, "It's a good thing you've got brown eyes, then, isn't it?"

I nodded. "Then, we're friends?"

King-Roy sat back down on his bed. "Just as long as you understand, Esther, we can't ever be *real* friends. We could never know each other as real friends, you know that, don't you?"

I stamped my foot just the way Sophia would do, and I said, "That's only because you won't let us. Of course we can be friends. We were friends until Ax and

Yvonne and Malcolm X got hold of you and turned you all around. We *are* friends, King-Roy, and if you'd actually clean those glasses of yours instead of smudging the grease around on them with your dirty handkerchief, you'd see the truth. You'd see that there are plenty of white people around willing to be your friend. But all you see when you see white is some fireman with a hose in his hands. And I'm not him!" I stamped my foot one more time and made my exit, just like a good dramatic actress would do.

THIRTY-THREE

The next two weeks were full of ups and downs. I enjoyed practicing my tap dancing, but I did it in secret, sometimes out in the pavilion and sometimes in the laundry room, or in my bedroom or the ballroom, depending on where I could get the most privacy. I wore socks instead of my saddle oxfords, so that no one would hear me, and sometimes I got King-Roy to watch me to see if I was doing it right. I also got him to teach me a few more steps that I thought would look impressive to my mother and father, which King-Roy did grudgingly, since he wanted to spend his whole life reading Nation of Islam stuff all of a sudden.

I watched Sophia and Stewart practice their parts after dinner, although most of the time we watched Stewart because Sophia thought she was already perfect and she was tired from working at the theater. I didn't have to take Sophia to the theater anymore after Wednesday and the funeral, which was good for me and bad for Stewart. Since Mother or Dad took Sophia to the theater, Stewart had no chance to take classes anymore, so he just practiced at home. He said he hoped that I was right that once my parents saw how good he was they'd approve of him taking lessons. I hoped I was right, too.

The funeral for Madeline was the saddest funeral in the whole world. It was much sadder than my grandparents' funerals. I cried and cried just thinking about how we were all there only because Mother made us come and not because we wanted to be there. And I cried because I wasn't sad she was dead. Well, I was sad, but not because I was going to miss her. That was it. I cried because I didn't miss her and I never would, and neither would anyone else standing around her casket except Mother.

On the way home from the funeral, I asked Mother why Madeline didn't have more friends, and Mother said, "She's always been a strange bird. She never really fit in anywhere. She was just a strange bird."

I poked my head up to look at myself in the rearview mirror, and I thought I saw a strange bird staring back at me.

My father caught my eyes in the mirror and said, "Esther, get your fat head out of the way, I can't see behind me," which was the way Dad always talked to everybody, and I never usually took offence. I knew I didn't really have a fat head, but that day I felt just like a goon. I felt like a big long-necked, fatheaded ostrich goon plopped down in the middle of a family of lovely swans.

As we approached the entrance to our driveway, I

looked across the street at Pip's house the way I always did, and I saw him out in the yard. I had called his house the week before, but his mother had said Pip was staying on in the Catskills a while longer. I rolled down my window and yelled out to him, but then Mother yelled at me to get my head back in the window before it got knocked off by the entrance gate, and anyway, Pip didn't even turn around and wave, so I pulled my head back in.

I asked my father if he would let me out so I could run over to Pip's to talk to him, and after Mother warned me not to scuff up my good shoes or tear my dress, they let me go.

I ran as fast as I could, calling to Pip as I ran, and finally he turned around and saw me, and all he did was kind of nod in my direction. That slowed me down. I walked the rest of the way over to where he stood leaning against his favorite climbing tree, which faced my favorite climbing tree, which was why they were our favorites. When I caught up to him, I hugged him and said, "I'm so glad you're back. How was your vacation? Did you have fun?"

Pip didn't hug me back. He gave me this careful kind of look as if checking me out, and he said, "Yeah, my vacation was fantastic. I don't know when I've ever had a better time in my life."

"Well, that's great. I sure missed you," I said.

"I bet you did," Pip replied, walking away from me toward his house.

"Hey, Pip," I said, trotting after him. "I did. I *did* miss you. What you saw in the ballroom that day was—"

Pip whirled around and said, while walking backward, "I'm in love with Randy, Esther. You may as well know. We're going steady."

"Going steady? You said you'd never do that. You're too young to go steady. What do you mean you're going steady? Have you kissed her?"

Pip didn't answer my questions. Instead he stopped walking and said, "And I'm going to the Hackley School in the fall."

"The Hackley School! That's all the way away in Tarrytown! That's a private school. You don't like private schools. And it's a boys' school. How can I go with you if it's a boys' school?"

"You can't. I'm going alone."

"But we said we'd always stay together. We were even going to go to the same college, remember? Hackley boys go to Harvard. You said you didn't want to go to Harvard. You said you didn't want to go to an Ivy League college."

I didn't know what to think. I didn't recognize the Pip in front of me at all. He looked the same, only taller and tanner than I usually thought of him as looking, but he sure wasn't acting like Pip.

"It's like your whole self has changed, Pip. Like you don't value the same things you used to value. Private schools and Harvard, and what will you do; will you board there? Will you stay at Hackley all the time and only come home on weekends, or will your parents drive you there every morning? Pip, how could you do this?"

Pip shrugged and said, "Things change, Esther." Then he turned around and walked again toward his house.

"I know!" I yelled, following behind him. "I know things change! Everybody changes! The whole world is changing! I know it, okay? Remember? I know it. And I'm getting left behind. I can't go to Hackley. If you all of a sudden have to go to a private school, at least pick one that I can go to, too, Pip."

"What for?" Pip said, his voice cold.

I stopped walking. "Pip!"

Pip turned around and said, "You've changed, too, Esther. You're not being left behind. You're just going in another direction. We both are."

"What? No, I'm not. I'm not going in any direction. I want to go with you. Pip, I want to go with you."

Pip shrugged again. "Well, you can't, and I don't want you to, anyway." He turned and walked up the steps to his house with his hands dug deep into his safari shorts.

I called after him. "Why are you so mad at me? What have I done? That time in the ballroom with King-Roy, I was just comforting him. His sister had died, Pip. I was just comforting him."

While I was explaining all this, Pip opened the door

of his house and stepped inside and let the screen door slam behind him so that my last words, "I was just comforting him," I said to myself.

I called after him, "Pip!" I ran up the steps and opened the screen door and yelled into the foyer, "Oh yeah, well we're moving to California, anyway, in case you didn't know. Just in case you didn't know."

Pip's father, Dr. Masters, stuck his head out of the living room and glowered at me. "Esther, we're in the middle of a meeting here."

"Sorry," I said. I backed away, holding the screen door so that it didn't slam after I had backed through it. Once I made it back out onto the porch, I turned around and ran home, and while I ran I wondered, if I was being the change I wished to see in the world, why did I keep seeing changes I didn't wish to see?

THIRTY-FOUR

I was so upset by Pip's news that I had forgotten to invite him to our show. I wanted him to see me tap dance. Maybe he would like me again if he saw me dance and he thought I was good. I wanted Laura and Kathy to see me, too. I wanted to impress them, but I knew they wouldn't be home until the thirty-first of August.

I called Pip's house the next day, knowing Pip wouldn't come to the phone unless it was for him. I didn't want to speak to him until after he had seen me dance, so I just asked his mother to tell Pip that he was invited to our show on Saturday the twenty-fourth.

By the end of the week, I got a letter from King-Roy's momma and so did King-Roy and so did my mother.

I opened my letter and my twenty-dollar bill fell out. I knew that meant that she wasn't coming, and I flopped down at the kitchen table and thought how everything was going wrong in my life. Then I heard both King-Roy and Mother calling to me, and I yelled out that I was in the kitchen. Mother and King-Roy both reached the pantry door entrance at the same time and tried to fit through the doorway together, so that for a moment they got stuck. But then King-Roy backed up and let Mother go first. King-Roy almost shoved her through, though, to get at me and have his say. Both of them held their letters from Mrs. Johnson in their hands, and they were both talking, or, I should say, *yelling* at me at the same time.

As far as I could make out, this is what they said.

KING-ROY: Esther, Momma says that you invited her to the March in Washington.

MOTHER: Esther, Luray says that you invited her to that march in Washington.

KING-ROY: How could you do that without asking me first?

MOTHER: How could you do that without asking my permission?

KING-ROY: Do you realize what you've done? She's coming and she expects me to be there, too.

MOTHER: Somehow she got the notion that we are all going to be there. (Mother held up the letter and shook it at me) You told her we were going to be there, and now my hands are tied. She's already made the arrangements.

KING-ROY: (He shook his letter at me) She's already made the arrangements. She's got her tickets for the whole family. Everyone is coming, so now my hands are tied. I have to be there. I could be disqualified or excommunicated from the Nation for this.

MOTHER: Now we have to be there. Esther, I am fit
    to be tied, I'm so angry with you. The very
    notion! Wait till your father gets home!
KING-ROY: I'm fit to be tied I'm so angry with you.
    The very idea! Wait till Ax hears about this!

Both of them waved their letters in my face some
more and yelled at me till their veins popped out in their
necks, and then both of them left, trying to push back
through the door of the pantry at the same time again. I
watched them struggle together, neither one backing
down, so that they burst through into the pantry at the
same time and stumbled over one another and fell onto
the floor, with Mother in her pretty pink shift, and King-
Roy losing his glasses in the fall.

They looked like a comedy routine, but I didn't
laugh. I watched them collect themselves and leave, and
then I picked up my letter. I read that Mrs. Johnson had
been planning to come all along. Their whole church
was coming, and they had buses that would bring them,
so she didn't need my money, but it was very thoughtful
of me, she said. She also said that she looked forward to
meeting me and seeing my mother after so many years.
"It's been a long time, but at last your mother and I will
be able to walk hand in hand again, just like we used to
when we were little. Just as it says in the song, 'We'll
walk hand in hand, someday.'"

I decided once King-Roy and Mother had cooled
down a little bit, they'd be excited to be going, since

King-Roy would get to see his family again and Mother would get to see her old best friend. And then I realized that we were going; we were actually going to the march! My plan—my great idea—had worked. Maybe at least one thing would turn out right.

THIRTY-FIVE

Excitement was in the air. We had our performance coming up and then our trip to Washington DC. We planned to take two cars to the march—the 1947 Ford Super Deluxe station wagon, which King-Roy had fixed so that it ran forward again, and the new Plymouth Fury. Mother told me I would have to help her prepare the picnic baskets so that we'd have food and something to drink while we were in Washington, and I was to gather up umbrellas and raincoats and sweaters in case it was cool out or it rained. Then we had to go into town to buy sunglasses for me, in case it was sunny, and comfortable walking shoes for Mother, Sophia, and Beatrice. Mother and Beatrice didn't own anything comfortable enough to be on their feet in the heat or rain all day, and Sophia had outgrown her Keds. I had pointed out to Mother that my Keds had big holes in the toes, so I thought I should get a new pair, too, in navy this time, and Mother said, "If I bought you new sneakers every time you poked holes through the toes, I'd have to buy a new pair every week. You'll get new Keds when you grow out of the old ones."

I tried explaining to Mother that my feet had stopped growing years ago, but she wasn't interested. I could get sunglasses and that was all.

I didn't feel too bad, since the whole trip to Washington—my great idea—had become a big production, and even Dad and Monsieur Vichy had grown excited about it. They were going as observers, they said. Dad got his camera ready, and Monsieur Vichy bought a new notebook so that he could take notes.

King-Roy had become nervous because Malcolm X had announced that anyone who chose to go to the march would be asked to leave the mosque, which is where the Muslims prayed and gathered together. Malcolm X said he would give them ninety days to get out.

"I only just got in, and look what you've done to me, Esther," King-Roy said. "Look how you've messed things up for me."

"But don't you want to see your family?" I asked.

"Course I do. That's why it's such a mess. And don't think this is all gon' go well, either. There'll be riots and beatings, and then how will you feel, Esther? How's it gon' be when you realize you risked my life and maybe your own family's life just so you could be the change, as you keep saying. You'll be the change all right. You'll be the change from safe to dangerous, or maybe to deadly. Now you think about that. There could be hundreds of angry people at this march, Esther. You don't know what that's like. You don't know what could happen."

What King-Roy said was true; I didn't know what

could happen. I was afraid of riots and violence, and I guess so was Dad, because even though Mother had purchased the Keds for Sophia, he said Sophia and Stewart couldn't go and that he'd ask Daisy if she would stay home with them. Then he started to worry about me going and then about Mother going, and then he wanted to call the whole thing off and he called it a bad idea, after all.

When Mother told me this, I stormed into my father's study, a dark-paneled room with lots of leather-covered furniture and framed photographs and posters of his plays, and Hirschfeld drawings of actors and actresses all over the place. He was sitting on his desk and talking with Monsieur Vichy, but I burst in and interrupted them and said, "Dad, you can't call off the trip. I have to go. I have to be there. This is important to me. Don't you see? We're going to change things. We're going to make it right. I have to go."

My father wiped at his balding head with an angry swipe of his hand and said, "Esther, don't come barging into my study and tell me what you have to do. *I'll* tell *you* what you have to do. You turn yourself around and you go out the door and you knock like a proper young lady."

"Dad, could you for once stop training me to be a proper young lady and just listen to what I'm saying? Could you just listen to what I have to say, just this once? This is important to me. This is the most important thing in the world to me. We have a chance to change things. We can go to Washington and show

President Kennedy and everyone that we *all* want what's right. We *all* want Negroes to have their rights and their freedom."

My father made a fist and hit it on his desk. He said, "Esther, your mother told me all about your romantic notions about King-Roy. And I'll tell you now that you will never—"

"That's not fair. I don't want this just for King-Roy. I want it for our country. What kind of people are we if we're so mean and hateful to people just because they got black skin? It's not fair. It's not fair, is it, Dad? Don't you want to see Negroes and white people get along? Don't you want them to be able to vote like us and to be able to eat at any diner they want and get equal pay for equal jobs? Don't you?" I had begun to march back and forth in front of his desk, and the marching gave me energy.

My father said, "Esther, yes, of course I do, but there are other ways of handling this. You can write—"

"It's time to act, Dad," I said. "It's time to march, not write," I said, still marching myself. "Sometimes I think we have to come out from behind our desks and come out of our houses and just march. Don't you think so?"

I stopped in front of Dad's desk and watched my father shake his head. Then he said, "You're just too young. It's not your battle—"

"No, I'm not! I have to go, Dad. I have to go."

I wanted to cry but I didn't because that would just prove to my father that I was too young. I paced over to the windows, then back again, while Monsieur Vichy went, "Tsk, tsk, tsk," at me. I ignored him and turned back to my father and said, "Do you remember that postcard Pip once sent me from Washington, the one with President Kennedy on the front? Remember when he was visiting a pen pal there?"

My father leaned forward in his seat. "Esther, what does—"

"It said on it, 'Ask not what your country can do for you—ask what you can do for your country.' Well, this is it. This is what I can do. I want to be a part of a group of people who want to make a positive difference in this world. Dad, this is important. Don't you see that? This is the right thing to do. This march is the right thing. Why can't you see that?" I looked at him and then at Monsieur Vichy, who had some kind of amused look on his face that made me want to kick him.

"Dad," I said, returning to him, "King-Roy says it's too late. He says we're in a race war. He says there are no more nonviolent Negroes left, but I don't believe it. Dr. Martin Luther King Junior doesn't believe it, either."

My father raised his hand to stop me and opened his mouth to speak, but I kept right on talking.

"We can't let mean, hateful people be the ones who control how our country behaves. Gandhi says we have to be the change we want to see in the world. Well, if all we do is sit around and do nothing while all the angry white and black people fight it out, then that just must mean we want to see all the blood and hatred and bad things happen."

"Esther." My father stood up and I shut my mouth.

"Where did you get all these ideas? From King-Roy?"

"No, all King-Roy and I do is fight. I've been reading stuff and"—I shrugged—"I don't know, I've just been thinking about it a lot, I guess."

"Well, Esther, you've surprised me," my father said. He crossed his arms and pursed his lips and stared so hard at me, I felt squirmy. I didn't know what he was thinking.

"I've surprised myself, too," I said, looking down at my feet. I thought maybe that was the end of our conversation, because nobody said anything, so I started to back away, but then Dad set his hand on my head and said, "All right, we'll go to Washington. But you'll stay with me and you'll listen to everything I tell you to do, do you understand?"

I sprung up onto my tiptoes and hugged my father. "Yes! Thank you, thank you, thank you. I love you." I squeezed him and let go and said, "You'll see, Dad. This is going to be beautiful, a beautiful event."

"Beautiful, eh?" Monsieur Vichy said behind me.

I spun around. "Yes, beautiful! You'll see."

Monsieur Vichy nodded and picked up his unlit cigar and stuck it in his mouth. "We shall all see," he said.

I didn't know if he was agreeing with me or being sarcastic, but knowing him, I decided he was being his usual mean old self.

THIRTY-SIX

Our trip to Washington was back on for everyone except Sophia and Stewart, who didn't care about the march, anyway, and the day of our big performance had arrived.

Auntie Pie had taken an old dress of hers and fit it to me. It was a sleeveless dress with a scoop neck in two layers of yellow material. The lacy outer layer had yellow beading all over it, and near my right hip she had pinned a large white cloth rose. The dress hung straight down from my shoulders to below my knees, and when I walked and tapped, the lower skirt part danced about my legs and I felt like a real flapper girl. Auntie Pie even gave me a soft pearl-colored crocheted cap to wear on my head, and Beatrice pinned my hair up under it, leaving just a few side pieces out to make my hair look bobbed. She did my makeup for me just as we had planned, highlighting my eyes with eyeliner, shadow, and mascara, adding foundation and rouge to my cheeks, and coating my lips with red lipstick. When she had finished, she stood back and took a look at me.

"You're absolutely stunning, Esther," she said, and

her eyes got all watery, which made mine watery, too.

I turned to look at myself in the mirror, and I thought I looked pretty, really pretty. My eyes looked so big and my eyelashes so long, and the eye shadow brought out the golden lights in the brown iris part. My lips looked fat with so much lipstick on. I didn't like the sticky way the lipstick felt and it smelled funny and tasted bad, too, but when I stood back and took a look at the whole picture, I knew I looked beautiful. I wished that Laura and Kathy and all those boys who Pip said told him I was a goofball could see me. I felt so excited, I wanted to burst. I didn't want anyone in the family to see me until I came out to do my dance, so I snuck down to the library early while Beatrice got Stewart and Sophia ready for their performances.

Sophia wore a short green dress with lots of frilly stuff around the neck and sleeves, and she, too, had a white rose pinned to her dress.

Stewart wore tights and a green tunic top that made him look like Robin Hood for his first dance, and he planned to change to his swim trunks for the second one. He had made up both dances all by himself, and he used some classical Tschaikovsky music for Robin Hood. For his second dance, which was my favorite because it had lots of leaps and somersaults and in-the-air cartwheels, he used the song "Surfin' USA"—another reason it was my favorite. He bought the single of the song and said if after the dances Mother and Dad let him keep dancing, he'd give me the record to keep.

Our program that I typed up on Dad's typewriter looked like this:

```
    Welcome to a Saturday Afternoon of
            Entertainment Galore!

Starring: Sophia Young, Stewart Young,
   and Esther Young
Costumes: Hyacinth Jessup (Auntie Pie)
Makeup: Beatrice Bonham
Producer: Esther Young


                PART 1
           SOPHIA YOUNG SINGS!

1. "Wouldn't It Be Loverly"--from My Fair
   Lady
2. "I Feel Pretty"--from West Side Story
3. "Somewhere over the Rainbow"--from The
   Wizard of Oz

          SOPHIA YOUNG PERFORMS!

    Dorothy from The Wizard of Oz
(Co-starring Prissy, the Beast, as Toto)


                PART 2
          STEWART YOUNG DANCES!

            "Robin Hood"
         Music: Tschaikovsky
     Choreography: Stewart Young
```

```
              "Surfin' USA"
           Music: Beach Boys
     Choreography: Stewart Young


                 PART 3
        ESTHER YOUNG SURPRISES!

      Time step and variations
      Shim Sham and variations
     Music: "Stomping at the Savoy"

  Shoop Shoop--choreographed by King-Roy
                 Johnson
           Music: "In the Mood"


  We hope you enjoy the performance!!!!
```

When everyone had taken their seats, Beatrice knocked on the library door and told me they were ready. I took a peek and saw Sophia standing in the center of the room waiting for her cue while Mother and Dad, King-Roy, Monsieur Vichy, Auntie Pie, and Stewart sat against the wall in our folding wooden chairs, waiting with their programs in their laps. The only person I didn't see was Pip. I felt crushed that he hadn't come. I pulled back from the door and closed it and tried to compose myself so I wouldn't cry and make all my makeup run. When Sophia began her first number, I swallowed the lump that had formed in my throat and opened the door back up a crack to watch. Sophia sang and performed everything perfectly, as usual, and the only thing that went wrong was that the Beast had grabbed hold of Sophia's leg with her front paws and wouldn't let go. Finally Beatrice got her to behave and Sophia began again with her dramatic monologue, and when it was over everyone applauded and cheered for Sophia.

Sophia curtsied several times before she sat down in the seat I had set out for Pip, and then Stewart got up to perform his ballet. He looked back toward the library at me while Beatrice put the record on, and I could see by the wild look in his eyes that he was petrified. I stuck my hand out the door and showed him that my fingers were crossed for him, and he nodded at me. The music began and he started to move. His first few steps were wobbly, and I thought maybe he shouldn't have started with an arabesque since he had to balance on one foot to do it, which was too hard when you're so nervous, but once Stewart got leaping and turning, he loosened up, and then he held his next arabesque without a single tremor. He was beautiful. His curly hair flopped around and his cheeks got bright red and he looked just like an angel dancing.

I stuck my head out the door a little further to see if Mother and Dad liked Stewart's performance and I saw Mother sitting up ramrod straight with her lips pinched tight and Dad sitting with his hand rapidly tapping his knee, not in rhythm to the music.

"Come on, he's beautiful, can't you see it?" I asked under my breath.

Stewart finished his first dance with a grand tour jeté and landed on his right foot and held it while Beatrice turned down the music to make it sound like it was fading out. Stewart then took a bow and I shouted, "Hooray!" and clapped from inside the library, and everybody else did, too, but I could see that Mother and Dad still didn't look happy. Their claps were more polite than everyone else's.

Sophia stood up in the middle of the applause and said, "There will now be a five-minute intermission while Stewart changes for his next dance. Please enjoy the pound cake and juice we have set up in the solarium."

Before Sophia had finished her announcement, Auntie Pie had jumped up and headed for the solarium so she'd be first at the cake. The others moved more slowly, and before Mother or Dad could say anything to Stewart, he ran off to the library to join me and get changed for his next ballet.

"Did you see their faces?" Stewart said, still breathless and flushed from his performance when he came into the room.

I helped him off with his Robin Hood top. "They're just surprised. They need a bit of time to get used to it, that's all," I said.

"Dad looked like he wanted to yank me off the floor by my ear," Stewart said, pulling his swim trunks on over his tights. "I'm so nervous. Did you see how shaky I was?"

"You looked beautiful, Stewart."

Stewart scowled. "I don't want to look beautiful. Dad doesn't want to see that. I want to look strong and athletic."

I nodded and handed him the big cardboard surfboard Auntie Pie had made from an old refrigerator carton I had retrieved from our garage. She cut out the shape and Stewart painted it blue with the words SURFIN' USA in fat red letters running along its length. On the bottom, Auntie Pie had glued a surfboard-shaped piece of felt so that the board could slide across the ballroom floor at the end of Stewart's dance.

"You do look strong, and wait until they see you do that cartwheel without any hands. It's like you're flying, Stewart. They'll love it."

"I hope so." Stewart looked up at me, his worried eyes wide and innocent-looking, and I smiled and crossed my fingers on both hands and held them up.

"Good luck," I said.

Stewart ground some rosin into the bottoms of his ballet slippers so they wouldn't slip too much on the floor and gave me a lopsided smile. "Thanks," he said. He kissed me on the cheek. "You look really pretty, Esther. I'm sorry Pip didn't come."

I shrugged a shoulder and didn't say anything. A few seconds later we heard Sophia ringing the servants' buzzer, a button set in the wall of each room in the house, and Stewart turned and hurried out of the library with the painted surfboard under his arm.

I stood by the door and watched him take his place in the center of the room with the surfboard held up in front of him, shielding him from the audience. The room was so quiet, I could hear my heart pounding in my ears. Mother and Dad both sat with frozen death expressions on their faces, and I was glad that Stewart couldn't see them.

I said a quick prayer for him.

Then Beatrice started the record and Stewart stayed still and hidden during the short musical introduction, but as soon as the Beach Boys started singing, "If everybody had an ocean," Stewart exploded, first by pressing the surfboard to the floor and cartwheeling over it in one slick movement, and then springing up and leaping and turning and flying. He was just flying. Beatrice had turned the music up loud and it must have really energized Stewart, because I had never seen him leap so high. Beatrice began clapping to the music, and Auntie Pie and King-Roy joined in. Then Monsieur Vichy, Mother, and Dad started clapping, and Stewart really flew. He was wild and yet he was graceful. He was all over the room and yet he was in control; he was in total control. Toward the end he did a series of eight leap-turns in a great circle around the surfboard, and then he picked up the board and ran and slid across the room on it and finished with his arms paddling in the imaginary water as the Beach Boys' song faded.

Then he sprung up from the board and did a low bow while everyone, even Mother and Dad, stood up and cheered. Everyone, that is, except Sophia. She sat in her seat with her arms crossed and a worried pout on her face. But that didn't matter, Stewart was a rip-roaring success!

THIRTY-SEVEN

I let Stewart enjoy the limelight for a while longer but once the applause had died down and everyone had taken their seats, I signaled to King-Roy to announce me, which he had reluctantly agreed to do. But when he stood up and made his announcement, he did it right—with lots of excitement and pizzazz.

He said, "Announcing . . . the one and only . . . the greatest . . . the most talented tap dancer of them all—live from Westchester County, New York—Miss Esther Young!"

I heard the applause and I made my entrance just the way King-Roy had taught me, with shuffle steps out from the library to the center of the room. I looked at everyone smiling at me, and I smiled so wide back at them, I thought my mouth might rip apart.

"Why, Esther Josephine Young, look at you!" Mother said. "You're beautiful!" I looked at Dad and he whistled, and then I saw Monsieur Vichy's cigar drop right out of his mouth into his lap, and Auntie Pie clapped and nodded, and Stewart just glowed, and King-Roy's eyes looked wide in his head and he was nodding like Auntie Pie, and Sophia's eyes had turned to mean little slits, but I ignored her. This was my turn to shine.

I gave a little curtsy, and then when everyone had quieted down, I began with my time step. I made sure that I kept my upper body relaxed and my arms light and moving with the steps, and I saw King-Roy nodding his approval out of the corner of my eye. I finished with a twirl and another curtsy and everyone applauded and I signaled for Beatrice to start up "Stomping at the Savoy" for my Shim Sham. While I danced I could see that Mother and Dad and everyone were impressed. I was even so impressed with myself that I added some extra flourishes with my arms and my hips, and as King-Roy would say, I "really got down into it."

When I finished the Shim Sham, everyone cheered for me, and I just couldn't stand it, I felt so proud. I couldn't wait to show them the Shoop Shoop dance. It had a number of difficult rhythms and steps that I knew would surprise everybody when they saw that I could do them so well.

Before Beatrice put on the music, I said, "I would now like Mr. King-Roy Johnson to please join me in performing his very own Shoop Shoop dance."

Everyone cheered and so even though it wasn't in the plans, King-Roy stood up and walked over to me and whispered, "I'll get you for this," but I saw the light in his eyes, so I knew he was pleased I had asked him.

I signaled for Beatrice to start the music, and we waited eight counts while Sophia climbed into Mother's lap and got settled, and then we were off, kicking and tapping and swinging and shooping, and it was so much fun, I laughed out loud and so did King-Roy, but then in the middle of our "double wing" steps, I heard an ear-piercing scream.

I looked over at the audience, and I heard it again. Sophia screamed, "No! Stop it! Mother, make them stop! She's better than I am! Esther's better than I am!" She hopped off of Mother's lap and ran at me. "Stop it. You just stop it! You're ugly and stupid and a no-talent dumbo."

King-Roy and I had both stopped dancing and Beatrice had turned off the record player, and while Sophia ran at me, screaming, Mother jumped up and ran after her and grabbed her just before she rammed into me with her fists.

Mother picked Sophia up and said, "Shush, now, Sophia. It's all right. She's not better than you."

"She is. She's better. I don't know how to do that. I don't know how to do that dance," she wailed, and kicked in Mother's arms.

Mother spoke to Sophia as she carried her back to her seat. "Sophia, it doesn't matter. It's just a silly little tap dance. Anybody could learn it if they wanted to. It's nothing. It's nothing, Sophia, dear."

Everyone else had stood up by this time, and they gathered around Sophia to soothe her while she sobbed and choked and stole the show right out from under us. I looked over at King-Roy and he looked so angry, I thought he might march over to Sophia and Mother and strangle one of them, but he didn't. He marched right past them, through the solarium and the living room to the foyer, and then I heard his *tap-tap* feet marching all the way up the steps.

Mother kept telling Sophia that my dance was nothing, a silly little tap dance. She had called King-Roy's dance a silly nothing. She had called my efforts a silly nothing. I stood in the middle of the ballroom stunned and unable to move while Mother kept trying to soothe Sophia.

"It doesn't matter one whit," she said while Sophia kicked and cried some more. "You're our star. You'll always be our star, Sophia, honey."

Then Dad suggested Mother take Sophia up to her room while the rest of us cleaned up. The show was over. Because of Sophia, the show was over, and I didn't get to finish my fancy footwork tap dance.

I slapped over to the row of chairs and with all the noise and fury I could muster, I slammed the seats shut and hauled a couple of them off to the closet in the foyer. When I returned to the ballroom, I saw that Stewart and Dad were gone and I asked, "Where's Stewart and Dad?" and Monsieur Vichy pointed toward the library with his cigar. "In there. Your papa wanted to have a leetle talk with Stewart."

"Oh yeah?" I said, feeling more anger building up in me. I imagined my father telling Stewart that he couldn't dance ballet after all, and I felt like barging into the library and yelling my head off, but I decided to march on up to Sophia's room instead and yell my head off at Mother.

Beatrice had collected the record player and the records, and Auntie Pie had gathered up all the silly typed-up programs and was taking care of the food table, and Monsieur Vichy was hauling the rest of the chairs to the closet, so I decided to do just that, march into Sophia's room and give Mother and her both a piece of my mind. I headed toward the solarium, and Beatrice called after me, "You did a really nice job with everything, Esther."

Auntie Pie mumbled around the pound cake she had stuffed into her mouth, "Very impressive, dear."

"Well, you didn't get to even see the impressive part," I said, stopping to glare at Auntie Pie. "Nobody did because Sophia had to act the brat and spoil everything!"

I stormed off and charged up the stairs and down the hallway to Sophia's room, and there I found Mother cooing over the dear little precious Sophia, who lay on her side in the bed, choking on her leftover sobs.

"Mother!" I said.

Mother looked up at me. She put her finger to her mouth and shook her head. "Shh," she said. "Not now."

"But I want to talk to you, Mother."

Mother patted Sophia's back. "Not now, Esther. I just told you. Now is *not* a good time."

I put my hands on my hips and I felt my face just burning with rage. "It's not a good time? Not a good time!

When would be a good time, Mother, in the middle of someone's performance? In the middle of Sophia's play, maybe? Should I jump up *then* to have a talk with you?"

Sophia yelled over her shoulder. "Go away, Esther. I hate you."

"Oh yeah, spoiled baby brat."

"Esther, that's enough!" Mother stood up. "I do not need one of your scenes right now."

"One of my scenes? One of *my* scenes? Boy oh boy!" I stamped my foot. "That just takes the cake. *Why,* Mother, *why,* do you *always* tell me I'm making a scene, but when Sophia throws a tantrum, it's poor little precious Sophia? Why is that? I'd just really like to know, 'cause it looks to me like you've created a little monster over there." I pointed at Sophia's back, and Sophia rolled over and stuck her tongue out at me.

Looking at her lying on her frilly little princess bed with a gleam in her eyes, I just wanted to reach out and yank her up and shake her so hard all her little baby teeth would fall out.

Mother moved toward me, blocking my view of Sophia, and said, "Esther, I will not tell you again. Now is not a good time to talk; we'll have this conversation in private later." Mother took hold of the door as if she was going to close it in my face, but I stepped inside the room so that she couldn't do it.

"No, Mother. Now is just the right time to talk. I don't care that I'm making a scene. Who cares? I'll make a scene if I want. I want some answers."

Mother grabbed me by my arm and said through gritted teeth, "Sophia, I'll be back in a little while. Why don't you read a book? Will you do that, sweetheart?"

Then Mother, still with her hand around my arm, pulled me out of the room and led me down the hall to her bedroom saying, "Esther, I don't know when I've been so upset with you."

"It was about a week ago," I said. "You're always upset with me. How is it I'm in trouble when Sophia was the one who ruined the show? Why don't you ever say to Sophia that you don't know when you've ever been so upset with her? I'm upset with her every day. She's a monster, Mother. Everyone down at the theater thinks so, you know. How can you let her call me stupid all the time? Why do you let her?"

By this time we had arrived at my parents' room, and Mother pulled me inside and closed the door behind us.

"Esther," Mother began, after letting go of my arm, "you're a smart enough girl to understand that Sophia is a lot more delicate than you are. She's high-strung, do you understand? She's a little girl with a big girl's mind, and she feels everything more deeply, more painfully, than the rest of us do."

"So when she makes a scene, she's high-strung and we should all feel sorry for poor little Sophia, but when I make a scene, I get yelled at and told to shut up."

"Esther, I have never told you to shut up. I do not use that kind of language."

I ignored this and said, with my arms flailing wildly,

"And you—*you*, Mother—you tell her my dance is silly and that it's nothing. King-Roy's dance is nothing! You insulted both of us just so our dear little precious doesn't think someone might be better at dance or prettier or smarter than she is."

My mother stood with her arms folded and one toe tapping nervously on the floor and said to me, "I'm sure King-Roy understands completely."

"Oh, does he? Is that why he stormed off so fit to be tied, I thought he was going to strangle you?"

"Esther—"

"Am I supposed to act stupid and ugly just so Sophia doesn't have a conniption fit or a mental breakdown? Am I not allowed to have a dream? Is Stewart not allowed to have a dream? Is no one allowed to dream anything because it might upset Sophia? Is that why you always make me feel stupid and ashamed of myself? To protect the fragile Sophia?"

"Esther—"

"You can't control the whole world, Mother, you know. There are prettier and smarter and more talented people out there. You can't protect her forever."

"But I can protect her now, while she's still young, and so can you."

I stopped and glared at my mother. "Mother, I'm almost nine years older than she is. When is it my turn? Why didn't I ever get my turn?"

"Esther—"

"Did it ever occur to you that I don't want to be a

gym teacher and maybe I don't even want to be a mother or a wife, either? I mean, why can't *I* be a star? I could be one, you know. I could be an actress, too, you know," I said, my heart pounding hard in my chest as I prepared to tell Mother what had happened down at the theater during Sophia's auditions.

My mother smiled at me with a sad little smile, and said, "Esther, if you want to act in your high school's little plays you—"

I stamped my foot. "No, Mother, I mean I could be a real actress on Broadway. Is that so hard for you to believe? Well, it's true. At Sophia's audition, the casting director wanted me to play the part of Zelda. He wanted *me*!" I jabbed my thumb into my chest. "He said I was really good. And so did his assistant and Stewart and King-Roy."

Mother's brows drew together and she asked me, "When did you audition?"

"It happened by accident, but they said I was great. They wanted me to play Zelda."

My mother closed her eyes and waved her hand in front of her face as though brushing away a gnat. "I'm sure they knew you were Herbert Nelson Young's daughter."

I nodded. "Yeah, I told them I was, but that's not why they offered me the part. They practically insisted I take it, but I didn't. I didn't because I didn't want to hurt Sophia in case she didn't get her part. But now I think I should have taken it."

"I'm sure you were too afraid to take it," Mother said. "I'm sure it had nothing to do with Sophia's feelings." Mother looked away. She looked toward the windows, so I jumped sideways to get in her view again and I said, "No, Mother. I wasn't afraid at all. It had never even crossed my mind to take it. I guess you've got me trained so well to think so little of myself and only to think of Sophia that it never even occurred to me to take the part." This realization had just come to me as I spoke, and then as soon as I said it, I knew it to be true. Mother had trained me to play the supporting role to my brother and sister all my life, and finally the role had started to chafe. I looked into my mother's eyes and I thought I saw fear there. I didn't understand it. "Mother," I said, "why wouldn't you want me to be an actress? Why don't you ever give me credit for my dancing or when I sing?"

Mother said, "I just don't want you to get your feelings hurt."

"But you're the one who's hurting them. Why don't you ever think I'm good at anything? Why haven't you ever encouraged me the way you do Sophia or Stewart?"

Mother walked over to the windows that looked out over the front yard and the polar-bear rock and stood with her back to me. "This is nonsense. Of course I've encouraged you."

"To get better grades maybe, to take better care of my hair and clothes, to learn how to bake a cake, to look after Sophia and Stewart, make the beds, vacuum the foyer. Maybe you think you're encouraging me with these stupid things, but who cares about those? Those aren't anything to encourage me about, except maybe the good grades. But those aren't talents. Those aren't my dreams."

Mother whirled around and I saw tears in her eyes. "Well, they are mine, Esther. You have just described my life as a wife and mother. So what you think of as no talent and unworthy of dreams is all I have. I have taught you only what I know. I have given you all that I have to give. I don't teach Sophia these things. I don't teach her anything. I only try to protect her, and Stewart is like your father, so like your father, but you, Esther, you've always been most like me."

There isn't anything in this world my mother could have said that would have stunned me more. I had never in my life thought of myself as being anything like her, and here she was telling me, asking me, even, to agree to this, to agree to be like her, to live a life like hers, and I felt so sad and guilty because I knew inside that I couldn't live her life. I couldn't be her, just as I couldn't be like Kathy and Laura. I thought about this and I wondered if there was something wrong with me. What kind of strange bird was I?

I looked at my mother, standing by the windows, her head held high and proud, her eyes blinking at me, and all I could say was "I'm sorry." I didn't even know what I was sorry about; I just knew someone needed to say it.

THIRTY-EIGHT

After I left my mother in her bedroom, I went down to King-Roy's room to try to talk with him, but he didn't want to speak to me or to anyone else in the house. I could hear the anger and hurt in his voice when he told me to go away. "Esther, I got nothing to say to y'all. I got nothing to say. You go on, now, and don't you keep talking to me."

"We don't have to talk about what happened," I said. "We can talk about this book I'm reading. I'm reading a good book by James Baldwin—*The Fire Next Time*. Have you heard of it?"

"I got nothing to say."

"The librarian in town gave it to me. She knows all about you because I told her, and she said for me to read this book. It's new." I paused for a few seconds and listened at King-Roy's door. "King-Roy?"

"I got nothing to say."

"He's a Negro like you and he says how he wants freedom and justice but he doesn't want to lose his soul in the process of getting it. He doesn't want any Negro to lose his soul going after freedom, and he thinks that doing to the whites what they've done to you is beneath your dignity." I waited. "King-Roy?"

"I'm not listening to that."

"He wants to know what makes a white man so arrogant as to think a black man would want to be equal to him. He says to be equal to a white man isn't good enough."

"That's what Elijah Muhammad says, too."

"Yeah, this James Baldwin met Elijah Muhammad. He tells about it in this book. You want to read it?"

"I don't have time."

I leaned my head against King-Roy's door and I could smell the paint on it. I took a deep breath of the paint and then spoke, my lips almost touching the door. "Why don't you have time? What do you mean?"

"I don't have anything to say to you."

"Are you packing in there?" I asked, hearing King-Roy moving about. "Are you cleaning up? What are you doing?" I knocked on his door. "Can I come in?"

"No, now go away."

"But the march is just three days away. You're still going, aren't you?"

"I can leave for the march from Harlem."

"So you *are* leaving."

"My momma said living here for the summer would change my mind about white folks, but it hasn't changed anything. Not a thing. Not one blessed thing. I don't know how my momma and yours could ever have been friends. Your momma doesn't even see me as a person.

Calling my dance no account, she might just as well have said the same thing about me—it all comes to the same thing, anyway."

I heard something bang inside King-Roy's room.

I pounded my fist on the door. "She didn't mean to hurt you, or me, she just meant to protect Sophia." I lowered my voice. "I think she's afraid for her. She's so high-strung and all. But she doesn't have to worry about us, you see. She knows we can handle it. It's a compliment, really," I said, trying to explain to King-Roy what I didn't quite understand myself.

"Yeah, I know all about those kinds of compliments. That's the only kind white folks give a black man, ones that sound like insults."

"So you're going to run away?"

"Go away, now, Esther. I don't want to talk to you."

I pounded the door again. "You're always threatening to leave. That's what you do, isn't it? You leave. You run away. You always run away. Just like at that march last May."

King-Roy yanked open the door so fast, I didn't have time to pull back and I fell against him. At the same time that I fell, he said, "What did you just say?"

He pushed me off of him and glared at me, and I never saw him look so angry. I didn't know his mild-mannered face could get that mean-looking. His eyes smoldered and he jutted out his jaw, flared his nostrils, and held his body so rigid and puffed up, I thought he might strike me.

I backed away from him and straightened out the flapper dress I still had on. Then I said, "It's just that James Baldwin says that what we're all really afraid of in life is death, the *fact* of death. That's what we're running from. But he thinks we ought to face up to death, because that's the only sure thing in life. Isn't that something? And—and he thinks we ought to go on and earn our death by living our life and facing up to our problems with passion." I shook my fist in the air when I said the word *passion*.

King-Roy glared at me, his nostrils moving in and out. He was breathing hard. "So you think I'm a coward, too. All this time, you've been thinking I'm a coward?"

I backed away some more and came up against the opposite wall. I shook my head. "No, King-Roy."

"Why do you think I joined the Nation of Islam? So I could run away? So I could hide? So I wouldn't have to fight? The Nation is all about passion—passion for the Negro, passion for freedom and human dignity. What I see is that I'm not running away, Esther, I'm running *toward*. I'm going where I belong, and if you or my momma or anybody else can't understand that, if you gon' keep calling me a coward, well, you go on, 'cause it won't make a difference to me. I know just what I gotta do. I know who my people are, and they don't live here."

King-Roy took a step back and slammed the door, and I felt its reverberation run straight through my body.

THIRTY-NINE

I changed into a pair of shorts and a button-down shirt and spent the rest of that afternoon reading in my favorite climbing tree. I thought that if I stayed up in the tree, I could keep a lookout for Pip across the road and also keep an eye out for King-Roy in case he came out and said he was leaving for Harlem. I tried to convince myself that it would be all right if he left. I could still go visit him. I could visit him in Harlem and maybe learn how to skip double Dutch with those girls I saw skipping rope in the street. Maybe he would even come back out to our house for visits once he stopped hating everybody—if he ever did. I knew he'd be a lot happier in Harlem than here with us. Yes, it would be all right. It wouldn't be the end of the world.

When I finished my James Baldwin book, I closed it and thought about what he had said about being passionate about life and earning your death. I thought what he was saying was for us to take action and be passionate about the things that mattered to us in life and to try to make a difference in the world so when it was time for us to die, we wouldn't have any regrets and we'd be ready, we would have earned our time to die.

In my mind, this sounded like what Gandhi had said about being the change we wish to see in the world, and I decided this would be my philosophy of life. This was how I wanted to live my life, and when I thought about that, having a philosophy to live by, I thought it didn't matter so much that I wasn't like Laura and Kathy. Maybe what Pip had said was right. Maybe I was changing, too. Maybe I wasn't being left behind. Maybe I really was just going in a different direction.

Thinking about this made me think of Pip again, and I wished like anything we could get back to being friends. We had had plenty of fights over the years but never one that lasted almost the entire summer.

I looked across the road to his yard, huge and green and bright, and thought about going over and trying again to talk to him, but then I heard the phone ring in our house through the open windows in the living room and I thought it might be Pip. Maybe he had seen me up in the tree and that reminded him that he forgot to come to the performance today.

I stashed my book in the waistband of my pants and climbed down out of the tree. I walked across our lawn and the circular driveway, toward the house, listening out for someone calling me to the phone. I didn't hear anyone, so I decided it couldn't be Pip. I slowed down and took my time walking up to the porch and then I waited at the bottom of the steps. When I heard King-Roy's voice I figured Ax had called him up and I left.

I ran out to my polar bear and sat on the rock and dug at the holes in the toes of my Keds. I sat on the rock for a long time, and I watched the sun move lower and lower in the sky until it scattered its light in the branches of the trees. I stared at the light, the way it sparkled on this leaf and that and made the pine needles look as if they were made of light, and I got so deep into wondering what it would feel like to be the sun that I didn't hear King-Roy come up behind me. I didn't know he was there until he spoke.

He said, "I've come to say good-bye."

I startled, then turned around on the rock, feeling the rough granite pulling at my shorts. "So you're leaving now?" I asked, standing up and brushing off my bottom.

King-Roy nodded. "I'm going to Harlem tonight. I need to say good-bye to Ax and Yvonne and the others."

For a moment I felt a flutter of hope in my chest. Was he coming back? Did he like us after all? Was he saying good-bye and then coming back here to live with us? Had he and Mother made up?

I said, "So, does that mean—"

King-Roy interrupted me. "No, Esther. There's been some developments at home. I . . . I gotta go home."

I looked into King-Roy's eyes and it seemed as if he had already left. He seemed so sad or worried—I guessed he was both.

I moved down off the rock and stepped in closer to King-Roy. "Do you mean home to Alabama? What happened? What kind of developments?"

King-Roy drew in his breath and held it for a few seconds, then he let go of his breath and said, "A couple of nights ago my brother got beat up by a group of white men back behind a Mobil filling station. They told him if they couldn't get to me, they'd get to my family."

"What does that mean?" I asked. "Were they friends of that fireman that got killed?"

King-Roy jutted out his chin to keep it from quivering and nodded. "Must be."

"But King-Roy, if you go home, won't they do to you what they did to your brother? Won't they hurt you?"

King-Roy shook his head. "I'm not goin' home to Birmingham. I'm goin' to my aunt's home." He scratched his nose and looked away. "Momma didn't want to tell me about it, but last night somebody set fire to her house."

"A fire! Was anybody hurt?"

King-Roy turned back to look at me and said, "No. Momma and them were all down at the church, praying for my brother Cyril. That's the one they beat up. Nobody got hurt in the fire, but half the house is gone."

"Why would somebody set fire to your momma's house, King-Roy? How could they do that? They can't get away with something like that!"

King-Roy shrugged and gazed toward my climbing tree. "Looks like they can, 'cause they did."

I took King-Roy's hand and I said, "Well, that's going to change."

King-Roy looked at me with a flash of anger in his eyes. "I'm gon' make things change."

I nodded. "Me, too, King-Roy."

King-Roy slipped his hand out of mine and set both his hands on my shoulders and looked straight into my eyes. "Esther, listen to me. Don't you let yourself get hurt, you hear?"

"I won't," I said, looking straight back at him.

King-Roy shook my shoulders. "No, you listen here to me, now. You've got lots of great ideas in your head, and I had them, too, once, but nobody's playing nice. It doesn't matter what color you are; if you start marching for our side, they're gon' knock you down, you understand?"

I nodded.

He squeezed my arms and blinked his eyes really fast and said, "Esther, I don't want what happened to my sister to happen to you, and don't think just because you're white that's gon' get you any kind of protection. If y'all go on to Washington, you be careful, you hear?"

"Is that why you've been so mad at me? Were you worried about me?"

King-Roy let go of me and looked away, and I saw his jaw muscles clench up.

"You do care about me, King-Roy, don't you? You do."

King-Roy turned back to me and nodded. "Course I do." The corners of his mouth turned up as he tried to force a smile. "Esther, you're my ray of hope." His smile faded. "Even if I don't think change is gon' happen until a lot more people have died and paid for it, paid for our freedom with their lives, I'm glad someone still believes a peaceful revolution is possible." He shook his head. "But I can't believe in nonviolence and mass movements as a way of changing anything anymore. Not after losing my sister and . . . and everything else."

I looked down at the holes in my sneakers and said, "I'm sorry about your sister, King-Roy, and about what's happened to your brother, and to your mother's house."

King-Roy didn't say anything, and I looked up and saw him staring at the ground. He looked so miserable. I wanted so much to do something, anything to take his pain away, but I knew that his kind of pain ran too deep for my words to make a difference. Still, I tried.

I stood on tiptoe and gave King-Roy a kiss on the cheek and said, "Thank you."

He looked at me and lifted his hand as if he wanted to touch his cheek where I had kissed him, but he stopped, holding his hand in midair, and he asked, "What are you thanking me for?"

I tilted my head and tried to think of how to say what I felt. "I guess . . . I guess it's for waking me up. I think until you came to our house it was like I'd been asleep. It's like all my life I've been walking in my sleep, not really seeing anything, and then you came to stay and it's like just by knowing you I've come awake to the world. I see the whole world now when I look at you."

"And I think when I look at you," King-Roy said, reaching out and touching my hair, "I see the sun."

I smiled. "Really? I was just wondering before you came over here what it would be like to be the sun. I really was. I like that, thanks." I hugged King-Roy, grabbing him around his neck, and I said, "I'm going to add that to my philosophy of life—to live bright like the sun. Let's both of us do that."

I felt King-Roy's shoulders sag, so I stepped back to look at his face and I saw that it had clouded over with sadness again.

"What? What is it, King-Roy?"

King-Roy shook his head. "I was just remembering something."

"What?"

"My sister's favorite song. She sang it the day we marched. When she was getting dressed, I heard her singing it. 'This little light of mine, I'm gonna let it shine.'"

"Sing it for me, King-Roy."

King-Roy shook his head and looked all grouchy at me. "I'm not gon' sing it. You're always trying to get me to sing or dance or do something. When you gon' learn I'm not here just for your entertainment?"

"King-Roy, you're the grouchiest nice person I know."

Just then my mother came out of the house and stood on the porch and called out to us. "King-Roy, time for me to take you to the station."

I grabbed King-Roy's hand. "I'll go with you."

"No, Esther. I've already said my good-byes to everybody else, and your parents let me come out here to say good-bye to you alone. That's how I want it. We'll say our good-byes here. Anyway, I need to talk to your momma alone, too."

"Just don't expect an apology from her. Mother doesn't apologize. Maybe I should come with you so—"

King-Roy shook his head. "No, Esther, I'm not looking for an apology, and anyway, I want to remember you right here at this house, waving to me from your polar-bear rock."

"But we'll see each other again, won't we? I'll come visit you in Alabama and you'll come back here. Maybe someday you'll move to Harlem, after everything's settled."

"Maybe," King-Roy said, but he didn't look as if he meant it. His whole face went pale. I didn't know a black man's face could turn pale, but I saw it with my own eyes. Even the color in his lips had faded.

"King-Roy?" I said, taking his other hand in mine so that I held both of them.

King-Roy glanced out to where my mother stood waiting by the car, and then he turned back to me and said, "I gotta go now, Esther."

Then he grabbed my shoulders and hugged me and I hugged him and we held each other a long minute and I whispered to him, "I'll never forget you, King-Roy."

And King-Roy whispered back, squeezing me hard, "Yeah, I'll never forget you, either, Esther."

I watched King-Roy walk away from me, and my heart felt so heavy I had to sit down. My legs didn't want to support me anymore and they shook as I sat on my rock. I tried not to cry. I didn't want King-Roy's memory of me to be of me crying. I wanted to be his ray of hope. I wiped at my eyes and watched him grab his suitcase and a paper bag off the porch steps, say something to Mother, and then the two of them got into the car.

Mother drove around the grassy circle and out toward the gate, and I saw King-Roy looking at me. He waved and I jumped up and waved back and my tears spilled down my face as I shouted out, "Bye, King-Roy. I'll see you. I'll see you again soon. Be careful!"

The car had reached the gate, and I couldn't stand to see him leave. I ran toward the car, calling his name, and when I couldn't see him anymore, when they had turned out of the gate, I shouted, "Come back! Make sure you come back, King-Roy."

FORTY

Later, when I went inside the house for dinner, Stewart handed me his "Surfin' USA" record and smiled. "I'm taking ballet, thanks to you, Esther. Thanks for the best summer I've ever had. I know I owe you more than this."

I tried to return his smile, even though my happiness for him made me feel even more sorry for myself. I felt as though things were slipping away again, out of my grasp, and I was falling behind once more.

Then, at the dinner table, in the middle of my staring down at the plate of roast beef and mashed potatoes I didn't want to eat, Sophia said, "Well, at least now you all don't have to go to Washington."

I looked up at the guilty faces around me, then over at my mother and then my father, and I saw that they were giving each other the look. It's the look that says, *Which one of us is going to explain it to her?*

I dropped my fork. "No! We're still going, aren't we?"

"Esther," Mother said. "King-Roy won't be there. His mother can't come. There's no need—"

"No need? No *need*? Mother, I can't believe you're

saying this. How can you just back out? Dad"—I turned to my father—"how can you do this?"

"Esther, we're all tired. This has been a long summer. Maybe if I were younger, if we didn't have other responsibilities, if—"

"No!" I stood up. "I don't want to hear excuses. I've told you how I feel about this, Dad. You know how important this is to me. You just don't think my thoughts or the things that matter to me are important." I looked at my mother. "If I'm dancing, it's not important. If I want to do something or go somewhere to try to change the world, it doesn't matter. Well, it's important to me, and I matter to me. At least *I* matter to *me*."

Nobody said anything. They all just sat there gawking at me, so I left the table.

My father called me back but I paid no attention. As I was running up the stairs, I heard him say in his booming voice, "I'd just like to get through one meal in this house without a lot of high dramatics. Is that too much to ask around here? What? What?"

When I got to my room, I kicked off my shoes and flopped down on my bed and punched my pillow. I thought about how miserable the whole day had turned out and how I had thought it was going to be one of the best days of my life, and how King-Roy was gone and Pip didn't even show up for the show, and how that's what I get for trying to be the change, because what good did it do, anyway?

Over the next few days, I grew more and more

depressed as the time drew closer to the march. I hadn't heard anything from King-Roy, either. I didn't know if he had made it home, even. He and his family were staying with his aunt, and we didn't have her name or her number, so we couldn't call.

I spent most of my time walking in the woods, feeling sorry for myself. I ate my meals by myself, making lots of cheese and tomato sandwiches and taking them out to the woods with me to eat.

Then, on the afternoon before the march, while I was sitting out on a boulder in the woods near the big pond, thinking about all that I had seen in Harlem the day I had gone looking for King-Roy, and all the conversations I had had with King-Roy about blacks and whites and violence versus nonviolence, and all that I had read about civil rights and peaceful revolutions and Gandhi's words to be the change you wish to see in the world, I decided that I just had to go to Washington. If no one in my family wanted to go then I would go by myself. I would take the train; or if that cost more than the twenty dollars I had, I would take the bus, but I would be there. I couldn't force the rest of my family or anyone else to care just by arguing about it. I had to *really* be the change. I had to act on my convictions. Yes, I would go by myself.

Once I had made this decision, I climbed down off the boulder and ran back to the house to get ready. I needed to pack up some food, stuff a bag with a rain poncho and my new sunglasses and a thermos of water, and, most importantly, write a letter to Mother and Dad telling them that I had gone to Washington. I figured I could leave it on my pillow.

I planned to sneak out early in the morning and ride my bike to the train station. Then I would take the local train into the city and catch a train bound for Washington from there. The whole time I was making my preparations, my hands shook. I crept about the house, collecting my things like a criminal.

I felt so nervous and jittery that I didn't even see Monsieur Vichy coming into the kitchen, and I crashed right into him. I had my sack lunch and thermos in my hands and I was trying to make a quick getaway up the servants' stairs when we crashed and I dropped my bag. Monsieur Vichy and I both said something like "Ugh," and then he bent down and picked up his pince-nez and my sack and the hard-boiled egg that had rolled out from it.

"I hope there was nothing breakable in zis?" he said, handing me the bag and the egg.

I blushed and rolled the top of the bag down tighter, waiting until later to drop the egg back in it. I said, "Thanks," and then, "Oh, sorry for the crash."

Then I turned around and tried to open the door to the servants' stairs, but with my hands full, and my nerves in such a state, I couldn't manage it.

Monsieur Vichy, who stood there watching my attempts, finally said, "Allow me," and opened the door.

"Thanks," I said, trying to avoid his gaze. I felt that

he could see right through me and that he knew exactly what was in the bag and in the thermos and he knew exactly where I would be taking them, too.

I felt his eyes on my back while I climbed the stairs. It was a narrow staircase with poor lighting so I suppose Monsieur Vichy could just have been holding the door and watching me to make sure I arrived at the top without any more mishaps, but I didn't think so.

I hurried up the steps, tripping near the top and almost dropping the thermos, and then finally I burst through the top door and shouted down, "Thanks, again," and rushed through the servants' quarters and down the hallway to my room.

I stashed the egg back in the sack, and the sack and thermos with my other things in the beach bag, tossed it onto my bed, and then fell onto the bed next to it, panting and waiting for my heart to stop pounding in my ears. My whole body trembled. I felt frightened from defying my parents, and frightened about what I had planned to do, and frightened that Monsieur Vichy had guessed about the trip and was right that minute telling my parents all about it.

I heard footsteps in the hallway, but my heart beat so loudly I couldn't tell whose footsteps they were.

Then I heard a knock on my door.

I sat up. "I—I'm busy. Go away. I'm—I'm getting dressed," I said, grabbing a shirt off the floor and throwing it on over the shirt I already had on so that I would be telling the truth.

"It is I, Esther. It is Monsieur Vichy."

Monsieur Vichy! He knows! He had probably already told my parents. Or maybe he was coming to gloat about it first, to torment me with it.

I felt panicked. I saw the beach bag lying on the bed and I grabbed it and said, "Just a minute."

I tried to toss it under the bed, but it got stuck and I had to get down on my hands and knees and push it under. "Just a minute," I said again.

Then I remembered that I had shoved my French notebook under the bed and I thought about my play. Maybe he had just come for the play! It was the end of August, almost. Well I would just show him the play. I would distract him with the play.

"I'm coming," I shouted.

I reached under my bed for my notebook with the two lines of my play in it. I stood back up, tried to straighten out the page with my sticky, sweaty, nervous hands, and then, at last, I opened the door.

"Here you go," I said, shoving the notebook in his hands.

"But what is zis?"

"My play. There it is."

"Your play? But it is just—"

"You were right, Monsieur Vichy. Once again, you were right. Esther is *très stupide, non*? The family scandal, *non*?"

"I only—" he began.

I exploded, my arms flailing about, giving myself a

chance to expend some of my nervous energy and distract Monsieur Vichy at the same time. "How am I supposed to write a play when I know nothing about the world? I don't get it at all. Like, for instance, the other day, the day of the show, I thought it was going to be a beautiful, perfect day. I thought Mother would see me dance and... and she'd see me. She'd see *me*, Monsieur Vichy. I thought Pip would come over and King-Roy would still be here, and I thought we would all go to Washington." I blushed when I said the word *Washington*. I shouldn't have said it, I shouldn't have reminded him. I continued, trying to cover up, "But... but you see, what do I know? I know nothing. I'm too stupid. So how can I write a play?"

"So you gave up," Monsieur Vichy said in this matter-of-fact way, as if he had just said, "So, have some toast."

"I'm just admitting that you were right."

"But no," Monsieur Vichy said, shaking his head. "I do not sink I was right at all. Zee first step in understanding anysing is knowing what it is you do not know. It is zee one who believes he knows everysing who knows nossing. I see you have learned a great deal zis summer, and so have I, Esther dear."

That stopped me in my tracks, Monsieur Vichy calling me *dear*. I stared at him, stunned.

"You will write your play, Esther. You will write about zis summer, eh?"

"But I don't know—"

Monsieur Vichy shook his head and waved his hand at me. "A writer doesn't write because he knows; he writes because he wants to find out."

"Find out what?"

Monsieur Vichy tucked my notebook under his arm and pulled a fresh cigar out of his breast pocket and unwrapped it. "What it is you do not know, my dear. You write to find out what you do not know." He stuffed the wrapper in his pants pocket and the cigar in his mouth.

"But how do you do that?" I stepped in closer to Monsieur Vichy. I really wanted to know.

"You simply write. Tell your story of zis summer and you will see zat you know more zan you realized."

"I just tell the story?"

Monsieur Vichy nodded and handed me back my notebook. "*Oui,* yes, just tell the story. Zen we will see."

I looked down at my two sentences and imagined starting over and writing about King-Roy and Pip and going to Harlem and learning to tap dance, and then I looked up at Monsieur Vichy and I smiled. "I think I'd like to tell that story."

"But of course," Monsieur Vichy said, nodding. "But zat is not why I have come here. I did not come for your play."

"You didn't?" My heart skipped a beat.

"Esther, I have judged you incorrectly."

"You have?" I backed up and sat down in my desk chair. My legs felt too shaky for me to stay standing.

He nodded. "I have been watching you zis summer, and what I have seen has surprised me, indeed."

"It has?"

"Esther, you are a girl of great passion—zis I have known—but I have wondered in which direction zis passion would go. I sought perhaps you were a silly girl, driven by frivolous whims, but I have seen zat, in truth, you were just casting about for a sing worthy of your passion, a sing worthy of your energy."

"Oh," I said, and blushed.

"When you spoke to your father about zee march, I saw you had given great thought to zis idea and zee principles behind it."

I nodded. "Yes," I said, feeling suddenly defensive. "I have. When I went to Harlem, that time—that time I came home late and everybody was so angry with me— well, that's what started it. I think if everybody in this family could just go there and see how people are living, how poor they are because of how white people have cheated them, well, then, maybe *then* they'd see how important this march in Washington is."

I stared down at my bare feet and thought of the poor children down in Harlem who walked the dirty streets barefooted, and I looked back up at Monsieur Vichy, who was standing there rubbing at his big belly, and I asked, "Have you ever been to Harlem?"

Monsieur Vichy shook his head. "Never. But now I will have to go, *non*? Maybe you will go with me?"

"Yes. Yes, I will," I said, feeling confused but pleased.

"*Bien,*" he said, nodding and removing his unlit cigar from his mouth and staring at it a second. "But zat is not all I wanted to say to you. I thought, also, you did a very good job of planning and producing your show zee other afternoon. *Très bien! Très bien!* I did not know, even, zat you could dance."

"King-Roy taught me," I said.

Monsieur Vichy nodded and rolled his cigar between his thumb and forefinger. "*Oui.* He was good, also. He was very good; I could tell." Monsieur Vichy paused, and then he said, "I sink, Esther, zat you are a girl of many hidden talents, *non*? Our little Stewart has been telling me zat perhaps you act, as well, or perhaps directing is more your forte, like your papa."

I felt myself blush, and I dropped my head forward, letting my hair fall into my face.

"What I know is zis: You have convinced me, my dear, zat zis march is *très* important. I have learned from you, you see. And I believe now zat I must go to Washington."

I lifted my head and saw Monsieur Vichy smiling at me, his little brown eyes twinkling behind his pince-nez.

"But I have *un petit* problem, you see," he continued. "I feel I should need an escort. I need an American escort."

I jumped up from my chair. "Me? You need me? To go to Washington?"

"But of course, it is you. Who else would do?"

"Really? To Washington?" I threw my arms around

Monsieur Vichy. "Thank you! Oh, thank you! I take back all the mean things I ever said or thought about you. Thank you!"

"Esther, you are choking me," Monsieur Vichy said, patting at my back.

I let go and grinned at him with tears in my eyes.

Monsieur Vichy smiled back at me, and after straightening out his slightly squished cigar, he said, "Now, we will need to get to sleep early because we will have to leave very early in zee morning. Agreed?"

I nodded and clapped my hands.

"*Bien.* I will come wake you when it is time, zen."

Monsieur Vichy turned to leave, but I called him back.

"*Oui?*" he said.

"I—uh—you're a good person, Monsieur Vichy. I just wanted to say thank you . . . again."

Monsieur Vichy bowed. "It is *I* who sank *you,* my dear." He backed out the door and I closed it behind him. Then I took a flying leap onto my bed and jumped up and down on it with sheer joy in my heart. I was going to Washington.

FORTY-ONE

I didn't know if Monsieur Vichy had guessed that I had planned to go to Washington on my own or not, but after he left, I noticed that my letter to my parents, written in gigantic letters so they wouldn't miss it, had been sitting on the desktop, right in front of Monsieur Vichy the whole time he was in my room. I saw it clear as day while I was jumping on my bed. I jumped off and tore the letter into little pieces and threw it away. Then I pulled my beach bag out from under the bed, and dug into my chest of drawers for the clothes I would wear, and set all of this out on my desk, ready for the morning.

I felt so excited about the trip to Washington, I couldn't sleep. I grabbed my transistor radio, turned it on, and set it down close to my head on my pillow.

It seemed that every song that came on that night was meant for me. I heard, "Those Lazy Hazy Crazy Days of Summer," and "Our Day Will Come," and "I Will Follow Him," and "Can't Get Used to Losing You," and "Cast Your Fate to the Wind," and "Big Girls Don't Cry," and I cried through all of them. I cried because I was happy; then I cried because I was sad and missing

King-Roy and Pip and even Laura and Kathy. I moved
my radio off my pillow because I had cried so much I
had gotten my pillow wet and I thought I might electro-
cute myself. I tucked the radio under the sheet and listened to more songs and cried. The later the night got,
the slower and sadder the songs became, and at long last
I found myself drifting off to sleep to the heartbreaking
song "Blue on Blue."

My dreams that night frightened me. I dreamed I was
at the march, standing in front of the Lincoln Memorial
with my arms raised, when someone came up from behind me and clubbed me over the head. Then I dreamed
I got trampled by the crowd, and then I dreamed a fireman with glowing red eyes aimed his hose at me and fire
came out and burned half my body. Between each dream
I would wake up, remember the dream, and then fall
back to sleep. The last dream I remembered having,
I dreamed I met Martin Luther King Jr. and he looked
just like King-Roy.

Then I heard someone whispering to me, "Esther.
Esther, wake up."

I opened my eyes. It was still dark out. I looked at
the form in front of me, blinking a few times.

"Pip?" I said, trying to decide if I was awake or
asleep.

"Yeah, it's time to get up."

I rubbed my eyes. "Are we going running?"

"No, silly, we're going to Washington."

I sprung out of bed. "Washington! I have to get

dressed. I have to meet Monsieur Vichy. I have to get—"
I stopped and looked at Pip.

"What are you doing here?" I asked, starting to
come to my senses.

"I'm going with you to Washington. I'm going to
march."

"Pip!" I hugged him. Then I stood back and said, "I
had decided you hated me forever. You didn't come to
our show."

"I was jealous," Pip said. He switched on my bedside light and we both blinked at each other. "I was jealous of you and King-Roy," Pip said.

"But you can't be jealous. You have Randy. You're
going steady with her. I'm the one who's jealous." I
grabbed my clothes off of my desk and went into my
closet.

"You are?" Pip followed me and stood just outside
the door.

I stuck my head outside the closet. "Pip, we need to
get things straightened out about us."

"I don't," Pip said. "I'm in love with you, Esther, and
I always will be."

"But what about Randy?" I asked. I looked down
and noticed I had buttoned my dress wrong and had to
unbutton it and start all over.

"We're not going steady. I mean, we were, for a day,
but I knew I was just trying to get you out of my mind. I
wasn't really interested in Randy and she wasn't interested in me."

I pulled on a pair of shorts under my dress, the way I always did when I went to school, and stepped out of the closet and looked at Pip. "But she's so pretty," I said.

Pip nodded. "She was really pretty at first, but you know what, she got boring to look at really fast. Her face never changed. Once you saw it, well, that was it. Pretty once; boring twice." Pip shrugged.

I laughed. "Pip, I love you, but I guess what I'm afraid of is that if we decided to be boyfriend and girlfriend, then in a year or two, it would all be over and then I wouldn't have you as a friend anymore."

"We'll always be friends, Esther."

"We almost weren't this whole summer, Pip." I slipped on a pair of sandals because I had torn at the holes in my sneakers so much over the past few days, they were almost unwearable.

I continued with Pip. "So I think maybe if we just stay friends for now, then later, when we're older, when it counts more, if we're still, well, interested in each other, then we could do something like go steady."

I grabbed my beach bag off of my desk and checked inside to make sure I had everything. I slipped a comb into the bag so I could comb out my hair in the car.

Pip turned out the light and met me at the door. He whispered when he got right up to me, "I'll always love you. Always; there's no maybe or if about it for me." Then he leaned forward and kissed me right on the lips and my heart did a somersault and I dropped my beach bag on my feet and didn't even know it until the kiss was over.

Pip pulled away and I looked at him smiling at me in the dark and he said, "There, now you can't say I never kissed you."

"And now you'll be telling everyone in school about how you kissed me and that we're going steady, won't you?" I asked, trying to sound annoyed.

"I'm going to Hackley, remember?"

"No," I said, picking my beach bag up off my feet. "No, I forgot. I forgot about that, Pip. I don't understand. Why are you going there? I'll have no one in school this fall if you're not there."

Pip opened the door and we walked out into the hallway. The light was on, so it was easy to see, but I didn't notice this. I didn't notice that all the lights were on, in the hallway, and on the stairs, and in the foyer downstairs.

Pip and I walked down the hall, and Pip explained that his father wanted him to give Hackley a chance. He wanted Pip to get a private-school education just like he had had.

"But you're different," I said. "Didn't you explain that you were different from him? Didn't you tell him how you felt about elitism and all that?"

"I tried," Pip said.

We argued about his going to Hackley, all the way down the stairs, and when we reached the front door I stopped and looked around and said, "Why are all the lights on? What time is it? Where's Monsieur Vichy? And how did you know we were going to Washington, anyway?"

Pip took hold of the door handle and said, "It's three in the morning, and Stewart came over last night and told me. We had a good long conversation. He's a nice little kid. I've always liked him."

"Yeah, me too, but—"

"And smart, too."

"Yes, but—"

"And he's really proud of his big sister."

"Pip, what—"

Pip opened the front door and I heard a loud chorus of "Surprise!"

I jumped three feet in the air I was so surprised.

Mother, Dad, Monsieur Vichy, Beatrice, Auntie Pie, Stewart, and Sophia all stood before me on the porch, and they laughed and clapped when they saw how surprised I was.

"What's going on?" I asked, looking around at all their smiling faces and noticing they each held a home-made placard.

Mother said, "We're going to Washington, Esther. We're *all* going."

"We're going to support the Negroes and their march for freedom," Sophia said, holding up a placard that said, END SEGREGATION NOW, and Stewart, holding a placard that read FREEDOM IN '63, said, "And we're going to support you." He stepped forward and gave me a hug, and then everyone gathered around me, placards knocking against one another, and they hugged and patted me.

My father said, "Esther, thank you for all of your help this summer. Your mother and I couldn't have made it through without you."

I was smiling and giggling so much my face hurt. I didn't know what to think. "When did you all plan this?" I asked. "How—"

"It was Monsieur Vichy," my mother said. "He called a house meeting last night."

I didn't understand. "You had a house meeting without me?" I looked at Monsieur Vichy, who stood beaming down at me through his pince-nez, then back at my mother.

"We had a house meeting *about* you, Esther," Mother said, and Sophia added, "*All* about you. You were the star of the meeting."

My father patted my back. "Monsieur Vichy and Stewart reminded us of a few things that perhaps we hadn't paid enough attention to this summer."

"Namely, you," Stewart said, nodding.

Mother said, "This march is important to you, and we realized last night, with Monsieur Vichy's help, that this wasn't just a passing whim; you were serious about this. Your father even said you've been reading books about civil rights." Mother shook her head. "I didn't know."

Then Beatrice said, "I liked what you said, Esther, about being the change." She smiled. "I like that. This march should be important to all of us."

I didn't know what to think. I was so stunned, I just stood there grinning and blinking at everyone, and then Mother brought a pair of navy blue Keds out from behind her back and handed them to me, and I almost fell to the floor.

"New sneakers!" I said. "When did you get these?"

Mother laughed. "A long time ago. I bought them for when school starts; but maybe you could wear them today and make sure they fit just right."

"Thanks, Mother!" I said, still smiling so hard I was sure my face had gotten stuck and would never unfreeze.

I looked at everyone gathered around me and I felt so happy and so lucky to be surrounded by so many people who loved me. Then I thought of King-Roy, and I wondered where he was and if he was sleeping safely at his aunt's house somewhere in Alabama.

I felt a nudge from Auntie Pie, who jabbed me with her placard, which read, END POLICE BRUTALITY NOW! and she said, "Well, let's get going, Esther. Time's a-wasting."

Monsieur Vichy had stepped off the porch and stood waiting by the cars. He opened the door of the 1947 Ford Super Deluxe station wagon and said, "Esther, my dear, your coach awaits," and feeling just like the winning contestant on the *Queen for a Day* show, I walked down the steps and into my "coach."

FORTY-TWO

All nine of us piled into the two cars, along with the placards and the picnic lunches and the beach bags, and set out for Washington.

At the start of the trip, those of us in the station wagon talked about the march and about how my family had stayed up late into the night, planning their surprise, and the mood in the car was festive and exciting, but by the second hour, everyone grew sleepy and one by one fell asleep, except our driver, Monsieur Vichy, and me.

While everyone slept, Monsieur Vichy reached into the bag by his side and handed me what looked to be the script of a play.

"What is this?" I asked, my voice a whisper.

Monsieur Vichy smiled and said, "You have forgotten we made a bargain? Zis is my play with beginning, middle, and end. Open." He nodded at the script.

I turned the page and saw a dedication: *To Esther, with great admiration and affection.*

I looked up. "For me?" I said. "You dedicated it to me?"

Monsieur Vichy smiled. "Turn zee page."

I turned the page to the cast-of-characters list and I saw that the main character's name was Esther.

I looked up. "Monsieur Vichy, thank you," I said.

Monsieur Vichy made a bow with his head and said, "You were my muse, Esther. I believe it is my best play yet. I like zee beginning, middle, and end story."

"Me too." I leaned over and hugged him. "Thank you. I look forward to reading this."

Monsieur Vichy blushed and patted my leg. "Why don't you try to sleep now. We have a long day ahead of us."

I sat back in my seat and closed my eyes, believing I could never fall asleep—I felt too excited—but I was wrong. Before I knew it, we were in Baltimore, where we all seemed to come awake at the same time, and we wondered aloud what kind of day it would turn out to be. On the news, they had said that the organizers hoped as many as ten thousand people would show up, from all over the country. I couldn't imagine so many people gathered in one place.

We didn't talk about it, but I knew the idea of possible riots was on all of our minds, as well, and the mood in the car had become tense and alert.

I had heard on my radio that Malcolm X had changed his mind and had decided to come to Washington after all. All the black leaders would be there, so he would be, too. That made me wonder if Ax and Yvonne would be coming, along with other Nation of Islam members, and if their presence would change the tone of the march. Would they try to incite a riot?

I looked out my window and saw a bus go by with a banner on its side reading FREEDOM, and then another bus and another, all with the FREEDOM banner, all heading to Washington, all seven of them. I rolled down my window and cheered at them, raising my fist in the air. Several people cheered back, and I sat down in my seat and laughed. That broke the silence and the somber mood that had fallen on all of us in the car, and we started to talk again, and then we sang songs. Then as we pulled up outside of my father's friend's house in Georgetown, where we would leave our cars and catch a bus, I said a quick prayer under my breath for the success and safety of the march.

We arrived at the assembly grounds to check in soon after nine in the morning. We thought we would be early, but already people were pouring into the area. Everybody looked happy; and groups of people, linked arm in arm, walked along singing. Women in white uniforms sold us buttons to wear, for twenty-five cents, that said, MARCH ON WASHINGTON FOR JOBS AND FREEDOM, and in the center of the button was a black hand and a white hand joined together. When I saw that, I thought of King-Roy and me holding hands, and I wondered what was happening to him that day. Was he just then getting up and eating a plate of fried eggs?

I learned later, when we got home, what had happened to King-Roy on the day of the march.

King-Roy had joined his family and his aunt's family in Bessemer, Alabama. He had gotten up early that morning of the twenty-eighth of August and had eaten sausage and biscuits for breakfast and had gone off whistling with his cousin to buy a new fan for the back bedroom where King-Roy and his brothers and sisters slept.

Pip bought six of the MARCH ON WASHINGTON buttons and pinned them all over the front of his shirt. "I love a good button," he said, puffing up his chest to show me the final effect.

"You're going to clank when you walk," I said, and he replied, "Who would hear me? It's so noisy."

Pip was right. People were chanting and singing and talking and laughing, and more and more people kept arriving every minute. They came with picnic baskets and umbrellas and placards, wearing buttons and hats with freedom messages, and they were black and they were white and they looked poor and they looked wealthy, and the more people I saw crossing the lawns, moving toward the Washington Monument where we were to gather for the march, the more excited I became.

My mother looked at me and said, "Esther, are you all right? You look awfully flushed. It's hot out; you be sure to drink enough water."

"I'm just excited, Mother. Do you believe all the people? Can you believe it?"

Mother smiled and squeezed my arm. "This is good, Esther. I'm glad we came." My father, who walked behind me, reached out and tousled my hair and said, "We're all glad." And Monsieur Vichy said, "Zis will make a good ending to your story, zis march, *non*?" and he winked at me.

Then we heard an announcement about the start of some mid-morning entertainment, and a few minutes later Joan Baez, a folksinger, started singing, "Oh Freedom," then "We Shall Overcome," and we all sang together in one voice, and I could hardly get the words out, the lump in my throat was so large.

After Joan Baez sang we heard Bob Dylan and Peter, Paul, and Mary, and Odetta and other folksingers, and we sang and cheered and swayed and cried, and there were poetry readings and spiritual songs and a song I especially liked—"Blowin' in the Wind," which Peter, Paul, and Mary sang—and I could see that all of us, my family and everyone around us, felt so full of a mix of emotions, we just could hardly contain ourselves.

A large group of church people joined hands and started praising Jesus, and they invited us into the circle. We joined hands in the prayer group while over the loudspeaker someone kept asking for the singer Lena Horne. Then people started moving away from the monument. Our group also started moving, and the only thing I could do was to move, too, to start walking or get trampled. "Are we marching?" Pip asked, and Stewart and Sophia looked at me as if I had the answer.

"I guess so," I said, surprised that there had been no official announcement. We all just started walking, marching along the bank of the reflecting pool toward the Lincoln Memorial.

King-Roy and his cousin Robert took the shortcut through the woods, carrying the tall, standing fan between them. His cousin was a talker and he rambled on and on about New York, telling King-Roy all about it, as if he had been there and King-Roy hadn't, and King-Roy only half listened because he kept thinking he heard something, or someone, walking behind them. King-Roy looked back several times but never saw anyone.

The marching crowd had stopped singing and cheering and praying and chattering. We had become a more solemn group. Two elderly black women who walked beside Pip and me had tears rolling down their cheeks, and they walked leaning against one another beneath an umbrella to keep off the hot sun, dabbing at their noses with tissues.

I looked behind me, to smile at Mother and Dad and Beatrice, and I saw a man in a wheelchair, wheeling himself and wearing the most blissful expression on his face. I thought that if you mixed the two women's and this man's expressions together, it would reflect the way I felt at that moment, listening to the thousands and thousands of footsteps beside and behind and in front of me, all marching, all moving toward the Lincoln Memorial, all with the hope for unity and equality in our hearts.

A white teenager handed me a black marker, and I looked up at him, wondering what I was supposed to do with it. I saw an equals sign marked on his forehead and I nodded. I grabbed Pip's head and I marked his forehead with the symbol for equality, and then he marked mine, while people kept on marching past us. We caught up to my family again and I handed them the marker, and when all of us, including Auntie Pie, had our foreheads marked, we passed the marker on and kept walking. We walked slowly, hampered by the crowd and the heat. Beatrice held her umbrella over her head to ward off the sun. Mother, Sophia, and Auntie Pie wore straw hats, while my father and Monsieur Vichy wore berets. Stewart and I had on sunglasses and Pip wore a Yankees baseball cap, but all of us felt the heat. One white man up ahead of us a ways had fainted, and the crowd passed him over their heads toward one of the first-aid stations.

Although we hadn't come close to the Lincoln Memorial yet, we stopped marching and chose a spot under an elm tree for a place to set out our blanket and our picnic lunch.

Mother said, "We can listen to all the speeches right from here, even if we can't see anybody. At least we can keep cool."

We all agreed and we spread out our blanket under

one side of the elm, while another family—a black family from Philadelphia—spread their blanket out on the other side. Before long our two families had joined together, and we shared our salads and fruits and desserts, and our stories.

Sophia and Stewart managed to squeeze between the crowds of people seated along the reflecting pool so that they, too, could sit on the edge of the pool and dangle their legs in the water.

After our lunch, our new friend—James—and Pip and I climbed up in the elm tree and sat on the branches beneath the shade of the leaves and looked out over the great sea of people. I had never seen such a sight in my life. There had to be even more than ten thousand people there. James told us that he had heard at least thirty thousand people had come from Philadelphia alone. I looked out toward the Lincoln Memorial, where I knew the organizers were getting ready to speak, and I thought that they had to be dumbfounded by the crowds of people who had come to show their support for civil rights. I thought, too, of King-Roy. I wished that he could be with us to see that, yes, mass demonstrations could work. We could gather together full of goodwill and make a difference. How could this march not make a difference? I knew the civil rights bill would have to get passed after this.

King-Roy sat at the kitchen table, eating cold fried chicken and a Jell-O salad, enjoying the new standing fan blowing on his face. When the phone rang, he reached out and answered it, since he sat closest to it.

A voice on the other end asked, "Is King-Roy Johnson at home?"

King-Roy felt a sudden chill run down his spine. "Who needs to know?" he asked the voice.

"Just tell me, is he at home?"

King-Roy stood up from his chair and looked out the window into the empty front yard. "And I says, who needs to know?"

The man on the other end said, "Let's just say it's a friend of Mike Mallard's."

"Don't know no Mallards," King-Roy said. "And King-Roy ain't home. His home done got burned up." King-Roy slammed down the receiver and turned to face his family. His hands shook so badly he had to stuff them into the pockets of his pants to hold them still.

Pip, James, and I watched the people streaming past us, and then out of the blue there was a wave of applause and a voice sang out over the loudspeaker "The Star-Spangled Banner," and everyone stood up. Pip, James, and I stood up on our branches, and we sang, too. Then after we sat back down, the Archbishop of Washington offered an invocation, so we stood up again while he prayed for our nation and for the people to set aside their bitterness and hatred and fill their hearts with love. Below me every head was bowed, and I saw everywhere hands raised in the air, reaching toward God in heaven and asking Him to hear our prayers.

We sat back down again and a man named A. Philip Randolph began to speak. I had heard about him on the news. He was the man who had the original idea for the march. He had planned the march over twenty years earlier, but until this day he had not been able to make it work.

A. Philip Randolph called our march on Washington a moral revolution, and I cheered when he added that this march was not just for Negroes and their civil rights alone, but it included their white allies, as well, because how could anyone be free as long as someone was not?

Mr. Randolph told us that when we left later that day, we would be carrying the revolution home with us, and spreading it throughout the country, and that we would do so until every last person was free.

Everybody cheered, and oh, how I wished that King-Roy could have been there to hear him speak and to feel the power and the energy of all the people spread out for miles around the memorial, cheering and applauding and waving their arms in the air.

King-Roy ran back to the room he shared with his brothers and sisters and went to the closet where he had stashed his suitcase. He opened it and withdrew a paper bag from inside. He opened the bag and pulled out the gun Ax had given him. He set it down on the floor and reached into the bag and pulled out six bullets.

King-Roy's brother Cyril watched him from the top bunk bed in the opposite corner of the room. He knew that King-Roy didn't know he was there. Cyril sat up in bed, careful not to make a noise. He watched King-Roy get down on the floor and load the gun, his hands shaking and the bullets spilling to the floor twice before he could get the gun loaded. Then King-Roy stared down at the gun a long time, and Cyril could hear him mumbling to himself. "It sounded," Cyril later said, "like he was arguing with himself."

There was a knock at the door and Cyril and King-Roy both listened to a white man's voice asking to speak to King-Roy.

We heard more speeches, and then more singing, and I had grown uncomfortable up in the tree, so we all three climbed down and joined everyone on the blankets. We sat back in the shade of the tree and listened to the songs and the speeches, and my voice grew hoarse from cheering for the demand for Congress to pass the civil rights bill now, and cheering for the demand to unify the churches, and cheering for "freedom now!," and cheering for the declaration that women, too, would sit in and kneel in and line in and walk for freedom and the right for blacks to sit at any lunch counter and be served, and the right for all people—black or white—to vote, and the right for black children to go to the same good schools as any white child.

I cheered and I sang and I clapped my hands raw. I

jumped up and down and shouted and linked arms with perfect strangers. I carried on until I just wore myself out. Then I sat back down on the blanket, and the afternoon and the heat and the speeches wore on, and on, and more and more people kept moving toward the memorial. People just kept streaming past us. The movement never stopped.

King-Roy listened to his aunt tell the white man at the door that he wasn't there.

The white man said, "Well, now, I know for a fact that he is. We just want to talk with him, that's all."

Then King-Roy's mother said, "My boy did not kill your friend. He is not a murderer. He's a good boy."

The man said, "All right, then. Why don't you let your son tell us that? That's all we want to hear."

"Y'all go on and leave us be, now," King-Roy's aunt said. "He ain't done nothin'."

King-Roy gripped the gun in his hands and tucked it into the waistband of his pants.

"Now, you listen here," the man at the door said, his voice not even hinting at friendly anymore. "Y'all better go get your boy or you're goin' to find yourself in a whole lot more trouble than you are now, you hear?"

King-Roy moved toward the door, shouting, "I'm coming. You just leave my momma and my family alone."

King-Roy's momma shouted, "My son is not a murderer!"

And the white man said at the same time, his voice sounding closer, "Come on out, boy. We only want to talk to you."

King-Roy had stopped in the doorway of the bedroom. He lowered his head and paused a moment, then he pulled his gun out of his waistband, set it on the floor, and kicked it under the nearby cot.

As hoarse as we all were, and as sore as our hands were from clapping, and as tired and hot as we were from sitting in the sun all day, when Dr. Martin Luther King Jr. stood up to speak, we cheered and clapped for several minutes. I stood up for his speech, as if by standing I could see him better or hear him better, but I couldn't see him at all and I could hear him no better standing than sitting. Still, I stood on tiptoe and listened with the crowd, and when I heard him speak, it was like listening to a poem and a sermon and a rousing call to action all at once. I felt my heart rise up in my throat several times as he spoke of fighting with dignity and with discipline and without violence, but fighting without rest, too, until every Negro is granted his rights as a citizen.

His words were like a song, like a Negro spiritual, and they filled me with such hope, not just for the Negroes, but for every American. Every word he spoke, every dream he described, filled me with great hope for our country, and when he spoke at the end, proclaiming that someday all God's children would be able to join hands and sing, "Free at last! Free at last! Thank

God Almighty, we are free at last!" I felt not only the hope for that freedom, but the recognition that we had, all of us, black and white, been bound too long, and here was the man and the day that would set us all free. I jumped up and down and cheered and cried with the crowd, and the sound was deafening, and the sound was beautiful.

King-Roy went into the kitchen and saw a white man standing on the stoop of his aunt's house. Behind him, out in the dry dusty yard, stood three more white men.

"We just want to talk to you, boy," said the man on the stoop. "Why don't you step out here with us so we can talk in private."

Mrs. Johnson grabbed King-Roy's arm. "Baby, don't go with those men."

King-Roy looked back at his mother and said, "Momma, I'm not gon' run this time. I'll stand my ground. I haven't done anything wrong."

He said these last words loud enough for all the men to hear him. Then he pushed through the screen door and started walking toward the waiting men.

Before he reached them, one of the men shouted, "Look out! He's got a gun!"

For a moment King-Roy stood frozen, not knowing what was going on, then he heard a sound behind him and he turned and saw Cyril standing there with the gun in his hand. He had taken aim at one of the white men and when King-Roy saw this, he shouted, "No!" and jumped in front of the gun.

Four guns fired at the same time. All four bullets went into King-Roy's body. And the sound was deafening, and the sound was horrible.

FORTY-THREE

After King-Roy died and after my mother and I got back from his funeral and after crying for three days, I reread the book on Gandhi. I thought about all the people who died, including Gandhi, in order that his India might be free. I wondered how my being the change I wished to see in the world could really make a difference. What did it matter that more than two hundred and fifty thousand people marched on Washington in peace and unity if King-Roy was dead? I felt so defeated.

I mourned King-Roy's death the rest of summer vacation.

Monsieur Vichy had said that writers wrote their stories not because they understood the world, but because they wanted to find out what they didn't understand. So I started writing my story. I wrote all day long, and the story of the summer with King-Roy just spilled out onto the pages. I sat out in the pavilion with Pip, and I wrote and wrote, desperate to find some answers through my writing, while Pip sat beside me, reading the book on Gandhi or writing letters to his pen pals.

In mid-September, the day before school started, the church King-Roy had marched from on the day his sister and brother got blasted with a hose was bombed and four girls were killed.

I went into the principal's office early on that first day of school and asked if the principal could please announce a moment of silence and prayer for these girls and their families.

Mr. Allston, who already looked frazzled with his glasses down at the end of his nose and the last wispy strands of hair on his head sticking straight up in the air, looked at me a moment as though trying to focus, then said, "Miss Young, we don't even have any Negroes in this school. There aren't any in this whole town."

I said, "There was this summer. King-Roy Johnson was here. He was here." I tried to hold back the tears I felt brimming my eyes, and I swallowed hard before continuing. "And there will be Negroes living here someday. Someday they'll go to this very school."

Mr. Allston gave me this superior look and said, "This is a very wealthy community. No Negroes can even afford to live here. Now, why don't you get along to your homeroom? I have way too much to do right now. So if you'll excuse me." He tried to brush past me with his stack of papers, but I blocked his way.

I said, "They will live here in this town, in your neighborhood even, Mr. Allston.

"This past summer I went to the march on Washington. Did you see it on TV? Over two hundred and fifty thousand people were there in support of Negroes. Oh, yes, they will live here someday." I nodded.

Mr. Allston stared down at me and I saw a look of fear pass over his face. He shook his head and said, "Esther, I fail to see why you even care about this."

And I said, "Mr. Allston, I fail to see why you don't."

"Homeroom, Miss Young," he said, pushing me aside with a strong arm, then hurrying from his office.

I fell against his desk, but I recovered myself and shouted after him, "Just one moment of silence? You can't even give them that?"

The next day in school, I wore a black armband and told anybody who asked me about it why I wore it. I told them about King-Roy and the four girls in Alabama, and most people shrugged, and some laughed, but some were sorry and wore armbands, too.

In early October I started taking tap lessons. When I tap, I'm happy. How can I help it? The music is happy and the steps are happy. I think of King-Roy when I tap, and it's as if he's near me, just above my left shoulder, and he's smiling because he's dancing, too. I believe that when King-Roy danced, his true self, his true loving spirit bubbled up from within and, at least for a while, erased all the anger and confusion he carried inside, and his face shone with a deep joy that I never saw at any other time. That's the memory I hold closest to me, those dancing moments when King-Roy would let his guard down. I think dancing was the only time he ever felt free.

In late October, after giving it a try for one month, Pip left Hackley, and he's now going to school with me again. He claimed that the March on Washington gave him the courage to challenge his father's decision to place him in a private school. "I stood up for my rights and I won," he declared.

Pip and I are informally going steady. I don't know what that really means, and neither does Pip, so we discuss it while we run through the woods beside my house. One day, I'm determined to beat him again in our race around the pond.

Now it's November and I have finished my story. It's not a play, as I had promised Monsieur Vichy; it's just my story of this past summer. I thought when I had come to the end, I would understand the world more. I thought I would be able to make sense of King-Roy's death and his sister's death and the death of the four church girls, but I can't, and most of the world is still a mystery to me. What I have learned through telling my story is that I understand myself more. Monsieur Vichy says that it's only through knowing ourselves that we come to understand the world. If that's the case, I've still got a lot of me I have to figure out.

Today President Kennedy was shot while riding in an open car through Texas. In school we had our moment of silence. Afterward, when I went to the bathroom to get some tissue, I saw Kathy and Laura sitting up on the sinks, putting on makeup, two cigarettes balanced

on the edge of the porcelain soap dish and their purses
on the floor with the contents of them spilled out onto
the tiles.

When I came in, still crying from the moment of silence and with my nose running, they looked at me and
then at one another, and they giggled.

I looked at them and wondered, *When did I get so
old?*